ABOUT THE AUTHOR

Craig Holden is the author of three previous novels: *The River Sorrow*, *The Last Sanctuary*, and *Four Corners of Night*. He lives in Michigan.

CRAIG
HOLDEN

THE

JAZZ
BIRD

POCKET
BOOKS

LONDON • SYDNEY • NEW YORK • TOKYO • SINGAPORE • TORONTO

First published in Great Britain by Simon & Schuster UK Ltd, 2002
This edition published by Pocket Books, 2003
An imprint of Simon & Schuster UK Ltd
A Viacom company

1 3 5 7 9 10 8 6 4 2

Simon & Schuster UK Ltd
Africa House
64-78 Kingsway
London WC2B 6AH

www.simonsays.co.uk

Simon & Schuster Australia
Sydney

A CIP catalogue record for this book is available from
the British Library

ISBN 0-7434-6160-6

Printed and bound in Great Britain by
Bookmarque Ltd, Croydon, Surrey

For Stuart Arthur Holden

and

in memory of my grandparents,

Howard and Eleanora Leake

CONTENTS

Contents

nothing which we are to perceive in this
world equals the power of your intense
fragility: whose texture compels me with
the color of its countries, rendering death
and forever with each breathing

—e. e. cummings

I'm a little jazz bird
And I'm telling you to be one, too
For a little jazz bird
Is in heaven when it's singing blue
—Ira Gershwin

THE JAZZ BIRD

Prologue

OUT OF EDEN

HE FOUND HIMSELF ON THE GRASS OF A GREAT DEWY meadow surrounded by trees and violent outcroppings of rock and the high clear sky. It was October, he knew. It was 1927. The sharp air of the morning burned in his nostrils. He felt as if he had just awakened from a long and exhausting dream. Or been born. He breathed carefully and looked around and, realizing that he was alone, began to walk. The dew wetted his shoes.

Ahead, down a short slope, he saw a road they had driven many times. He came to it and stepped into it. A motorcar approached. He waved but it veered around him, its throaty electric horn blaring and distorting and fading as it went. The wind it generated whipped about him, spinning dirt into his eyes and chilling his wet feet and lower legs. He stepped back to the berm.

Other cars came. One finally slowed, and stopped. The driver leaned across. "Mr. Remus?" he said. "Is that you? Is everything all right?"

Remus got in. It was a Packard, a runner's car. Those big old, good old twin-sixes, heated up and retrofitted with extra water and gas and oil tanks and limo springs to bear the load of thirty cases of Remus's best, unpacked and hand-wrapped in newspaper, and stacked in where the backseat had been removed. They could cruise at ninety nonstop all the way from Cinci to Chi.

The man looked at him and waited. He was supposed to say where, he remembered. He was supposed to remember this man. He found that he could remember very little.

"The station," he said to the man he did not remember, who had stopped in Eden Park.

There was blood, after all. He hadn't noticed it before. A single shining spot of it on his trousers, near the zipper, over the region of his testicles. A round globule, thick in its relief, just beginning to coagulate. His suit was a good hard worsted, which is why it hadn't soaked in but sat there, beaded. He hadn't gotten any other blood on himself, that he'd seen anyway. It didn't matter. His fingers felt hot. He pressed the nails to his nose and inhaled and smelled the cordite, the back-blow, the burn there. Then he remembered and reached into the right pocket of his suit coat and found it, its barrel warm still. He wondered if it had burned a hole in the fabric.

Below them, the city lay in perfect definition in its basin against the river. So often it was shrouded, in cloud, in smoke, in haze, but today it showed itself, as if to make some point he couldn't quite grasp. They crossed the small pretty bridge and drove toward the edge of the park, through heavy trees just beginning to show their autumnal color. The trees too needed to display their vibrancy to him, to rub it in. We are so beautiful, they seemed to say. And alive.

The road held on to the lip of the cliff, high above the shining river and Kentucky beyond that, then came steeply down Mount Adams. They passed the reservoir and sped into the basin. He had emerged from one dream but suspected now that he had awakened into another. And that this was the one from which perhaps he would never escape.

As if it were some bizarre tour, the driver, this man he apparently knew, proceeded to take him past all the old places: Marcus's Front Street garage, the old lawyer Ring's office brownstone up the Eastern Row, then over to Race, within view of the dark building at the corner of Pearl. Where were they going? They'd already passed the Second District Station on Broadway. That would have done. Remus said nothing. He understood: it was a tour for his benefit. The driver must have known. (Soon they would all know. Everyone would know.) The driver knew, and he had passed his own sentence and was now administering it—you must look, the sentence read. You must remember it all as it happened and is happening and will happen together at once and in perpetuity. He watched it all unfold, the past in the present, here in Cincinnati and before that long ago in Chicago. It all seemed to be happening, still, though he was beginning to realize now that it was over.

MEN AND WOMEN HURRIED IN AND OUT. THE GREAT engines sat hidden inside the building but their exhalations rose in white clouds from high vents into the fine morning air. The man Remus did not remember pulled his Packard up to the arched doors. At the station. The depot. The Dixie Terminal.

Remus began to laugh. The man looked at him.

"I'm sorry," Remus said. "I'm sorry. I meant—no, no. This is fine. I thank you so very much."

"Sure thing, Mr. Remus. Anything for you, sir."

When the man pulled away, Remus waved at a cab. As he did, he put his other hand into his jacket pocket and felt the hammer, the mother-of-pearl handle, the now-cool barrel. Without looking, he removed it. It fit almost entirely within his hand. He dropped it into the trash receptacle on the curb.

"This is the wrong station, you see," Remus began, when he got in the new machine. "The authorities—"

The driver glanced back at him.

"The police station," said Remus. "Take me there."

DISCOVERY

BLACK FOR MOURNING

ALREADY, THE TELEPHONE IN THE STUDY WAS RINGING. They had just come in the front door from a glorious month at the family cottage at Murray Bay, Quebec: the clear frigid water with its walleye and bass and muskie, the autumn trees, the brisk air, the children. Ten years they'd been married, Charlie and Eleanor Taft, but instead of a second honeymoon they'd chosen to take the children along, and it had so been the right thing.

Charlie carried a couple of bags, though the staff was unloading most of them. Now he dropped them in the doorway and raced to catch the call.

"Charlie," Eleanor said. "You're still on your holiday! How important—" But he was gone.

"Taft," he said. It was one of his assistant prosecutors. As the man spoke, Charlie watched through the front window.

"Samuel!" Eleanor called.

Sam paused on the running board of the Pierce-Arrow as he reached up toward the canoe tied to the rooftop, his cuffs extending out from his coat sleeves. Charlie had always noticed how dark those white cuffs made Samuel's skin look, as dark, almost, as a Negro's. He was the darkest Asian Charlie had ever seen. He'd come to work for the family when they lived in Manila, in 1904, when Charlie's father was governor there, under Roosevelt, when Charlie was six and Samuel was seven and orphaned.

"Can you come move these, please?" Eleanor said. "Charlie's blocked the way."

"Yes, ma'am."

"I see," Charlie said into the phone. "Give me half an hour."

When he came out, Eleanor said, "What is it, dear? You look pale."

"George Remus," he said. "You remember him?"

"The bootlegger."

"That's him."

"I met his wife, once. Lovely lady. Imogene. She hosted a luncheon at the Sinton—"

"He's just shot her to death. In Eden Park."

"Oh my God. Charlie."

"On the way to the divorce court."

Eleanor sat down on the sheet-covered Queen Anne sofa.

"They're taking him back up there, now," Charlie said. "To the park. I'm sorry, but I should go—"

"Of course you should, dear," she said. Sweet, pretty Ellie.

"I'm sorry. All this—" He waved around at the mess of the closed-up house.

"Never mind it," she said. "We'll get it taken care of. You go. Oh, that poor woman."

"Yes—"

"Charlie, this will be very big, won't it?" She understood these things implicitly. She simply knew, and how she did he did not quite understand, for he told her little.

"Yes, dear, it will. If he chooses to fight it."

They were both silent a moment, contemplating this. Charles P. Taft II, third child, second son, of former governor, ambassador, judge, and U.S. president, now Supreme Court chief justice, William Howard Taft, had a straight road to the very top, wherever that was—the Senate, the federal judiciary, even perhaps the presidency. His major competition was his own brother, Robert, editor-in-chief now of the *Enquirer*. But Charlie held his own, and his election, at only twenty-nine, to prosecuting attorney last year in this, their home city, proved it. Still, it was one step at a time, and now the next step was this. This, coming off the last step, which had been a stumble, a locked-up case of another bootlegger-murderer, "Fat" Wrassman, who had gunned a man down in a speakeasy. He'd been defended by a one-time assistant prosecutor named Carl Elston. Though the police pressed for aggravated homicide, Charlie wanted a conviction for first degree. He'd have won it, too, if the main witness to the shooting hadn't disappeared the day before he was to testify. In the end, Elston tied them up in knots, and Wrassman had walked.

So now it was to be Remus, the bootlegger lawyer. And who, Charlie knew, had become something of a publicity hound these past few years. This would be national news. Except for the finale of Lindbergh's cross-country publicity tour, this might be the biggest news. He'd have to call the chief justice and let him know before it hit the papers.

"It will," he said again to his wife.

"Then it's an opportunity," she said. "Isn't that what your father would say?"

"That's just right," he said. "A chance to shine."

"There's the thing," she said. "My Charlie." She stood up and placed her hand on the back of his neck and kissed him lightly on the lips.

"The end of the honeymoon," he said, and she smiled at him.

He had lost the Wrassman case, but the public gave him that. He was young and new and, though that didn't excuse anything, they'd give him one, anyway. But this, this was too big, and he had already played the grace card. This one had to be a win, however it turned. Maybe Remus would confess and look for some plea. Life instead of death. The public would buy that. Remus was a kind of hero to a lot of these people. As long as he went away, Charlie didn't care. But if Remus fought, it could be ugly. Charlie had no doubt that Remus would fight. And he had no illusions that he could let this one slip away. The election wasn't for another three years, but they'd never forget.

When he came downstairs after changing, Ellie said, "Your black suit."

It had become his custom since the election to wear black when visiting the dead. So Charlie didn't need to tell her that, in addition to going to the crime scene while the police questioned Remus there, he was also going to pay a visit to the morgue.

♣ ♣ ♣

EDEN PARK DRIVE CAME SOUTH INTO THE PARK FROM the crown of Mount Adams, then halfway down its descent curved nearly 180 degrees back to the north, to its intersection with Fulton at the reservoir, before leaving the park to the west. Here, just after the curve, the detectives watched as Remus planted his feet, formed his hand into a gun, and mimicked the recoiling of the weapon. Charlie spotted Frank Dodge hovering away from the group, beyond the gazebo, toward the edge of the reservoir, out of Remus's view. Dodge was the Justice Department agent who had hounded Remus clear to the federal penitentiary for whiskey violations. It was in the aftermath of this that Imogene Remus had come to him to plead for her husband's early release. Ultimately, she left Remus and became one of Dodge's star informants.

Later that afternoon, as Charlie fought his way through the crowd that had formed outside the doors on the south side of the courthouse that led most directly to the county morgue in the basement, he saw Dodge again, standing at the double doors, watching out over the crowd.

"Amazing, this," Charlie said.

"Everybody likes a freak show."

"Are you going in?"

Dodge nodded, but only moved to take a Lucky Strike pack from his pocket. He fingered the last one free and crumpled the packet and threw it on the ground. Charlie struck his lighter and held it out. Dodge leaned forward.

"They called me, you know. First," Dodge said.

♣ ♣ ♣

HE'D BEEN LYING ON HIS BED, SMOKING A CIGARETTE, when a cop he knew phoned. "The crazy bastard's done it. He just plugged her in Eden Park!"

"Who?"

"Remus. His wife. They took her to Bethesda."

At the hospital, he found her friend Laura sitting on a bench in the hallway, hands pressed between her knees. She just shook her head when she saw him. He tried to get back to Imogene, but they wouldn't let him. "It's too late, pal," a doctor finally told him. "I'm sorry."

CHARLIE SAID, "I HEARD SOMEONE CAME INTO THE precinct house and started screaming at him. You hear about that?"

"No."

"Well, come on." Charlie knocked on the door.

Though the labs were downstairs, the smells of the business of that place seeped up to the landing. The men walked down in silence and then along the marbled length of the dim main corridor. It was only when they came to the double doors at the end, where the smells were strongest, that Dodge said, "You're going to go for the chair, aren't you?"

"We'll see, Frank. It's awfully early."

"I mean, if ever there was a case for it—" A steady ticking came from somewhere deep within the great building. "They say she wore black. Did you hear that?"

"No."

"To a divorce." Dodge shook his head. "I assume I'll testify?"

"I imagine," Charlie said. "I mean, we're not there yet—"

"No, I understand. What I mean is, even though I may testify, I want you to use me if you need some leg-work."

"Good," Charlie said. "Yes. Thank you, Frank." He smiled. He had once thought Dodge looked very young, though he was ten years older than Charlie, nearly Remus's age. Now, though, Dodge looked to be in his fifties, with violet smudges beneath his eyes and a tightly drawn mouth. He had been handsome, and had held that for a longer time than many men, but it was gone now. It was not an easy job being an untouchable in a world where both sides, the law and the outlaws, despised you.

"Right now," Charlie said, "let us go in and see to this poor woman." Dodge held the door for him.

HE PICKED UP AN *ENQUIRER* ON THE STREET. A COPY WAITED at home, but he wanted to read during the ride. The story, of course, was front and center. A file photo of the thick-necked Remus, wearing a homburg, and one of Imogene. Charlie looked at her for some time before he began to read, comparing this vital image with the sad blue face, the opaque, half-opened eyes he had just observed. She was pretty, to be sure, but there was another quality, of guile, of mystery, or danger, especially in her eyes. The story described the sensational events of the morning, then filled in the background of the couple: Remus, forty-two, the one-time wealthiest bootlegger in the nation; Imogene, thirty-two, his young bride, his second wife, a war widow herself, and the daughter of a prominent local lawyer named Alfred Ring, who had also died tragically, seven years earlier.

Charlie read a few lines further then came back to this. He'd known Alfred Ring, or had at least met him. It was some years ago. And he remembered later hearing about the death from his father, but that would have been when he was back in New Haven, in law school, after his return from the war. Then, with a start, he sat forward and said, "Oh, God."

"Sir?" said Samuel, from the front.

"I met her."

"Pardon?"

"What?" Charlie said. "I'm sorry, Sam. Talking to myself."

He sat back. And as if through some conjuring trick, an image of that long distant afternoon came back to him as clearly as if he were seeing it now. He had been perhaps sixteen, a year from Yale, from meeting Eleanor, a few years from the horrors of France. It was at a reception in his aunt and uncle's downtown Cincinnati mansion, undoubtedly in honor of his father's presence in the city that the family considered its home, though Charlie had himself lived here only occasionally.

He remembered little of the affair, held as always in the great music room, except the image of this young woman on the porch beyond the series of portals in the east wall. He'd been watching her, staring really, since she had come in. Though she was older, and, he learned, engaged, he couldn't stop himself. As she leaned against the railing overlooking the gardens, her hair lifted in the breezes passing through the open house, and the sunlight seemed to gather itself around her head in a kind of golden bonnet. At that moment she looked up at him.

He remembered flushing and looking away, then chastising himself for acting this way. Later, she came over and introduced herself. She was simply pleasant, he remembered, and bright, and interested most in the myriad places he'd visited around the world. She told him how lucky he was, an adjective he'd grown sick of hearing by the age of six. When she said it, though, it hadn't sounded condescending or admonitory, but wistful, full of her own longing. She had been to London last year, she said, her first trip to Europe, and she couldn't wait to go back.

He tossed the paper aside and watched out the window. Ellie had mentioned meeting her once, at a luncheon. As Imogene Remus. She'd been nearly as well known as her husband, at the peak of their power. Charlie had heard of her, though he'd never paid much attention and certainly never made the connection to the girl he once met. How was it, he wondered, that he'd never put together these facts, that this woman was the daughter of a friend of his father's? But then he realized that that wasn't really the question. It was, How had this well-bred girl, this fortunate daughter, gone from the top of Cincinnati society to being the moll of a bootlegger, to end up being shot dead in the street? That was a journey Charlie could hardly begin to fathom.

As Sam pulled into the drive, Charlie picked up the paper, tore off the corner with her photo, and tucked it into his case.

✸ ✸ ✸

HE FOUND ELEANOR AT THE DINING ROOM TABLE, HER LIPS
tight with disgust. She said, "They're saying she was
pregnant."

He nodded and shrugged. He hadn't heard that.

"Was she, Charlie?"

"I don't have the report yet. I don't know."

"And he was drunk? It's disgusting."

"Where are you hearing this?"

She pointed at the stack of papers on the table. The
tabloid on top screamed out "whiskey killer!" She
said, "I was at Elder Street today, the Findlay Market.
It's all anyone's talking about. Someone said he tried
to kill himself in the jail but they stopped him. Maybe
they shouldn't have."

Charlie put his hands on her shoulders. "That
part," he said, "we'll take care of soon enough."

THE SWIMMER

IN THE EVENING THEY MOVED HIM FROM A HOLDING CELL in the precinct house to the county jail on the upper floors of the courthouse. Now, in the night, alone, he wondered where everyone was. He had lawyers. Then he remembered that they had quit, the last of them, in exasperation at his endless criticism. But surely someone should have come.

Of course, most of them were gone now. Marcus and Stratton and Landau and Hess and Gherum were gone. Zoline and Jess Smith and President Harding. Fowler the valet. All gone. But Conners was not gone. Babe was not gone. At least he didn't think so.

He remembered Babe driving him into the park and that when he'd looked around, later, the car was gone. Babe must have got scared and ran. Well, good for him. Remus hoped Babe was out there in the world, running still.

He had a cell to himself, a wooden bench, a single blanket, wool but thin. No pillow. No mattress or sheets upon the hard bench. The brick walls glowed cold. His shoulder, especially, ached. Sitting up took some pressure off it. He wedged himself into a corner and dozed and woke back into damp darkness, shivering harder and aching more deeply as the night wore on.

At one of her magnificent parties, the bright lighting made his eyes water. He looked at all the fine people in their fine clothing. He stood at the head of a table as long as a tennis court and held up a glass. The guests grew silent. He offered them well-chosen words of hope and good cheer. They smiled and offered their glasses to him.

The staff brought the food then, course after course of finely wrought delicacies in the form of wide flat bowls of a swirled orange and yellow soup, twisted knuckles of warm breads, selections of delicate and exotic appetizers. He could name none of them, though she had told him half a dozen times the names of each. It mattered to her to name what they had constructed, to name each particular element of it, as if by so doing, by cataloging and ordering, it could somehow be preserved. Escargot, he remembered then. Chewy grubs marinated in hot garlic butter, and threaded back into perfect shells. He had laughed at this indulgence, the stuffing of dead mollusks into new shells, so that one could simply have the pleasure of taking the tiny fork in hand and pulling them out again, of feeling the slight suck of the vacuum they had formed.

God, he was cold. He'd always lived for the cold, for the waters or the black nights. But this creeping insidious jailhouse chill was not that. You needed to move. If you could move, you could let it pull you in and just go where it took you, and come out better for it at the end.

Once it had been the pier by the grounds of the old world's fair in South Chicago. As he shed the heavy woolen trousers and jacket his mother still dressed him in (though he was nearly fourteen), he gazed out across the unbounded expanse of it. The flat gray swells rose and fell as if the whole thing were some breathing, many-lunged creature, each lung expanding and contracting separately but in complex synchronicity. He'd never tried it this early. Small floes of ice still dotted the surface.

As he walked from the pier toward the stone breakwater to the north, his feet left scalloped depressions in the dirty sand. In the summer, he could swim for two hours, but now it would be enough just to make it from the breakwater to the pier. A quarter of a mile. Nothing, really, except in this cold.

The lake slapped at the end of the wall. The perpetual wind, frigid, heavy with moisture, whipped about him. He shivered, breathing, looking. Nothing. Nothing. His mind blank, in the way he could make it. He dove.

Oh, the ice of it, the blinding, numbing frigidity. The gray water hugged him to its bosom, sucked him down and squeezed him as his mother did sometimes, so tightly he couldn't breathe. His mind dimmed; he saw sparkles, then darkness, until the ice shot through clear to his spine, to his heart and brain and the core of his gut, and burned, and he came back.

He broke through a swell into the gray light, into the air. The swells lifted him. The great gray city, his city, Chicago, lay before him. A rail ran along the shoreline, the steam from a locomotive coming toward him. Farther up haze rolled from the mouth of the river, from the factories and foundries and refineries that lined it. Beyond that he could not see, but he knew what was there—the green money haze of Lincoln Park, the part of the city that did not belong to him. Not yet.

He broke toward the pier, arms cutting, legs grinding, face turning between the lighter gray of the air and the darker gray of the water. He swam to stay alive. But halfway across he knew he wasn't going to make it. He felt his muscles locking up, and he suddenly couldn't breathe. He stopped and trod, gasping, looking up at the dimming sky. He had never been so frightened. He imagined his body, gray now as the water, slowly sinking, spinning, to the eternal warmth at the bottom. That vision made him move against the pain. Then he forgot where he was, forgot how to breathe, and inhaled the fishy, greasy water, and choked.

Then he was crawling onto the pier's rough planking. The water he vomited steamed on the wood. He felt hands rubbing him, a coat thrown over him.

"Crazy damn kid." A man walking in the fairgrounds had seen him go in. The man rubbed until George began to feel his arms again, until he could walk back to the bench and get dressed.

He looked back out over the gray water.

"You try that again," the man said, "they'll be tossing the hooks for you."

He knew he'd had no business going in. He loved to swim, but that hadn't been why. It was something else, a thing he needed to understand. To try. To know he could do. He was alive. He hid a smile. His arms and his legs burned as the blood and the feeling returned.

IN THE MORNING, A DEPUTY CARRYING A STEEL RING OF keys opened the barred door and motioned for him to follow. They entered a stairwell. Up a flight, on the top floor, they passed along a narrow walkway between storage cages full of furniture and file cabinets and boxes and racks of uniforms, and through a doorway into a small suite. The deputy backed out and closed the door behind him. Remus didn't understand.

One of the rooms held a bare mattress on a frame, the other an old deeply stuffed cracked-leather sofa. In the bathroom, he ran water until it warmed, then held his hands under it and worked the stiffness from his knuckles. There were no towels, so he wiped them on his trousers, which were filthy anyway.

The door opened. A man in a brown suit came in. "Mr. Remus," he said. "Sheriff Anderson. It's been some time." He held out his hand, which Remus took, though he did not recognize the name nor remember the man's face.

"How is this? It's not luxury, but—"

"I don't understand—"

"Well, exactly," the sheriff said. "I apologize for all that last night. I didn't understand at first, either."

"One gets what one deserves."

"Deserves," Anderson said. "Exactly. You put my two children through the university, sir. Are you aware of that?"

"I . . . wasn't," Remus said.

Anderson nodded solemnly. "These rooms are yours for as long as you're with us. Think of what you'll be needing."

Remus looked around at the space. What would one need? He felt his wet trousers. "Towels," he said.

Anderson laughed. "You can even have a telephone installed, if you like. You'll have to arrange for the billing, of course."

"Of course," Remus said. "I . . . thank you for this."

"Not at all," said the sheriff. "Oh, you have a visitor, a Mr. Conners."

Remus felt his throat tighten. Conners had always been the best of them. It turned out he'd been at the precinct house, unaware that Remus had been moved until early this morning. They embraced. Conners put his hands on Remus's face and shook him and said, "What have you done, George Remus?"

A deputy brought in a low table and a pot of hot coffee. As Conners poured, he said, "We have to talk."

"Yes," said Remus. "I don't really remember it."

"You confessed."

"Yes."

Conners told him what he knew, which was only spotty.

Remus remembered a detective coming back to his cell in the precinct house and saying, "Well, you've done it. She's dead." When the detective led him back into the central booking chamber, someone screamed at him, "You killer! You crazy bastard!" and tried to get to him, but the detective hustled him away, down a hallway toward a quiet room where they could talk.

Now it was a new day. The coffee was warm. Now he would begin to figure out what to do.

Conners said, "The press wants to know . . ."

"I'll talk to them."

"Do you think it's wise?" Conners was silent a moment, then said, "The sheriff said you have a preliminary hearing at one."

"Do you remember him?"

"Anderson? Yes," Conners said. "Very well, actually. You?"

"No. But he was a good man, wasn't he?"

"He was good."

"He must have been," said Remus.

AT HIS ARRAIGNMENT IN THE MUNICIPAL COURT, HE FELT strong. He spoke clearly and held the judge in his gaze. He clasped his hands behind his back. He remembered this, the beat of the world inside the bar.

"Your Honor," he said. "I plead not guilty." He heard the rustle of the pages of the reporters behind him. Oh, he felt the strength of it all now coming together within him.

Later, at the press conference, he wore the same navy suit but had changed into a silk shirt and a fine pale yellow tie. He looked at each reporter in turn as they stared collectively back.

"George Remus is not insane," he declared. "I am responsible for my actions. What I did was justified, and that shall be my defense. Morally justifiable homicide."

As to the question of counsel, he claimed he had no

money for lawyers. Yet he held up two telegrams, one from the noted Chicago criminal lawyer W. W. O'Brien (a partner of Clarence Darrow), and the other from the former Chicago federal prosecutor Hugh Daly, both offering their services at no charge.

"Regardless of money, Remus's lawyer shall be Remus," he declared. "It's my life in the balance. I'll defend myself."

At the hearing, he'd made the same pronouncement.

"Can you remain unbiased, unaffected by your emotions?" the judge had asked.

"No good lawyer remains unaffected by his emotions, Your Honor."

"It's a very difficult undertaking you propose, Mr. Remus," the judge said. "To be fair to oneself—"

"Judge, I can only say that it's as if I'm two separate beings. As if Remus the defendant exists there, and Remus the lawyer stands here. I cannot explain it except to say that one role does not trespass upon the other. That my emotions, thoughts, powers of reason, are somehow entirely separated."

"Mr. Taft?" the judge said.

"The state has no objection," said Charlie. "Mr. Remus, the lawyer, should know that we're convening a new grand jury on Monday, and that his client will be its first order of business."

"We thank you," Remus said, glancing over.

"Also, Your Honor," said Charlie, "the state is arranging for an alienist to examine Mr. Remus at the earliest possible date. Certainly this week."

"We ask the court to waive such examination,"

Remus replied immediately. "Whoever would suggest Remus is insane, that's who needs the examination."

Though he was topic "A" at the grand jury proceedings, Remus went nowhere near it. They didn't need him to know what he'd done. At the end of that week, the indictment came down as expected: that George Remus did kill and murder his wife, Imogene.

TEARDROPS

ELEANOR PEEKED BETWEEN THE DRAPES AS CHARLIE ate breakfast, but said nothing. They'd already discussed it the day before.

"Why do they come here, Charlie?"

"Maybe they think I'll talk to them here."

"You're not going to, though?"

"No," he said.

"Your father's right."

"As always."

"My dear son," the latest letter from the chief justice began. "Because your opponent has clearly chosen to try this case in the media, the temptation must be great for you to do the same. Resist it. Not only will it cheapen your image, it will weaken your chances. The element of mystery, of never letting the defense get itself quite set against your strategy, is valuable above all else. I have great faith in you, Charles." It was signed, simply, "Your father."

At the front door, Eleanor held the lapels of his overcoat. She drew him to her and leaned her face against his chest. He kissed the top of her head. The children were all in bed still.

"Kiss them for me," he said.

When he stepped out, he surprised them. It was only seven; he usually left at seven-thirty or eight. But that quickly they were upon him, pressing in, shouting questions, scribbling on their little pads. Cameras snapped and flashed though the papers had already run this photo—The Prosecutor Leaving for Work.

"Please, Mr. Taft, any statement," one shouted.

He stopped. "Here's a statement," he said. "Get off my lawn. If you have any hopes of communication from this office, stay away from my house."

They stared at him. In the first moment he thought it was in reaction to his rebuke, that he'd made some small headway. But then he knew they were just waiting for something else, having succeeded in getting him to speak at all.

He shoved through them toward Samuel, who waited at the rear door of the Pierce-Arrow.

IN THE QUIET OF THE BACKSEAT, CHARLIE OPENED THE morning's *Enquirer*. It was true, what his father said—Remus was using the media. The Remus press conference had been a circus, the man, turned out in his fine suit, acting like a fool. A defense of morally justifiable homicide. They'd had a good laugh around the office at that. Walt Sibbald, Charlie's first assistant, had already worked up a Remus impersonation.

"Well," he said, blowing out his cheeks to mimic Remus's size, and aping the self-important tone, "what can I say? The lady just . . . needed killin'. That's all there was to it. Any jury'll see that."

Charlie smiled and folded the paper. In his office

waited a stack of others: the Cincinnati *Post* and *Times-Star* as well as dailies from St. Louis and Columbus and Toledo and Lansing and Chicago. Remus's man, Conners, had men in these cities searching for possessions or cash that Imogene had allegedly stashed in warehouses and safe deposit boxes, and which Remus claimed belonged to him. The press had taken to following the men around, speculating on what they might find.

As they came into downtown, he looked at the paper again. *a dry autumn,* it said. Hadn't rained in two weeks. A thought occurred to him, a thing he'd neglected to do, for some reason. As they approached Court Street, Charlie leaned forward and said, "Sam, how would you feel about a morning of hooky?"

"That's fine, sir."

"You remember where the shooting happened?"

"The lady, Mrs. Remus?"

"Yes."

"I believe I do."

"Let's go there."

They followed Seventh east until it turned into Gilbert Avenue and started up Mount Adams. The gears of the great car sang as it climbed. Sam turned onto Eden Park Drive, passed the museum, then slowed as they came to the reservoir.

"This is fine. Thank you, Sam," Charlie said. He got out and walked past the gazebo, across the road, and a little ways up the hillside, then stopped. It was still quiet, the real rush hour not having quite begun. Before long these roads would be jammed with traffic heading down.

As he stood looking back at the spot, he tried to imagine it: the taxi run off the road, women screaming, other motorcars stopped all around, the drivers watching, the muscular Remus leering, Imogene running for her life as he fired. What must it be like to see a thing like that? He'd seen plenty of killing, himself, more than any ten men ever deserved to see. He had fought the Boche near Chaumont as an artillery gunner, and later as an officer at Verdun. And he had killed more of them than he cared to count. But that was different, killing men who were coming to kill you, men who threatened nothing less than the free world as it was known, aggressors, oppressors, murderers. Huns. That was one thing. But shooting an unarmed woman, a pretty, well-dressed, elegant woman, in the middle of rush hour in the middle of Eden Park in the middle of Cincinnati, Ohio, my God, he thought, that was another thing altogether, and one he just could not comprehend. What could possibly drive a man to it?

He walked back toward the road.

Could a festering hatred grow so foul that it blinded you to all consequences? Given that you had it in you to kill and that you had decided irrevocably to do it, wouldn't it make sense, at least, to be discreet? To allow yourself at least some possibility of escape?

Remus, who had been so cloaked, so covert, at the beginning of his criminal career, had become a grandstander toward the end. That, too, was a foreign impulse to Charlie. But perhaps that inclination, combined with the hatred, the sense of loss and jealousy and bitterness, explained it. He needed not just to kill her, but to do it publicly, to demonstrate the depth of his agony, the extent of her betrayal. To paint himself as the victim, in some pathetic way.

Or was it something else, a sudden rage so explosive that it was simply uncontrollable? Again, this was not an emotion Charlie could re-create in himself. He could only imagine it abstractly. Even after seeing his friends and comrades slaughtered, he had killed with icy calculation. There had been no room in France for other emotions. The men who let them come either died or cracked.

Or insanity, he supposed. That might explain it. But he wasn't going to allow that, not in this case. Remus was no more insane than any other man on the street that morning. He hadn't tried to play that card yet, but the possibility still floated out there. The game was still very new.

Charlie made a note to talk with Walt about this question of motivation. It intrigued him.

A gust of wind came up and whistled in the treetops. He knelt at the curb and listened again. A motorcar passed.

He saw it, then. On a rounded cobblestone. There had been no rain. A dark splash, a tear-shaped stain. Blood. He had not bothered to look for it before, when he was here. Its apex pointed to the south. She had run this way. A chill passed through him, and a shudder of the excitement of discovery, of touching a hidden thing.

He waited for another machine to pass, then stepped into the road and bent over. Here, another stain a few stones farther up. And there, another, beyond that. Connecting dots. A car came and pulled abruptly into the oncoming lane with a toot of its horn. He did not look up at it. Here, now, a large black splash, the size of a man's fist. No teardrop this. He squatted and brushed his fingers over it.

The teardrops resumed. More splashes. He followed until the trail ended abruptly. This must be where she was loaded into the vehicle that took her in.

He straightened and felt a slight wave of dizziness. Sam watched him through the glass of the Pierce-Arrow fifty yards back. The wind whispered. Remus must have walked off somewhere in here, up this hill.

It occurred to him that Remus was a Hun.

She had worn black, Dodge said. To a divorce.

What in Christ's name would possess a man to do this?

He waved Sam forward.

"The Alms," he said as he got in.

"A TERRIBLE BUSINESS," THE MANAGER WAS SAYING. "Terrible. She was a longtime resident. We knew her well."

"How long?" Charlie asked.

"Oh, on and off for years. She closed up the house, you know, sometime after he, Mr. Remus, went to prison. In '24 or '25. This became her home, in Cincinnati."

"I know the detectives must have interviewed you on the morning of the shooting."

"No. Wasn't here, I'm afraid. Happenstance. Didn't see a thing. Heard about it when I got back."

"Well, anyway, can you show me the room?"

Charlie followed the manager into the elevator. He said, "Did you ever see him?"

"Who?"

"Remus?"

"Oh, well, yes."

"He visited her?"

"Well, now, years earlier, in '20, perhaps, or '21, there was a time when she stayed here. He put her up, paid all the bills, for a couple of months."

"Is that right?"

"Yessir. Up 'til they were married. I was the assistant manager back then."

THEY SAT TOGETHER IN THE RESTAURANT OR THE LOBBY, hands clasped, heads together. She'd laugh at the things he said, a delighted, girlish laugh. He just watched her, as if to assure himself she were real. You could see them there often, like that.

Sometimes she'd disappear. Then a few minutes later he'd be gone, too. You were to think he'd left, but of course he hadn't. The assistant manager knew where he'd gone. Others knew, as well. It was against the law, a violation of the Mann Act, but what could they do? Mr. Remus paid the hotel a lot of money. It bought, among other things, a certain blindness.

WHAT STRUCK CHARLIE FIRST WAS THE SUN POURING through the windows of the breakfast alcove. That was why she'd chosen it. She knew the hotel well and she had money, so she would have told them where to put her. A nice southeast corner suite that caught the luxurious morning sunlight.

Directly beneath the window sat a small wicker breakfast table and chairs. Across from the alcove, a chintz sofa and chair, a desk and lamp, then a separate bedroom. A comfortable space. According to Remus, she'd stolen millions of his dollars.

The bedroom floor was piled with clothing the detectives had stripped from the armoire. The bureau drawers stood open. They were stuffed with more clothing, except one, which was filled with shoes. Her purses had been emptied onto the bed.

In the bathroom, the stuff of a woman's toilet—makeup, brushes, soap, perfume, a conditioning salve for younger-looking skin—lay scattered on the counter. Her mess or the detectives'? A floral scent lingered. He bent and sniffed the perfume atomizer with its little cloth bulb. Lilac. He looked at himself in the mirror, straightened his tie.

In the room he took off his coat and laid it on the back of the chintz chair. In the bedroom again, he stood, looking. Some of her undergarments hung from the third bureau drawer. He wondered if the detectives had taken any special interest in them, held them up to each other, whistled maybe. What a humiliation, to have your life exposed. But that was just death. Every death was ignominious.

On the bed, he saw, it was not just the contents of the purses. A carved wooden box lay overturned as well, its lid beside it. He moved it. Two photographs lay beneath it. In the first a mother and a father stood on either side of a pony, upon which sat a girl of perhaps ten. It was the lawyer Ring and his wife and his daughter, Imogene. None of them smiled, but they did not look unhappy. The second photograph was of a smiling uniformed soldier, an Enfield resting in his arms. Her first husband. Eleanor had an almost identical shot of Charlie somewhere among her possessions.

Next to the photographs lay a small book with a green leather binding and a leather band with a metal clasp that fit into a lock attached to the front. The band had been cut. The first entry was dated March 15, 1920, the last, May 23, 1921. That's why the detectives had left it. It didn't concern them.

She would have been twenty-five, twenty-six, years old.

Charlie carried it out to the wicker glass-topped table in the alcove in the lovely cascading rails of light. He sat in a wicker chair and crossed his legs, and read:

Monday, March 15, 1920

I need to walk, especially when I can't help being in this city. To be out of the stuffiness, in the air, the rain, the light, to breathe . . .

Sometimes Laura walks with me. After I retrieve her from Father's offices, we window shop along the Eastern Row, then walk west into the city center. Traffic is terribly heavy, streams of motorcars and horse carriages and the electric streetcars, and I wonder sometimes what will happen, one day, when it all just gets so busy no one can move . . .

A FINE BORDEAUX

FARTHER NORTH THEY WENT, SOMETIMES CLEAR TO THE Findlay Market past the hawking vendors with their carts of fruit or bread or fish or flowers or vegetables, and the people shouting and dealing and trading and carrying baskets of the goods they'd purchased. Sometimes they spent the entire time just walking, hungry only for talk and sometimes not even that, for Laura knew everything, more even than Father and Mother, so what need was there to talk of it? So much was in the past now, receding faster and faster each day into history where it would stay forever. But what the past had wrought had left her here, alone but bound, frustrated, unhappy. Sometimes she felt sorry for herself. She told Laura she was horrible and spoiled and Laura should just tell her to stop it, and sometimes Laura did.

Laura was five years older. She was thirty and she'd worked for Imogene's father for ten years. From the beginning, when Imogene was still practically a girl, Imogene had worshiped her, and Laura had taken her in, shared confidences, listened. It had changed between them, of course, as Imogene grew up and found her place in the world, which was a very different place than Laura's, but they had remained close, and there were still things Imogene told Laura that no one else knew.

ON WEDNESDAY IT WAS TO BE THE SINTON—GOOD FOOD, sublime food, was as much a release sometimes as walking.

She arrived at the offices at noon. Laura was finishing something so she sat outside the oak balustrade where the clients waited. She had a view back into a conference room where this new client, George Remus, sat alone, writing, waiting no doubt for Father. She knew from the way Father spoke of Remus that he was pleased to have him, which simply meant that Remus would generate plenty of income. He was in some lucrative business or other.

A radiator hissed and high overhead a wooden fan forced the heated air back down, but it already felt hot and dry. Outside a streetcar passed loudly and in its wake, the sounds of traffic—the wheezy percolations of motorcars, the clacking of hooves and the heavy rumble of wagons, the voices of the pedestrians who risked their very lives passing through it all—rose together and were amplified in the high domed plaster and wood overhead. She watched Mr. Remus working when suddenly he looked up at her, directly into her eyes. She looked away for a moment, then back. She smiled, and he nodded. He continued to look. She did not feel that she could look away. It was rude to stare, but he seemed to imply nothing by it nor did he seem self-conscious, he just looked, regarding, as if he were thinking of something far away, as if they were both far away, someplace else altogether.

"Imogene. A word?" It was her father. She followed him back, rolling her eyes at Laura as she passed. Laura smiled.

He shut his office door and said, "One A.M.?"

"Father?"

"And your mother tells me she smelled liquor on your clothing, and cigarette smoke."

"Does it strike you as odd that Mother sniffs my clothing? It does me."

"Imogene," he said. "You're out with these sorts of . . . people who . . ."

"Just because it's illegal now—" She knew he kept bottles of it locked away in his study.

"It's not the legality, but the sort of person who drinks it in public, who goes to these places."

"I don't know what you mean. I go to hear the music. I'm certainly not getting drunk, if that's what you're asking."

"Music." He didn't even like her to play rags on the piano at home. He said, "You have a station in this city, Imogene. You've suffered a terrible tragedy, but it doesn't excuse . . . this sort of thing. And now that you're living under my roof again—"

"Perhaps I shouldn't."

"Don't be insolent. I'm just asking you to have a little courtesy, to show a little decency. That's all."

Someone knocked, then immediately opened the door. It was this man, Remus. "I apologize," he said, "but I'm pressed, Alfred. If I could leave this, perhaps you could ring me—"

"Yes, yes," Ring said. "Of course. Leave it with Laura, will you?"

Remus hung in the doorway a moment, looking at her. He simply stared, as he had before. She felt compelled to say something, but as she opened her mouth, he shut the door.

"New client," her father said.

"So you've said. You should have introduced us."

"He's no one you want to meet."

"Really."

"No. In fact . . . no."

"I see."

"Just please think about what I've said, Imogene. I know how difficult it's been—"

"No, Father," she said. "You don't. But I won't go anymore." A lie, but God, she couldn't stand to listen to him sometimes. "The last thing I want is to make you and Mother uncomfortable."

Outside, she slipped her arm through Laura's as they walked.

"So," Laura said. "What did the mysterious Mr. Remus have to say?"

"Why, nothing at all. I think he's a bit rude."

THE GRAND CAFÉ IN THE SINTON HOTEL WAS HER favorite, especially with Laura, though Laura couldn't afford it too often. It was not the fact of being seen there, of rubbing shoulders with the right ladies in the right hats. She loved the staff, the assuredness of a waiter's hand, the slight crackling of his starched sleeve, the white gloves of the captain, Jean, who knew her of course and bowed just slightly; she loved the food, the grilled lamb chops or the roasted tenderloin or the smoked salmon, always perfect and always too much so she and Laura split the main course; she loved the room itself, the high ceiling with its colored-glass skylight and the corner pillars of terra-cotta embedded with Rookwood tiles and the huge painted murals high up on the walls and the marble squares of the floor. It all seemed to dampen unnecessary noise, so that you could talk and not be overheard, your words rising straight up into the air.

Jean, who was French, bowed and the hatted ladies looked up. Jean showed them to the back of the high open room, to a corner banquette where you sat to eat and talk but not to be seen. The special today was a brioche of capon livers with new peas. They ordered that. Normally she didn't care much for chicken liver, but the way they sautéed it and then tucked it into the crumbly crust with sweet onions and peppers and spices was wonderful and she knew Laura loved it.

Laura spread white butter on a piece of the good warm bread. "I miss the Bordeaux," she said. They had always split a bottle, which was a little much for lunch but once a month it was a fine thing to do. Then in January Prohibition came in.

"They could probably get you some," Imogene said. "I mean, who would care?"

"They wouldn't," Laura said. "They can't."

Imogene waved at Jean.

"What if you get caught?" said Laura. "What do they do to you?"

"Oh, not much, I hear. A fine or something."

Jean came over and leaned down. "We so miss the wine," Imogene said. "Is it at all possible—?"

"I'm sorry, madame," Jean said. Imogene smiled and nodded.

Laura sipped at her tea, which was not Bordeaux, and said, "He is very mysterious, though, isn't he? Remus, I mean."

"Are we still talking about him?"

"No one knows exactly what it is he does."

"I'm sure he's just another boring businessman, Laura."

"They say he's a criminal."

Imogene laughed.

"I know this," Laura said. "He works at all kinds of strange hours. Your father has people running halfway through the night up to his rooms here."

"Here?" Imogene said. "He lives at the Sinton?"

"Oh, yes, in a suite. He doesn't even have a proper office. I hear he's quite well off, but they say all he does is work. He's obsessed with it. It's just that no one knows what 'it' is."

The order came. The smell of the liver with its spices was so rich she felt the saliva run in her mouth and she wasn't even particularly hungry, but even if she had been she could have simply breathed in that smell and it would have been enough. Jean made sure the waiter set the dish between them and that they each got a clean white plate. When it was ready, he served, lifting the delicate slices of brioche with serving forks and setting them on the plates, then lifting the onion and other bits of goodness too and setting that on the slices.

As they ate, Jean came back carrying a white porcelain teapot. He nodded at a waiter, who cleared away the identical one already on their table, and their cups, and set down clean ones.

"Courtesy of . . . the gentleman," Jean said, and nodded toward the arched entranceway where Remus stood, watching them.

Imogene said, "I don't understand."

Jean poured. The tea that came out had the hue of venous blood. Jean said softly, "A fine Bordeaux." He held his hand out, palm down, to indicate the desirability of discretion, and said, *"Bon appétit."*

Imogene looked again at the doorway, but it was empty now.

A LAWYER'S LAWYER

CONNERS BROUGHT IN A MAN IN A WELL-TAILORED TWEED suit with a gold fob and a homburg pressed firmly on his head.

"George," Conners said. "I think . . . I want you to—"

"Carl Elston," the man said.

Remus looked at the man's face, and at the hand he offered. "What is this?" he said. "Mr. Conners, what are you doing?" Elston, of course, was the attorney who had recently defeated Charlie Taft on behalf of the gangster Fat Wrassman.

"Listen," Conners said. "Listen to him, George."

"I am my attorney."

"It's a smart strategy," Elston said. He smiled, took off the homburg, and sat down on the leather sofa. He wore his hair oiled and combed back from his rounded, puffy face. His eyes were set too close together, though they shined with the spark Remus had always looked for in his men. Remus knew good men. Elston shifted a little, settling himself, draped one leg casually across the other, and stretched an arm along the back of the sofa.

"Please," said Remus, standing before him. "Make yourself comfortable."

"Smart but for one thing," the attorney, Elston, said, "and you know it well, Mr. Remus. That old saw—the lawyer who represents himself has a fool for a client."

"That'll be all, Mr. Elston," said Remus. "Thank you for your time."

"How are you going to do the legwork?" Elston uncrossed his legs and leaned forward, bracing his forearms on his thighs. "You've been denied bond. You're stuck here, comfortable as these rooms may be. Mr. Conners has shown me the list of depositions you want gathered. That's dozens, maybe hundreds, of hours of work right there, and all over the country. Also, excuse my saying it, but it's been a good long time since you've argued before a jury. Then there's the simple fact that this is your life. I read what you said to the judge, but in the end, you're not two people, sir, and you know it. Somewhere you're going to be blinded to a misstep. Maybe only once. But once is all Charlie Taft will need."

"*I* represent George Remus."

Elston's eyes flicked to Conners, then back. "I said that's fine, a good strategy. But you need a co-counsel, someone as quick and aggressive as yourself, but who is not yourself. Or you won't survive." He leaned back again. "I don't need the work, Mr. Remus. This case will preoccupy whoever takes it for several months. I don't have those months to spare. But it interests me. You interest me. The situation interests me."

"I'm sure the national exposure hasn't crossed your mind."

"So what if it has? I'm the best criminal lawyer in this city. I'm offering you my services. Not, though, I should say, gratis, as your Chicago friends have. I'm expensive. My initial retainer for a murder is a thousand dollars. If it's true, as you've said publicly, that you have no money, then I shouldn't have troubled you."

"I'm sure that if Conners hadn't assured you we might find your fee somewhere, you wouldn't have bothered coming up. It happens that the notion of a co-counsel has crossed my mind, largely, as you say, because of the constraints on my situation."

Remus looked hard into the bright, too-close eyes. He could smell the hair oil, which he did not like. "I'll be arraigned now that the grand jury has indicted," he said.

"Chester Shook will get the case."

"You know this?"

Elston nodded.

Remus regarded the man for several moments, then pulled a straight chair around from the table and sat.

"How—"

"It doesn't matter. He's not as bad as you could have done, though he was a prosecutor, so we have to assume he'll lean that way. He usually does. Still, he's fair enough."

Remus was silent, thinking. He stood again and looked out the barred window over the city.

Elston said, "You were a trial lawyer, once."

"Yes."

"I understand you were successful."

"Sometimes. Sometimes not. When you lose at

criminal law, though, Mr. Elston, it's not like losing at other endeavors."

"That's why I try not to do it."

"I couldn't do it any longer," Remus said. "I lost enough. My last client was a man named Gillenbeck, a lawyer himself who came home one afternoon, shot his wife, then made love to her. No one denied his insanity, yet they sentenced him to hang."

Oh, he had raged for this crazy man. The Chicago judges hated him, anyway. He screamed in their court-rooms, sweated, threw papers. He did his own jail time, for contempt, and paid hundreds in fines. Fuck them, was his motto. The people loved him. And so he screamed for Leo Gillenbeck, and appealed, and pled. And failed.

"He hanged?"

"In early '19. I remember it . . . vividly."

The wind had raced so quickly over the walls and through the open ports of the lookouts and turrets at Joliet that it moaned. Gillenbeck looked serenely out over them, having no idea where he was. The exe-cutioner lowered the mask and cinched the noose and stood stiffly at the iron lever. Gillenbeck's father wept. The warden nodded. It seemed, finally, so sud-den that Remus nearly yelled. Gillenbeck plunged toward the earth but was stopped several feet short of it with a sharp commingled cracking of rope and cer-vical vertebrae. The large leg muscles contracted, sending waves up the rope. Then it was silent but for the wind and Gillenbeck's father's sobbing. Remus breathed in the smell of that fetid place. And he knew he was finished.

"So, just like that, you walked away from your whole life?"

"It had already begun to crumble. Inside me, it had crumbled long before that." He'd come home at night and look at his wife, Lillian, a stocky, healthy woman, five years his senior, and at his beautiful daughter, Romola, and know that it had died. He'd come so far—a pharmacist at seventeen, the owner of two stores by twenty, law school, a practice, this house, this child. And he wept, because what he'd achieved was already done, past. It didn't matter. It never mattered, what you had. All that mattered was what was out there in the world still. That's what drove him, what had always driven him, from the North Chicago tenements to the drug counter to law school. And now, again. It would drive him to Cincinnati, where he had glimpsed the newest, greatest possibility.

"And you came here to sell whiskey."

"What I did was not, technically, illegal."

Conners, who'd listened silently until then, said, "You can't imagine it. What George foresaw here, what he understood, was nothing less than genius."

Later, as he was getting ready to leave, Elston said, "We'll need to talk about that morning, in the park."

"I can't remember it."

Elston had stood up, but he sat back down and was quiet for a long time. Remus started to say something, but Elston said, "It's all right." He put his hand on Remus's knee. "Don't think about it. Let me handle it."

"Yes," Remus said. "Yes. But if I can't—"

"It doesn't matter. Trust me."

After they had gone, as he lay in the quiet, the city humming far below, its lights playing across the ceiling, he thought, it does matter. To remember. He could remember years ago, moments so clear it felt as if he could touch them.

In the beginning, her hair was a dark blond, almost exactly the color of a type of fried honey cake they sold in a bakery he'd discovered on Eighth Street. She wore it cut sharply across the forehead in bangs, then on an angle along her cheek. Her skin was so clear and pale that even from across the office he could make out the blush in her cheeks. Her eyes, he thought, were dark.

It was only after their third or fourth encounter that she spoke to him. He'd stopped up to leave some documents with Laura and found Imogene sitting in the waiting area.

She stood up. She said, "I've been remiss in not thanking you. For your gift the other week."

She smelled of lilacs. "It was nothing . . ."

"On the contrary. We enjoyed it very much."

He saw that he'd been wrong. They were not dark, her eyes, though not pale either, but a medium-toned gray highlighted by bright flecks. The first time, before he realized who she was, he'd seen something in those eyes, glimpsed some depth, felt some connection that was new to him. Also, he'd remembered her as particularly slender, but saw now that she had what one might call a healthy bosom, rounded and well-defined. And her ankle-length skirt did nothing to hide her hips and posterior; rather it and the wide sash girding her waist set them off in such a manner that he found he could not, after all, look at her for very long.

"We haven't actually met. I'm George Remus."

"From Chicago," she said. "You were a lawyer there, no?"

"Does your father let you read all his clients' files, or just the interesting ones?"

She lifted the end of the sash around her waist and examined it. "Am I being terribly rude?"

"Not at all. You seem very good at being rude."

This evoked from her a short, bell-like laugh. Then her father cleared his throat from the doorway of his office. Imogene excused herself.

He knew what Ring thought of him—a dirty Hun, peasant stock who'd happened to fall into some money. Of course Ring took it. They all took it. But no one liked the Boche anymore, not after the war. Even this city, which was so full of Germans, had just Anglicized all the old Teutonic street names. Bremen Street became Republic. Frankfurt Avenue became Connecticut. Berlin became Woodrow.

He knew what he was, and what Imogene was. Beyond that, he knew only that there was something odd in her life, some wrinkle he hadn't yet identified, and that he couldn't help but think of her. The thoughts were such a mixture of the lovely and the painful—her voice and her scent juxtaposed with the snotty, spoiled look she got sometimes and the obvious fact that she saw him as dirt under her shoes— that it was somehow more pleasant, or perhaps more bearable, than if he had believed he might truly have a chance with her.

As he lay in his Sinton suite and tried to conjure her face, though, he got only pieces. Her mouth came to him—the word *ripe,* tawdry as he thought that sounded, came to mind. He saw a variegated eye with its narrow, well-groomed brow.

Now, all these remarkable years later, on the cot in his jailhouse suite, he found it happening in reverse. She was disappearing. That face was leaving him, with a wink, a fleeting smile.

The sensation reminded him of the time when he was five and they'd just come over from Friedeburg, the seven of them, to live in three tiny rooms in the black building with the black sweating hallways where the smells of piss and fish and cabbage hung like shrouds, and their uncle, the pharmacist, would come to visit. He lived with his American wife and son in a brick house with a yard and never brought them to the tenements. But whenever he came, he'd take a sharp new one-dollar note from his billfold and hold it at the end and instruct each of them in turn to place their thumb and forefinger on either side of it, at the center. If they were quick and caught it after he let go, they could keep it. Such a simple thing. A dollar. A fortune.

You are vatching are you not? he would say.

They would concentrate with all their will.

Vatch, he would say. Focus. Conzentrate. You must pay attention. Are you vatching? And it was gone, past their fingers, riding the air back and forth in lazy waves to the floor.

MOTIONS

THE SIZE OF THE PACK OF REPORTERS OUTSIDE HIS HOUSE had increased. As Charlie pressed past them toward the car, a single voice rose above the din: "Have you heard Elston's moved to have the insanity laws overturned?"

Charlie stopped. He said, "What did you say?"

Now they had drawn blood. They shouted and pushed. He shoved through them. But they grew hysterical, knocking into him, making him stumble. Samuel held out his arms, blocking them, so Charlie could throw himself into the rear of the machine.

Then it was quiet. But Charlie hadn't heard them anymore. He was lost in the thought of what this meant if what the reporter said was true: that Remus, who had yet to enter a formal plea to the grand jury's indictment, was changing his defense.

THE OFFICES OF THE HAMILTON COUNTY PROSECUTING attorney, on the second floor of the county courthouse, were a linear series of some dozen rooms. Each was spacious and well appointed, though the one at the end of the hall, the chief's, was the largest and nicest. It was actually a two-room suite, but the main chamber itself was easily four hundred square feet, with high, arched, many-paned windows running from ceiling to floor. The walls were paneled with a thick veneer of wormy chestnut, and the desk and other furniture had all been cut and milled from a single lot of finely grained Ohio black walnut.

As Charlie passed through the outer receptionist's vestibule, he found both of his secretaries, Walt Sibbald, several of the assistant prosecutors, and the mayor's press secretary waiting. They had apparently heard, too. And like the reporters, they all, except Walt, began flinging questions at him. Walt merely inclined his head toward Charlie's office door.

Charlie held up his hands until they grew quiet. "I'll speak with Walt, alone," he said. "Then we'll begin."

CHARLIE WAS BUILT PROPORTIONALLY, WITH A PLEASING BALanced look, a kind of athletic tension to his step, and a body that appeared both compact and lithe. Walter, some said, looked like a young and struggling tree. He was very tall and round-shouldered and exceedingly slender but for the startlingly prominent dual protrusions of his Adam's apple and nose. He wore round spectacles, favored drab flannel suits and knitted argyle vests, and looked, it was agreed, more like a professor of Latin than a prosecutor. And yet, in the beginning, Walter had been Charlie's Trojan horse. When defenders first saw him, they assumed they'd been given a gift. It was only after Walter had systematically and dispassionately ripped them apart that they realized otherwise. Of course now, after a year in office, Walter was nearly as well known as Charlie.

When they were seated, Charlie behind the massive desk, Walt with his legs crossed in one of the leather chairs across from it, Charlie said, "The press were at the house at six."

"I know."

"I think—are they at your house, too?"

Walt nodded.

"All right. I'll move for a gag order. Remus knows exactly what he's doing, whipping them up like this."

Walter peered over the tops of his spectacles at his notes. He said, "Looks like we're in for a bit of a fight after all."

One of the girls knocked and came in with a coffee tray. When she had gone, Charlie said, "Have you thought much about his motivation? Remus's? Do you wonder what was in his mind?"

Walt nodded and set his pad on the broad arm of the chair. "Something's turned up."

Charlie watched him a moment, then said, "What do you mean?"

"Listen—Remus's wife left him while he was in prison. She stole most of his money, so he says. And she was perhaps seeing other men. He's complained about this to anyone who'd listen, especially the press, and yet he's done nothing about it. He wouldn't even help his lawyers prepare a case for divorce. And then, on the morning of that divorce, just like that, he decides to gun her down. What happened?"

From the hallway came the noises of bodies moving: feet, voices, laughter—reporters. The place was in chaos. He'd have to see about restoring some order. Remus was not the only case in Hamilton County. He said, "Are you suggesting there was a reason he killed her? Beyond simply rage or revenge?"

"Remus is a very smart man, and very controlled. He was a good lawyer and a better bootlegger. He found ways of working the system no one dreamed of. You don't gross eighty million dollars in four years by accident. Imagine if you read in the papers that Henry Ford had shot his wife to death. Would you immediately assume it was in a rage of passion?"

"Not Ford."

"You'd think he had something concrete to gain by it, wouldn't you? Something huge. Either that, or he was insane."

Charlie made a sound in his throat.

Walt said, "We know of the meeting in the room." A waiter had testified to the grand jury that he'd delivered four dinners to Remus's Sinton Hotel suite on the evening of October 5, the night before the murder. "Now, here's the thing. Late last night, a detective turned up a cook at the Alms Hotel. On the evening of October fifth, it turns out, when this cook went outside to smoke, he saw a black Cadillac brougham come past several times."

Charlie leaned forward.

"He claims to have recognized George Remus in the backseat."

Charlie slapped the desk. "They tried to do it the night before. That's premeditation. And conspiracy. His procrastination in helping his lawyers build the divorce case—that's why. He knew she'd be dead."

"But why?" Walt said. "Was it the money? Was killing her a way to get it back? I suppose it's possible. Maybe he needed her dead while they were still married."

"But then he must know where it is, if in fact she stole it. I doubt that he does."

"I don't really think there was much money left anyway."

"No, I don't either," said Charlie. "So what else did he have to gain?"

Walt uncrossed his legs and picked up the pad. "I don't know. But if we can find out and demonstrate that, along with a conspiracy, there's not a chance an insanity defense will hold."

"It won't be easy, Walt, digging up something like that. And you know as well as I do that the insanity defense won't hold anyway, especially if we show conspiracy." Charlie propped his elbows on the desk and pressed his fingers to his mouth.

Walter said, simply, "Twelve citizens."

Charlie opened the humidor on his desk and selected an Uppmann. He said, "You're right." In his drawer, he found the silver cutter Eleanor had given him for one of their anniversaries, and clipped the end. "We need to put every nail in the coffin. Let's look into this."

Now, for the first time, Walt smiled.

Charlie lit a match and sucked until the end of the Uppmann glowed evenly. He took it from his mouth and said, "Start with the woman who was with her, this Laura Peterson. They were close for years. Talk to Frank Dodge. He knows the situation as well as anyone. Maybe Imogene said something to him."

"Documents," Walt said. "The Senate testimony, the original whiskey trials and the appeals, the indictments, even the interviews. When he finally started to open up, he really opened."

"There was that series in the St. Louis paper last year, I remember. Read that again."

"I have. It's amazing what he did. But he happened to have been both a pharmacist and then a defense lawyer in a city that went dry two years before the country, giving him plenty of experience with bootleggers. He was perfectly positioned."

"You can say that about any of them—Ford or Carnegie or Gary. But they're the ones who did it, who saw it."

"There's the thing," Walt said. "The vision. Can you imagine sitting in your law office one day and suddenly realizing, from your readings of the Volstead Act and your connections, that you'd hit upon the formula for millions?"

The "formula" was that Volstead allowed for the purchase of wholesale whiskey by pharmaceutical corporations. Each company was allotted a certain number of withdrawal certificates, but many didn't need all they had a right to. Remus simply went around and negotiated to buy up the excess. He moved to Cincinnati because it lay within a hundred miles of 80 percent of the nation's distilleries.

"And then that he kept it hidden for so long."

"He paid everybody," Charlie said. "And I mean everybody."

"Except Dodge."

Charlie drew on the cigar. "Work on motivation,

but let's keep our focus on proving this conspiracy. We need that. So let's push, hard. Knock heads if we need to. I think we should involve Mr. Basler."

Clyde Basler, an assistant PA and former street cop, was the antithesis of Walt Sibbald—squat and muscular, coarse, harsh, physical, confrontational, threatening—except that they were both fine craftsmen in the courtroom.

"I've spoken with him. He's ready. What about this motion, the insanity laws?"

"It's nonsense. Nothing'll come of it. They're running, Walt. We need to press now, before they get any more organized."

JUDGE SHOOK, WHOM CHARLIE KNEW WELL, ALLOWED CARL Elston to mount a long, carefully reasoned argument against the new Ohio insanity laws. They were unconstitutional on three fronts, Elston claimed, as Remus sat stonily beside him: first, the fact that only nine of the twelve jurors at the sanity hearing needed to decide the defendant was sane to disallow the defense; second, that if the defendant was found to be sane, this benefited the prosecution but not the defense; finally, that requiring a defendant to expose his defense before the trial was tantamount to making him testify against himself. They were interesting arguments. Shook listened for nearly an hour.

At the conclusion, he said, "Anything else? Anyone?"

Charlie cleared his throat. This was perhaps not the best time, but time mattered. "Your Honor, the state has a motion as well. We ask that a gag be imposed upon all participants in this proceeding. The case is being tried in the papers, the jury pool poisoned—"

"I thought you were a Yalie," Elston said.

"I beg your pardon."

"I thought you went to Yale. A good school, I understand. Top-notch. One would think they'd require you to take a course in constitutional law. On top of these insanity laws, now you're going to suspend our First Amendment rights as well?"

"That's enough," the judge said. Charlie assumed he'd retire to consider the motions. Instead, he sat and thought for all of thirty seconds, then denied Elston's motion to overturn the insanity laws. Under the law, he added, the defense had another forty-eight hours to formally enter a plea.

"As for the gag order," he said, "I'm denying that, too. Good day, gentlemen."

Elston and Remus rose and left without another word. Charlie's eyes locked with Shook's for just a moment. In the hallway, of course, the press waited. Charlie recognized only a few of them as local reporters.

Outside, on the stone steps of the Main Street side of the building, Elston and Remus were holding forth again. Remus's irritating voice boomed on about constitutional challenges and the miscarriage of justice. Charlie tried to slip past, though some of the reporters spotted him. Samuel waited with the Pierce-Arrow. Charlie settled back into the leather seat and closed his eyes.

So Remus would face the panel of alienists. And they would determine that he was perfectly sane, and that would be the end of it. There would be no defense left to the man.

Something bothered Charlie, though. Like a seed stuck in his teeth, it distracted him. Just days earlier, while still purportedly planning his defense of justifiable homicide, Remus had filed motions with the court to allow him to collect depositions from around the country concerning the events of the years leading up to the murder and the alleged betrayals and crimes Imogene had committed. Charlie hadn't bothered to object.

Now he wondered if these depositions really had something to do with the insanity plea. His heartbeat quickened. He cracked open the window. It had been a ruse, he saw, a trick. They pushed the motions through before revealing their true defense strategy. That was why it had surprised him to learn so soon of the motion to overturn the laws. He'd let them dupe him.

Well, then, he thought, let them run around. Let Remus spend every damned dollar he had left. It would all come to nothing. Remus was a killer, and he'd be dead, himself, Charlie calculated, inside six months. And rightly so.

The children were playing in the front yard. They shouted when the car pulled in, and ran to him and grabbed at his pant legs. It was too chilly, he thought. They should be inside. But he knelt on the lawn and embraced each of them in turn, then left them to play a little longer. Inside, the house smelled of roasted pork and fresh bread. He found his wife in the kitchen, stirring something on the gas range. Eugenie, the frizzy-haired girl they'd recently hired, was setting the table in the dining room. Charlie came up behind Eleanor and put his arms around her.

"Careful," she said.

"Smells good."

"I'm glad."

"The food, too."

"Oh, very nice," she said. "Charlie?"

"Mmm?"

"I was thinking—"

"Again?"

She turned her face and lowered her voice, so Eugenie couldn't hear. "Maybe we should get the children down early. Is that possible?"

"I suppose," he said.

"That way," she said. "We could turn in early, too. I imagine you must be terribly tired."

"Not really—" he started, but she had inserted the end of her tongue in his ear, then, and so he understood.

BUT AFTER DINNER, WHILE ELLIE HELPED EUGENIE GET THE children ready, Charlie slipped into the study to read a little more. He had taken Imogene's diary from her room.

Later, Eleanor called him. He said he'd be right up. But by the time he finally went, she lay asleep on top of the throw on their bed, still in her clothes. He unbuttoned her dress and sat her up to take it off.

"Waited," she said, huskily.

"I know," he said. "I'm sorry."

He pulled the sheet back, then let her down and

covered her. He knelt beside the bed and leaned into
her face and smelled her breath and her throat. Then
he went back down to read some more:

April 20, 1920

    At an after-the-theater supper party in the
Sinton's Mezzanine Gallery, beneath the high
arched windows and the statuary and the gods
and angels above us on the domed ceilings, we
were served. The only shame of it was that I'd
been seated next to Mary Norris . . .

THE MAKER

STILL, IN SPITE OF HERSELF, SHE LOVED THESE EVENINGS. The tables were fitted in between the two-story windows with their massive scarlet brocaded draperies, and it was a cross between an elegant restaurant and a party, with people wandering here and there, stopping to chat, mixing. The theater itself had been fine, the Olympic as impressive and the performances as accomplished as ever, but it was these gatherings afterward that felt important. She knew they weren't, and on any other day she was tired of all of these people she knew so well, and of this city, and of all the same old things. But these evenings crackled.

"And so Constance said she was busy, you know," Mary Norris was saying, "that she had a *previous* engagement . . ."

Mary and Imogene had gone to all the same schools, and Mary's father was an important client of Imogene's father's. Mary either complained interminably, or talked about other people. She knew everything.

" . . . but you know it wasn't true. It's that clod husband of hers. She couldn't drag him to anything that mattered. Well, then, you know what I heard?" She leaned over and whispered, "She's pregnant again. Again! That's how those people are, you know. The women, my God, they're just seen as breeding cows or something." Mary sat back and caught her breath and rolled her eyes. "Well, that's what she gets for marrying into a family like that. They're just so . . . ethnic."

Imogene nodded and smiled and stifled a yawn.

Later, as she stood alone at the edge of the great balcony, looking out over the winding oval staircase and the busy corridor below, George Remus passed beneath her. He wore an overcoat, and he was headed toward the lobby.

She watched until he passed from her sight. Then, without thought, without bothering even to collect her wrap, Imogene ran after him. Outside, the night was clear. Up Ogden Place she could just make out his curious stride, the slightly bowed legs, the arms swinging away from the body. He seemed to her almost grotesquely powerful.

The night was clear. She stayed a block behind, losing him in the dark shadows of buildings then finding him again as he passed beneath a street lamp or as the headlights of a car washed over him. He appeared to be headed for Father's offices. She felt disappointed and terribly foolish. But it didn't matter. Before long, she'd be leaving for France, where she'd have to contemplate the horrible things that had happened there, but then there would be Paris, wonderful Paris, and anyway she would be gone from this awful place.

Remus went past the offices on Broadway, to Fifth,

then east to Fuller, then south again, clear down the slope from the basin to the rough flats alongside the river. This was strange. There were no houses here. On Front he pounded on the high doors of a garage. They cracked open and he slipped inside.

She lifted her dress and crossed into the muddy wasteland of rail sidings and loading zones and boxcars that lay toward Water Street, between Front and the levee. In the darkness, she waited.

A machine passed. Then the garage doors opened. Yellow light spilled onto the cobbles and a moment later three motortrucks roared out. The last stopped, a man hopped out and shut the doors, then leapt aboard again. Someone shouted. The convoy left, and she was alone in that fetid wasteland.

As she hurried west across the dark flats, something moved. A man, very near her, said something and laughed. She tripped. The ground hit her face. She felt dazed, thick. She heard footsteps. She got up and ran now, out into Front Street, then to Fuller and up the hill clear to the top, to Fifth.

Her skin was damp, her heart thudding. She had torn the dress. Her cheek ached, and her knees and the palms of her hands burned. She had a good long walk back to the Sinton, but the night was cool. She trembled and hurt and she needed to think. She could not imagine what she had just witnessed.

NO ONE KNEW HIS NAME. PEOPLE WHO OUGHT TO HAVE AT least heard about a new businessman in town knew nothing. Except for the work he brought her father (whom she could never ask) it was as if he didn't exist in Cincinnati. She cared nothing about Remus himself. But the thought of his transparency irritated her.

THOUGH IT WAS DANGEROUS, SHE WENT TO THE Magnolia Club alone now. She'd once brought Laura, who'd hated it, and came a few times with other friends, but they just got drunk and stupid. She sat at a wobbly table and nursed a neat whiskey that burned in her mouth. After a glass, she began to feel a spinning in her head and chest and an opening in her mind. The music, which was, in itself, mediocre, really, flowed better and faster and she felt herself lifting with it, eyes closed, head nodding, faintly smiling. She sat at the front so they blew it right into her face. She liked it that way, loud and hot and steamy, the pasty saxophone player cracking notes and straining to reach heights that were beyond him, the Negro piano man smacking out sloppy chords, the trumpeter with his heartless, colorless tone, and a skinny girl singing flat and sharp, but all of that made up for by the drummer, also a Negro, who made you cry sometimes, God he could beat it, his hands crossing over, whacking one tom then flip-flopping to another, a quiet brushstroke when it was needed, then a hot hopping banging syncopated double-time that made you want to get up and shake whatever you had to shake.

The club was in a basement deep below a restaurant on Magnolia at Vine, in Over-the-Rhine, with blue lights and a ceiling so low that a man had to duck and smoke hanging thick between the rafters and sweating stone walls that stank of mold and whiskey and cigarettes and she closed her eyes and shook her head and sometimes it made her so happy she could hardly breathe, but she never got up to dance or shake like some, she liked to just sit and sip and listen and nod to the bad music and the good good rhythm.

SHE OPENED HER EYES THERE ONE NIGHT AND SAW A MAN talking with the fat owner near the bar. The owner laughed and the man turned. It was Remus. The owner walked him toward the back and they went out. When the owner came back, she caught him and pointed and said, "You know that man?" He looked at her, smiling, not confirming or denying, and said, "Vy?" in his German accent.

"I . . . I'm a friend of his."

"Really. Of hiss?"

She nodded.

"Who iss he?"

"George Remus," she said.

The owner pursed his mouth. "So?"

"If he's . . . coming back, I wanted to buy him a drink."

The owner laughed. "You don't know him. He never touches it."

"Then what—"

"Enjoy. It's a good party he makes. You understand? For you to enjoy." He laughed again.

She went up the steep narrow staircase holding the slender iron railing, toward the light of the nighttime city and the cool air and the quiet. She came out into an alley alongside the building. In one direction lay Vine Street. In the other, darker, direction was a brick warehouse and trucks and voices. She walked toward it, careful to stay out of the low light that came from the doorway.

From the darkness alongside one of the trucks, she saw men lit only by lanterns, standing around some wooden crates as another man worked at one with an angle iron. He removed a bottle from it, yanked the cork with his teeth, and tipped it back. His larynx leapt and fell. The soft light refracted through the whiskey and broke into tiny amber swirls.

"We thank y'all, Mr. Marcus," one said to a man on the truck.

"Don't thank me," Marcus said. He pointed around, then turned and looked and said, "The hell'd he go?"

Something moved behind her. A low voice said, "Nice night, isn't it?" Remus stood so close she could smell him. Beads of perspiration wetted his hairline and the bridge of his nose.

Her chest hurt. She said, "You're bootleggers."

"You figured that out?"

"Does my father know?"

"Ask him."

"What are you . . . Are you going to do anything to me?"

His eyes brightened and he smiled. "I suppose I could have the men tie you up and chuck you in the river."

"Maybe I deserve it. This is none of my business."

"Really? The way you've been following me, it sure seems like your business."

"You— Will you tell my father?"

He looked down the alley at the traffic on Vine, then walked toward it, away from the men. She followed him.

"What I do, Imogene," he said, "is not technically illegal. I go with these men for the adventure, really, the ride. It reminds me of something . . . of swimming, actually. The night coming, the cold air. But I'm not a whiskey runner, if that's what you're thinking."

"I'm not thinking anything, Mr. Remus. It's your business, not mine."

"Well, you're obviously curious, so let me explain. What I do is all just paperwork. With the government."

"The government knows about this?"

"In a manner of speaking, and up to a certain point, yes."

"Whiskey is illegal."

"When these men take it in their trucks and sell it, that is illegal. What I do is not."

She looked at him in the darkness. "You sound tired," she said. She touched his hair. She did it without stopping to think. It was soft and damp. "I hope you don't hate me for following you. I should be ashamed."

"But are you?"

"I should be." She smiled.

He smiled too. And then his smile left and he did an odd thing. He gripped her arm and squeezed. He squeezed hard. He pulled her close to him and pushed his nose behind her ear. He pressed it into her hair and against her skull and he sniffed her.

She felt his breath hot on her ear, in her hair, and

she knew in that moment there was a great danger in this man, greater than any she had ever been so near, and it frightened her. But at the same time she felt a deep liquid warmth spreading through herself, a feeling she remembered distantly from her youth, from when she had first met poor Malcolm and would walk to his house without telling anyone where she was going. She had felt it then, this river, but not like this, not this powerfully. Nothing like this.

"Mr. Remus, you're hurting me," she said.

Into her ear, his breath hot and moist, he whispered, "Don't follow me again."

She would not. In a week she would be on a ship bound for Calais and then a train for Paris, and so for a time it would not be possible. And then it would have become only what once was.

She watched him walk back up the alley, and watched the men greet him. The one who had opened the bottle shook his hand solemnly. She knew then that what the owner had said was true, that this was the man who made the party. All the others, the ones you saw—the drivers and the buyers and the sellers and the owners and the musicians—were just players. But Remus, the maker, was so far above it all that hardly anyone even knew he was there.

OPENING
ARGUMENTS

SKIRMISHES

CHARLIE GREW TIRED OF READING THE PAPERS, BUT IT WAS the simplest way of following the movements of the new Remus machine. In D.C., Carl Elston was photographed on the steps of the Capitol Building holding the fruits of the access he'd been granted to Remus's Justice Department files. In New York, he posed with Senator Fiorello La Guardia, an old Remus chum who'd given a long deposition regarding, among other topics, Remus's fine character and the evils of a Justice Department that had hounded him. Meanwhile, George Conners continued his midwestern quest for Imogene's phantom loot.

The insanity hearing was set for November 14. Elston, in between trips, had been fighting it mightily in the press, and had formally petitioned the appellate court to overturn Judge Shook's ruling. In the meantime, the three court-appointed alienists reported that they'd had little time to examine Remus because he claimed he was so busy preparing his defense. When he did allow them in, he was distracted by his texts and telephone calls and barely paid them any attention.

One morning in early November, Walt knocked on Charlie's door and slid into a chair.

Charlie said, "You hear the one about the horse that goes into a saloon and orders a drink?"

"No."

"Bartender says, 'What's wrong?' 'Nothing,' the horse says. 'No?' says the bartender. 'Then why the long face?'"

Walt suppressed a smile, then said glumly, "They accepted the petition."

"Who?" Charlie said, but of course he knew. The appellate court had agreed to hear Elston's argument on the insanity laws. It would take months to come before them, and even if they declined to overturn, Elston and Remus could push it clear to the state Supreme Court. This gambit had bought Remus nearly two years after the whiskey trials in 1922. It could do the same here.

"In a year," Walt said, when they'd discussed it earlier, "the heat goes out of the thing. The outrage isn't there anymore, not like it is now. Remus has all that time to wage his public-relations war. It changes everything."

Charlie rolled a cigar between his fingers, then set it on the desk. He pressed his fingertips to his lips.

It was Walt who finally said, "We may need to deal, Charlie."

"Then I'll need something, Walt," said Charlie, feeling hot now, leaning across his desk. "I'm not going in there with nothing but Remus's recanted confession, not if we have to do it this way."

Walter looked out the high windows at the thin

light, a habit he had when he was stymied or upset. He said, "We're working on it, Charlie. That's all I can tell you. Clyde Basler's putting in as many hours as he can spare, and we've got a couple detectives on it as well."

"Clear Basler's desk," said Charlie. "Reassign his other cases. Get us half a dozen detectives, full-time. If you have trouble, I'll call the commissioner directly. How about Dodge?"

"Clyde's talking to him this afternoon. He talked with this Laura Peterson a couple days ago, at the Alms. Nothing much. She knows of no men Imogene was seeing, nothing about the money. She says Remus was nuts when he killed her. We'll work with her on the language."

"Did you say the Alms?" Charlie asked.

Walt nodded.

Charlie walked to the high window and looked out. He didn't notice, a few minutes later, when Walt left.

IMOGENE, IT TURNED OUT, HAD PAID TWO MONTHS AHEAD for not only her own room, but one for Laura Peterson as well.

"She was always generous to me," Laura said.

Laura's room, though nice, was smaller and didn't have the light of Imogene's. Charlie laid his coat over a chair at a side table that held a tray with a steaming teapot and two cups.

"I need help on this," he said.

"I've told it so many times."

"Not just that morning. I want to understand Remus. What motivated him. What may have caused him to finally do this. And I need to understand her."

"Why?"

"I could say that it might lead me to something on Remus. I could say I'm looking for a clue in her past. But the fact is, Miss Peterson, I'm just interested."

"Isn't that unusual for a prosecutor?"

"Is it? I don't know. Maybe." He nodded at the teacups. "I see you're expecting someone. I won't be long."

"I'm not," she said. "They always bring two. Would you care for some?"

As she poured, he sat down, then said, "You knew her a long time."

"I met her when she was fifteen."

"And you knew her first husband."

"Of course." She set the pot down and sat across from him.

"Was he anything like Remus?"

She looked surprised. "Remus?" she said. "Not at all." Then she laughed. "Though you know I used to tell her that, in the beginning. There was a passing physical resemblance, I suppose. I said it mostly to tease her."

"She met him in '20? Remus, I mean."

"Mmm. That's right. Early '20."

"So a year and half after her husband was killed."

She leaned toward him a little and tilted her head. "But he wasn't killed. At least not right away."

"She wasn't still married when she started seeing Remus?"

"Well—" Laura twisted the napkin in her lap, "it was a complicated situation."

"I know some things, Miss Peterson. More than you

might expect. That Remus was a client of her father's. That she knew very well what he did for a living. I'm just trying to see it all for what it was. Do you understand?"

Laura sipped her tea. She said, "She'd gone to France, you see, after they met. She didn't come back until the end of that summer. One afternoon, in the early fall, we went for a walk. Instead of going into the downtown, she took me toward the river. Why she would want to walk there, I had no idea."

IMOGENE LED HER TO FRONT STREET, TO A ROUGH GARAGE with high open bay doors where a man in a suit stood smoking in the doorway and looking out toward the river. He was small, with dusky skin and pointed yellow teeth. Inside, several motortrucks were parked in a line along one wall. Haphazard piles of truck parts punctuated neat stacks of wooden crates. The man said, "He's crazy, you know. All the traffic out there. And that water's cold." He spoke without looking at them, as if he'd expected their arrival.

A group of men stood at the levee. Laura followed Imogene toward them across Water Street and the rails and pitted truck roads of the lower river flats that stunk of oil and coal and the deeper piscine odor of the river. Some of the men wore suits. Others were rail workers, truckers, dockhands. They had been watching the river, but turned to look at these two incongruous women. Then someone shouted, "There!" and pointed over the water.

As she looked, Laura could just discern, far out in the middle of the river, the form of a swimming man.

"How long has he been in?" Imogene said.

"An hour," said one of the men.

"Who is it?" asked Laura.

"Mr. Remus," said Imogene.

As he approached them, he slowed not at all. He seemed, in fact, to grow stronger. Laura saw that the water transformed this strange ungainly man, this Remus, into something beautiful. He moved as fluidly as his medium, one powerful stroke after another, head rotating just enough to sip at the air.

A small motorboat of burnished red mahogany passed near him and someone on board pointed and the others rushed to the side to see. As they passed, their wake lifted him above the level of the river's surface, then dropped him. He swam through it without a break. As he approached the dock, a huge man, as big as any man Laura had ever seen, went forward to help him out and drape a rough blanket over his shoulders. The spectators applauded.

Remus gave them a sweeping theatrical bow. He wore a short-sleeved outfit of broad navy-and-white stripes. The solidity of his body, which was not so apparent in his suits, was revealed now—the heaviness in the shoulders and the arms amplified by the striping of the fabric, the ribbed belly beneath it. His chest heaved as he smiled around at the men. Then he saw Imogene. The smiled vanished. He came over.

"Miss . . . Ring?" he said.

She flushed. "Please," she said. "Call me Imogene."

"Imogene, then. So how was the world? France, wasn't it?"

"Fair," she said.

"Only fair."

"Fair is not a bad thing, I think."

"I suppose not."

She reached forward, placed her hand on his, and said, "You're shivering."

"How can I . . ." he said. "Did you want something? Or did you just happen to be strolling on the waterfront?"

She laughed, then said, "There's a charity ball to be held next week that I'm afraid I'm bound to attend. I wondered if you'd do me the favor of escorting me."

Laura didn't know who was the more shocked, herself or Remus. He merely opened his mouth. Laura said, "Imogene—"

Imogene looked at her and smiled.

Remus said, "I—um, had a conversation or two about you while you were away. Mutual acquaintances. I wonder what your husband might think of my escorting you."

She wavered not at all. "You didn't do enough conversing, Mr. Remus," she replied. "My husband, you see, cannot think. He received a parting gift from your former countrymen at the Meuse-Argonne, just ten days before the surrender. It was a large shell, we were told, though he was not too near it and he was barely hit. A single sliver penetrated his skull and lodged somewhere in his forebrain. He lives in a sanatorium up north of here, near Oxford. I'll be glad to take you to meet him sometime. His name is Malcolm Coffey, by the way. He drools, but he's friendly enough."

Remus took a step back and looked at the river, at

the new bridges and the old steam paddler that had come in while he swam. He opened his mouth and closed it, then said, "You went—"

"It's all just pretty fields, now, Mr. Remus. It happened in one of them. Which one doesn't make any difference."

"I'm sorry. I had no idea."

"No," she said. "Well, now you have. I cannot date other men, of course. But I can at least enjoy their company. You're an interesting sort of person. I think you'd make what will otherwise be a dreadfully dull night into something enlivening."

Imogene had told Laura what she'd discovered—that Remus, the specter, supplied the city with whiskey. Now she was asking him to come out into the daylight of her society, to expose himself to a world he didn't need and probably mistrusted.

And yet, Laura wondered, did it also entice him, this man who lived in the city's most glamorous hotel, who dressed himself in the finest clothes, who paid one of the city's most expensive lawyers to push routine papers of incorporation and taxation? Remus liked the stuff of wealth. In Chicago, he merely made a good living. Here, he had at least begun, apparently, to make a fortune. Now, in a gesture, he was being offered a kind of entrée to the society that went with it.

At the same time, Imogene knew what it would do to her parents, their married daughter being seen in formal company with this man who was not only a criminal, but, perhaps worse, of the immigrant classes. It was some cruel game, Laura thought, that Imogene had concocted out of her boredom and her dissatisfaction and her anger and her nihilistic desire to repudiate her parents.

And yet, Laura saw, too, what passed between them. Imogene reached out again and placed her hand on his, and again he began to tremble. The color came back up in Imogene's face, and her lips parted as she gazed at him. Laura had seen this look some years before when Imogene, as a girl, had used Laura's company as cover to meet with a nineteen-year-old man named Malcolm Coffey.

"So he went," Charlie said.

"Of course he did," said Laura. "How could he not?"

"It was a great risk for them both, in its way, I suppose. I wonder if the danger wasn't part of the attraction."

"I thought at first that that was much of it. But I believe Remus could have lived happily without any more danger in his life. Imogene's reasons were more complicated."

"This is helpful," Charlie said.

"I still don't understand why."

"I don't either," he said. "I don't know."

Walt and Basler were waiting for him in his office. He read the excitement on their faces.

"I talked to Dodge," Basler said. "Nothing at first— did he know of any men friends of hers, did she ever talk about the money? He didn't recall anything. So I went fishing, told him what we were after. He thought about it. Said she'd never said anything directly but she had mentioned something a few months ago concerning an old case. In September of 1920, a Kentucky sheriff vanished. Bootleggers, they figured, but there was no way to investigate it. Dodge said he vaguely remembered the case when she mentioned it. Anyway, she said she knew exactly what happened to that poor man, and when the time came, when it would do her some good, she was going to let the world know.

"He said at the time it didn't make much sense to him. But he noodled it around, you know, now and then. Since the killing, it hadn't occurred to him, until today, 'til we talked. Get this, Charlie—he says he thinks, now, that she was planning on fingering Remus at the divorce hearing for the disappearance and murder of that sheriff. It was some plan she had to get him."

Charlie looked from Basler to Walt. "Is he serious?"

"I don't know why else he'd say it. He's got nothing concrete, but he seems pretty damned sure of the notion."

"There's your motive," said Walt.

"Find out," Charlie said. "Who was on the case. Anyone Imogene might have talked to about it. Someone in the old Remus organization who might talk. This could be a home run."

IN A *POST* PHOTO, CONNERS MUGGED BEFORE A COLUMBUS garage where some of Remus's possessions, including his legal library, some furniture, and much of his clothing, had been discovered.

In Toledo, he was interviewed about a storage

locker that Remus had petitioned to have drilled open. The story had intrigued Charlie in spite of himself. The papers not only covered the story but also the bookies' line on the contents. Charlie laughed when he found a *Blade* on his desk that declared: "BOX A BUST!"

GROUNDWORK

THE COURTROOM HAD TWENTY-FOOT CEILINGS, WOODEN floors and benches, and slatted wood blinds on the high arched windows. Sound echoed, especially the voice of George Remus when it was lifted in anger. Shook's bench was little more than a desk set upon a dais a foot or so off the ground. When the lawyers approached, they stood above him; Walt Sibbald had to stoop to converse. The effect was that the judge appeared as a part of the continuum of the defense and the prosecution rather than the presiding power. Of course, he did preside. He oversaw all aspects of the proceedings, from the behavior of the attorneys to the seating of spectators and the press, whom he accommodated and who became great fans of his. Though he banned all the paraphernalia of modern reportage from his room—telegraphic equipment, wires, cameras, flashes, typewriters—he had managed to commandeer the courtroom next door solely for use by reporters.

Elston stood and said, "We have a motion, Your Honor, involving this log of Mr. Remus's visitors, the time of their arrival and departure . . ." The sheriff, on

Taft's order, had begun requiring Remus's visitors to sign a ledger. When Remus found out, he'd destroyed his room in the ensuing rage.

"Mr. Taft?"

"Your Honor, the sheriff of this county has the right to impose any rule he sees fit. Also, if he has a prisoner whom he reasonably believes may be visited by persons wanted under the law, he has the right to record their names and, if warrants have been issued, to secure their arrest."

"In the case of common criminals, yes," Elston said. "This is the case, first of all, Your Honor, of a man fighting clearly and directly for his own life, and second, a man who is acting as his own counsel. It may well be that there are witnesses crucial to the defense who will speak to no one but Mr. Remus, and yet who feel that they cannot allow the sheriff to record their name. And so the defense of this man's life is jeopardized. Would you allow Mr. Taft to post a deputy outside the door of my office, say, to record anyone I might interview on Mr. Remus's behalf?"

"Judge—" Charlie said, but Shook held up both hands to quiet the room.

"The sheriff has a right to keep such a list. But I hereby order him to turn any such lists over directly to the court, not to the state. The court will then decide what, if anything, is to be done with them, and in a manner that is not prejudicial to either side. That's the end of it. Is there anything else?"

"There is," Walt said.

"How did I know that, Mr. Sibbald?"

The room laughed as one body, Remus and Elston

included. The judge smiled and waited until it had settled again, then looked at the prosecution table.

"Your Honor, this regards the depositions Mr. Remus's legal team has been collecting. Most of those we've had a chance to read concern events that happened years ago. We therefore move to deny their admissibility on the grounds that they're irrelevant."

"You'll have to be specific."

Walt said, "Let's take for instance the testimony of the warden of the federal prison in Atlanta, where Mr. Remus was held for nearly two years beginning in January of 1924. Unless Mr. Remus is going to make the claim that his insanity stretches back that far, then we fail to see how this is relevant to the defense of insanity. Rather, we believe that the purpose is simply to introduce testimony that will induce sympathy for Mr. Remus."

"Mr. Elston."

"Judge, this is a very simple thing—"

"We can only hope."

Again the room echoed with tittering. Shook hammered, then nodded at Elston.

"It's a process, Your Honor, of the gradual but inexorable breakdown of George Remus's will and psyche that happened over the time period mentioned by Mr. Sibbald. A process that began with Mr. Remus's losing control of everything in his life—his property, his business, his money, even his marriage—and ended in his losing these things altogether. A process of his becoming aware of one disturbing fact after another, in a manner that added up to nothing less than a kind of torture. It is our contention that the collective result of these events and revelations was the mental breakdown that led, in the end, to the commission of Mr. Remus's regrettable act."

"Regrettable act," Sibbald said, "indeed."

Shook pressed his hands together, and pressed the edges of his fingers to his lips. He looked out over the crowd and said nothing for a full minute. The crowd grew gradually quieter until there was no sound in the room but breathing and the ticking of a ceiling fan far overhead.

"I'm afraid," Shook said, "we'll have to consider each deposition in turn, as the trial unfolds. But since this is a case in which a man's life is at stake, Mr. Sibbald, the court must be lenient toward their admission. In the case of this particular deposition, of the warden at Atlanta, I'm inclined to allow it. If I should feel at any time, however, that this is abused, I'll stop it, and if it continues, I will disallow the use of these depositions altogether. Is that clear?"

"Also," said Sibbald, "in the case of the Atlanta deposition, the defense has submitted only a part of it. The state feels that if it's to be admitted, it should all be admitted, including the section in which the warden states that Remus was punished for stealing food and giving it to other prisoners."

"Objection!" Elston said.

"No." Remus rose and placed his hand on his attorney's shoulder. He said, "The defense will withdraw that objection. Let it all be admitted."

Remus saw Charlie Taft smile at this. He felt the blackness begin to fall. He pointed his finger and said, through gritted teeth, "Laugh now, Taft, while you still can."

"That's enough, Mr. Remus," said the judge.

All three evening editions covered Remus's victories. The *Sun* proclaimed: "TWO SWINGS, TWO HITS FOR REMUS—DEFENSE SCORES POINTS IN EARLY INNINGS."

THAT EVENING, A DEPUTY UNLOCKED THE DOOR TO Remus's suite. Conners poked his head in. "You have a guest, George," he said.

"Well, I'd rather not—" Remus began, but Conners opened the door and motioned in a young woman. Remus stood up. His eyes stung. "Romola," he said, and held out his arms to his daughter. She wept, too. Conners stepped back out.

"Oh, baby," Remus said. "I have missed you. I need you."

"I meant to come sooner. I should have been here."

"It's fine," he said. "I've been busy, and you're here now."

She was twenty-one and beautiful in a way her mother had never been. In the years after he left Chicago, Remus had seen her, of course, had been a father to her. She often came to Cincinnati to stay with him.

"How is your mother?" he said.

"She wishes the best for you. A *Tribune* reporter came out to get her impressions. Have you seen that piece?"

"No."

"I'll find it for you. She told him there was no question you should be found not guilty. That if you did it, you did it to save yourself, and what man should go to jail for that?"

"She said that?"

"She did."

Remus smiled and took his daughter into his arms again. "Welcome to my new mansion," he said.

CONNERS AND REMUS HAD MET IN FEBRUARY OF 1920 when Conners, a former Treasury agent then in real estate, heard about this new businessman and arranged to show him the old Lackland estate at the corner of Eighth Street and Hermosa, in Price Hill. It was a huge, aging brick mansion surrounded by out-buildings and set in a private ten-acre park. Boards covered the windows. Remus declined to make an offer, but he liked this man Conners so much that he offered him a job. In a matter of months, Conners had become second only to Marcus in the hierarchy.

In late September, a week after Imogene's charity ball, Conners again opened the padlocked gate. At the dance, the subject of real estate had come up, and Remus mentioned this grand old place he'd seen, now in disrepair. A symbol, he claimed, of what Prohibition had done to the local businessman, for the Lack-lands had been brewers. (This notwithstanding the fact that the family had sold out years before the new laws.) Imogene's eyes had widened and she gripped his coat sleeve. She'd grown up not far from there, in Delhi Hills, and had been friends with several of the many Lackland children. It made her sorry to think of that warm, busy house lying deserted now, but she was curious about it. So Remus had Conners arrange for her to see it.

As the three of them crossed the overgrown

grounds, Conners said, "The ask is a quarter million, but it'd need that much again put into it."

"I'm still not buying," said Remus. The other two laughed.

The foyer floor was marble. Beyond that wide wood planking lay dingy and peeling and warped where water had leaked in. Some of the wool carpeting had begun to rot.

"It's still magnificent," Imogene said.

"Would you like a tour?" asked Conners.

"I'd rather remember my way through it. Do you mind?"

"I'll be on the porch."

She took Remus into rooms she'd played in, showed him hidden staircases and closets and dumb-waiters. She led him up to the cupola, from which they could see most of Price Hill. Afterward, when she went out to see the grounds, Remus found Conners on the front porch, smoking. As the two stood watching out across the expanse of the unkempt lawn, Imogene came into their view, walking along the iron fence at the southern property line.

Remus said, "Tell me about the distillery."

"We sign next week."

John Marcus had introduced Remus that summer to two New York racketeers who controlled the water-front over in Covington and Newport. They agreed to invest four hundred thousand dollars in his business. Part of that money would now make a down payment on the purchase of the Fleischmann distillery in River-side, which held over thirty thousand cases in its ware-house.

"Have you thought," Remus said, "about how we're going to get those cases out?" The Treasury Department gauger, whose job it was to monitor all withdrawals, came with the deal, of course, and the paperwork still had to be in order.

"That's your trick," said Conners.

"It's no trick," Remus said. "But there aren't enough certificates on the market right now, and besides that, they're getting expensive. We've been driving the price up, I'm afraid. I want you to buy a drugstore."

Conners looked over at him. "They're around, but they're mostly small storefronts, not much cash flow."

"I don't care about cash flow. Buy one. I'll have Ring create a new holding company."

"And then?"

"He'll execute a transfer of title, file some new articles of incorporation, and the Little Neighborhood Pharmacy will become Ohio Pharmaceutical Supply."

Conners thought for a moment before it came to him.

"My God," he said.

Remus laughed.

"You can apply directly to the government for certificates. You'll be able to withdraw for almost nothing. And, since you'll own the distillery, you can sell it to yourself. Mr. Remus, that is frankly brilliant."

"It is at least elegant, Mr. Conners. At least elegant. The beauty of it is that there's no limit to the number of corporations we can create, or whiskey we can manufacture."

"We'll expand. The entire Midwest."

"The problem then becomes transportation. Whiskey's limited to a percentage of a company's business. We'll need to purchase pharmaceutical supplies and ship them to establish a paper trail. For that, and for the whiskey itself, trucks won't be enough. At Imogene's dance, I met a man named Harry Stratton, a vice president of the American Express."

"Trains. But will he help us?"

"He's also the part owner of a restaurant that does a healthy backroom business. Marcus's people have sold to him, so he knew my name. I want you to meet with him."

Imogene appeared and said, "Are you two solving all the world's problems?"

"Nearly," said Conners.

"Well, keep some for later so you don't get bored." She came up the steps. "I do love this old place," she said. She slipped a hand under Remus's arm and hugged it to her. "Thank you."

Remus felt a great warmth course through him. He had not seen her since the dance but had not failed to think of her since then at least every few minutes. It had come to him, in his contemplations, that a woman with her intelligence and beauty and spirit and self-assurance could become, in and of herself, a man's impetus. His catalyst. His reason. As it stood, he had himself only ambition, aimed generally upward, and a curiosity as to what he could get away with. But she could inspire anything. And justify it. And sweeten it. And, by so sweetening, jeopardize it as well. But having tasted a hint of what might be, he had come to realize that there was nothing else he wanted so much as her.

"It seems," said Conners, "that your high society agrees with my boss."

"Is that so? I thought he looked uncomfortable in a tuxedo."

"Well, it turns out there's a certain, uh, ancillary value to these kinds of dos."

She laughed. "Well, there's a startling insight."

Remus said, "I think that was her motivation all along. She felt sorry for our humble little enterprise and wanted to help."

She laughed again, then said, "And *I* think Mr. Remus has a taste for the life."

Conners nodded. Remus could see the possibilities clicking in those hard eyes.

A DEAL

"HOW LONG HAS IT BEEN?" CHARLIE ASKED. HE'D COME
by the First Precinct house on his way into the office.
Clyde Basler had met him at the front desk and led
him to a sweltering little room in the back where a
very large man sat at a table. Though the man's name
was Russell Klegg, he went by Babe. He was cuffed to
the table leg. The cuff cut into the flesh of his wrist,
and the huge hand looked swollen and gray. One
entire side of his face, from the eye to the jaw, was
badly bruised. His fattened lips were crusted with
blood.

In the room as well were a detective and a uniformed cop.

"Three o'clock yesterday afternoon," the detective
said.

"Has he had anything to drink?"

"No."

"Take the cuff off," said Charlie. "Get him some
water and a wet cloth. This is not meant to be a torture session, gentlemen. I said press him. I didn't say
kill him."

The big man looked up at him. His eyes were

hooded and heavy with exhaustion and pain and delirium, but they showed no sign that the beatings had had any effect other than to steel him. This Babe looked like a man who could take more pain than all the cops in Cincinnati had to give.

In the hallway, Basler said, "Seventeen hours, not a thing."

Later, when the man was more comfortable, Charlie and Basler went in. Babe rubbed an index finger across his forehead and flicked the sweat onto the tabletop, then rubbed the swollen hand. He did not look at them.

"Mr. Klegg," said Basler, "you ready to talk?" Basler was built a little like Remus, Charlie thought, muscular with heavy brows and a strong jaw. He seemed always to sneer. He was a valuable man to have in certain situations.

"I a'ready talked lots," Babe said.

"But now we want the truth," Basler said. "We need to know what went on in Remus's hotel room the night before the shooting."

"I dunno. Mr. Remus and Mr. Conners talked a lot."

"About what?"

"I dunno. Money."

"Tell Mr. Taft what you said about the whiskey."

"If they could get some'a the whiskey Mizz Remus had stole. They was a warehouse Mr. Remus had, and she had 'em lock it up."

"And Mr. Remus was angry about it."

"Yeah."

"You drove Mr. Remus to her hotel that night," Charlie said.

The Babe looked up.

Charlie spoke softly and slowly. He said, "They call you Babe, don't they?"

Babe nodded.

Basler said, "I explained to Mr. Klegg that he's looking at a charge of conspiracy to commit."

"I'll make you a promise," said Charlie. "If you tell us what happened, whatever Mr. Remus put you up to, I'll guarantee you walk out of here a free man. Understand?"

"I unner'stan. But I dunno what'a tell. He jus' said, 'Drive me there.'"

"To the hotel? The night before the murder?"

"Yeah."

"To see her?"

"I guess."

"To kill her."

Babe shrugged.

"Didn't Remus and Conners plan it out? How they were going to gun her down? Or how Remus, at least, was going to do it? Did you discuss hiring someone? A gunman?"

"I dunno nothin' 'bout that."

"Look," Basler said. "We can leave right now, let the detectives start in on you all over."

Charlie looked up at Basler and shook his head. He put his hand on Babe's shoulder and said, "You must be hungry."

Babe nodded.

"We'll get you some good hot food as soon as this is over. Sausages and eggs and toast. Coffee."

The man's head hung down toward the table. He

shook it a little. Charlie saw his shoulders fall in on themselves, as the tension that had held there for so long let go. Charlie had seen it before. It was like a wire snapping when it went. You could almost hear the recoil. Charlie pulled a chair up close to the big stinking man and leaned into his sweat and his pain, and whispered, "What do you say, Big Babe? This can all be over."

"Yeah," Babe said. "I'll tell."

"Thatta boy," said Charlie. He nodded at Basler, who went out and came back with the detective.

"All right," Charlie said. "Let's get on with it."

Babe looked at Basler and said, "Wha' you said before."

"I said? It doesn't matter what I said. It's what you say."

"I say wha' you said. 'Bout Mr. Remus."

"What did I say?"

" 'Bout drivin' him."

"To kill her? The night before?"

"Yeah. That."

"He wanted to kill her then?"

"Maybe so."

"Did he or didn't he?"

Babe looked down at the table and shook his head again. Then he said, "Sure."

"And they planned it out, he and Mr. Conners?" said Basler.

"Sure, that, too."

The detective slid a stack of blank paper across and took a thick black pen from his jacket. "Write it out."

"Can't," Babe said.

"What're your hands broken?"

"Can't write."

"Can't write?"

"Can't read, neither."

Basler huffed and swore, but Charlie said it was all right. The detective would write it down.

"You overheard Mr. Remus talking with Mr. Conners about killing his wife," said Basler. "Is that correct?"

"Yessir."

"What was said?"

"I dunno."

"Listen, you've got to help us. That's the deal."

"'I oughtta do it once an' f'rall.'"

"Mr. Remus said that?"

Babe nodded.

The detective wrote. And so it went on.

Later, Basler said, "Babe, we want to ask you now about why Remus planned on killing her."

Babe sat with his head down, shaking it.

"You must have some idea. Did Remus think he could get his money back by killing her? Was he jealous?" Basler cleared his throat. "Was he afraid of something?"

Babe looked up.

Charlie said, "Did Mrs. Remus know something that could hurt Mr. Remus?"

Babe looked from Basler to Charlie, thought a moment, then said, "He was mad at her. He din' say nothin' that night. But in the mornin' he said something 'bout her talking 'bout somebody gettin' killed, and Frank Dodge."

"What about Dodge?"

"He knew 'bout it, I guess."

Charlie sat very still. "Who'd she talk to? Remus?"

"I dunno. He said she was gonna tell the lawyers."

"At the divorce proceeding."

Babe nodded.

"Who was killed, Babe?"

He shook his head.

"Do you know of anyone in the past who was killed?"

Babe laughed.

"Had Remus killed someone, or ordered him killed, that Imogene would have known about?"

"Mr. Remus didn' like killin'. He said they was other ways."

"Did he ever kill a sheriff?"

Babe stopped at this, and they all saw it. Charlie knew. It was that moment when you named it, and everything changed.

"You're protected. I gave you my word, Babe."

Babe stared off. He said, "It'd got pretty bad."

"What had?"

"It was after the two Jews come in and we got bigger."

"The partners, you mean. The rackets men from New York."

"Yeah."

"So this was in, what, late '20?"

"I guess."

"Mr. Remus was escorting Imogene, then."

"Oh, yeah," Babe said. "Lots. I drove 'em sometime. Her father, old man Ring, was angry 'bout it so we kep' it hid."

"Where'd you drive them?"

"Restaurants. The park. The Magnolia Club."

"She liked jazz."

"Mr. Remus hated the place. After, he'd swear 'bout the noise an' stink of it."

"But he put up with it for her, did he?"

"Yeah."

Basler and the detective were looking at Charlie. "Anyway," he said. "What was bad?"

"Hijackers. They start hittin' our trucks, takin' hundreds a cases. Mr. Remus screamed and yelled. He told Conners and Mr. Marcus to find out. One night 'Jew' John made us wait. They brought a man in. I seen him around."

"Deputy Nick Callett, from Covington?"

Babe nodded.

MARCUS STRADDLED A WOODEN CHAIR, HIS ARMS HANGING over the back. He wore a pale gray gabardine suit with a pink rose in the lapel, a white linen shirt, and a scarlet necktie. His fingernails were buffed and shined and appeared, at a certain angle, against his dusky brown skin, to have been coated with polish. The effect of his arms hanging, the pooling blood, heightened this phenomenon. His cuffs extended from the gray jacket, and gold links shined in the light of the single lamp hanging down over the man who sat across the table from him. Beyond them, other men moved in the shadows of the Front Street garage.

Marcus said, "You hearing about this Man O' War? What a piece of flesh!" The great horse had won every race he'd entered that year, and had just been retired to stud.

From somewhere beyond the light, Babe said, "Sure."

"What you guess an animal like that's worth?"

"Chrise," Babe said. "Maybe fi'ty?"

Someone whistled.

"I heard a hundred," said the man across the table. Like Marcus, he was small and thin and dark-skinned, though for this they bore little resemblance to one another. He was fine-featured, sharp-edged. His hands rested on the table, his wrists crossed, as if they were bound.

"Yeah?" said Marcus. "You heard that?" Marcus, with his hollow, pock-marked cheeks and small, badly yellowed teeth, smiled. His smile was a famous, frightening thing. The man across from him closed his eyes.

"You hear everything, don't you, Nicky. You got some big ears. Why don't you tell us, we can get on."

"I don't know, Jew John," the man said.

Outside, on Front Street, a cold rain fell. It fell farther out on the river flats and beyond that on the great dark river.

"Christ," Marcus said. "A hundred g's for a fuckin' horse. Who'd believe that?" He tapped his heels against the wide planking of the floor. "So, Deputy Nick," he said. "We've paid you some good money."

Nicky Callett nodded.

"But now we're gettin' moved in on, you look the other way."

"It's not like that."

"Listen," Marcus said. "You want to butter your

bread on both sides, go ahead. I just gotta know who it is."

"I understand, Mr. Marcus," he said. "I do. But you gotta understand—"

"I don't gotta understand nothin'!" Marcus said, his horrible face inflaming. "Except who the fuck is jumpin' my trucks! And how do they know where my trucks are gonna be? And how do they know just when we're moving quantity? And how do they know we're withdrawing from the Fleischmann in Riverside so that they're sitting there waiting when we come out? Huh, Nick? How the *fuck* do they know all this?"

For just a moment, Callett's own face changed. Something passed over it.

Marcus shoved his chair back and stood up. Babe came out of the shadows and over to the table and rested upon it the hams at the end of his arms. "This is jus' bid'ness, Nick. We know it ain't you tellin', 'cause you don't know all the stuff. We just need'a know who. Tha's all. You our pal, ain't that right, Jew John?" As he spoke Babe placed his large hands over Nicky's much smaller ones, and slipped his fingers around the slender wrists.

Nicky pulled, but pulling against the Babe was like pulling at a parked truck. He screamed. The men in the shadows watched. The sound echoed off the wooden floorboards and the motortrucks and the wooden crates. It echoed out into the night and down the flats and out across the water toward Kentucky.

"Shh," Babe said. "Nicky. We jus' wanna know who."

Marcus came up from behind and touched Nicky's shoulder, and he screamed again, throaty, panicked.

Marcus laughed. Some of the men laughed. Babe smiled at him, a soft, sweet, little boy smile. "Shh," he said.

Marcus touched the back of Nicky's neck. Nicky jumped again, but did not scream this time. "What're you gonna do?" he said.

"We gotta know, tha's all," Babe said.

From the shadows came a hissing, then the sound of ignition, and the blue flame of a welding torch lighted the darkness.

"What kind of sick bastards—"

"Jus' tell us who, Nicky," said Babe.

"Tell you who?" Callett said. "It's you, you assholes. Nobody's in here. How's a guy supposed to keep it straight, huh? You all running around behind each other's backs."

Babe looked down at him.

"Look in your own house, Jew John," Callett said, into the air. "That's all I have to say to you."

Marcus roared as he lifted a three-foot-long tire iron. He gripped it with both hands at the angled end, and stepped, and planted his foot and swung with all his strength and snapped through into the back of Nicky's head. The bar rang with the impact. Babe let go of Nicky's hands and held him up by his lapels. Blood ran from the wound down Nicky's back and soaked through his suit.

A couple of the men produced a large, open wooden barrel that smelled sweetly of whiskey. A series of one-inch holes had been drilled in a ring around its belly. The men lifted Nicky's flaccid body and lowered it headfirst into the barrel. They maneuvered it until it

curled and folded in such a way that they could bend
the legs and fit them in as well. They added a long
length of heavy chain for weight, and resealed the top.

A little while later a motorboat carrying the two
men and the barrel left from one of the piers down on
the levee. It headed out into the river, in the rain,
toward Kentucky, and then turned upstream, into the
current. Later, it came back with the two men, but not
the barrel.

CHARLIE SAID, "REMUS WASN'T THERE?"

"But it's true, isn't it," Basler said, "that Marcus was
as loyal to Remus then as Conners was?"

Babe nodded.

"Marcus did whatever Remus told him to do?"

"Yeah."

"You said Remus screamed at them. He said to find
out who was double-crossing them and take care of it,
right? What's that mean, Babe? To take care of it?"

Babe looked at the tabletop.

"It means get rid of them, right?"

Babe nodded.

"Remus ordered Marcus to do it. Doesn't that
make sense?"

Babe continued to nod.

LATER THAT WEEK, A DETECTIVE BROUGHT A WOMAN
named Mary Hubbard to Charlie's office. Charlie
knew of her. During the whiskey trials she'd been
dubbed Old Mother Hubbard. Her husband, Eli, a
driver, had died suddenly days before he was to have
testified against Remus. At that time, his wife's accu-

sations against Remus and Marcus were suppressed by the defense.

"I could've sent 'em away forever," she told Charlie. "I know what horrible things they done. Like they done to my poor Eli."

"And this Kentucky sheriff—"

"I heard about it from Eli. He said that poor man jus' got caught in the middle and they sicced that mad dog Marcus on him."

"Who did?"

"Well, Remus and Conners," said Mary Hubbard. "Who else?"

The next day Walt took an offer to Elston: they would allow Remus to defend his claim of insanity without the alienists' ruling beforehand. In return, the trial had to start as soon as possible. Elston and Remus agreed in principle. Judge Shook imposed his own conditions: first, that the panel of alienists would be present throughout the trial and could stop it at any time, even over the judge's objections, if they felt unanimously that Remus was insane; second, that they would be allowed to make a ruling as to his sanity during the course of the trial, and to be questioned on the stand as to their findings. Elston tried to object, but Remus overrode him, not only agreeing to accept the findings of the court-appointed alienists, but declaring he would not bring in any of his own to offer testimony for the defense.

Shook declared that the original date for the insanity hearing, November 14, in less than two weeks, would now be the opening day of the murder trial of George Remus.

Afterward, the press waited as usual. "It's a war," Walt had said. And in a war, Charlie well knew, you did whatever ugly things you had to to win.

"I'm sorry, Father," he whispered into the still air of that great building, knowing that the chief justice would feel a bitter disappointment when he learned of Charlie's capitulation. He went out toward Court Street. They ran to him. When they were still, he said, "The state of Ohio would like to make a statement."

When Charlie got back to the offices, Walt waved a newspaper. He said, "They found one here, at the Third National. A bank box in her name. Remus has filed a petition to open it."

"Pull a warrant," said Charlie, "but keep it quiet. If the petition's granted, I want first crack."

Late that evening, long after darkness had fallen, Eleanor called him to say that his children would at least like to see him for a few minutes before they went to bed. He said of course, he'd come right home. But he sat in the darkened room, with only the desk lamp on, and opened the diary.

August 28, 1920

Laura called. Something was wrong. George came in to sign some incorporation papers, but when he arrived he acted strangely. His arm was in a sling and he had a terrible gash on his fore-head, but it was something beyond that. Father finally put him in a car and sent him back to the Sinton. But Laura knew that something inside him was not right . . .

PARTNERS

THE DOOR TO THE HOTEL SUITE STOOD OPEN. BABE SAT BY the window. "Is Mr. Remus in?" Imogene asked him.

He waved a hand toward the bedroom door. She knocked, then opened it. Oh God, she was frightened when she found him lying half off the bed, soaked with sweat, his face burning. A line of horrible black sutures ran down onto his forehead. When she tried to move him just a little and bumped his right arm he cried out even in his delirium at the pain. Why was no one taking care of him?

She called out, "Babe, get me cold water and a cloth quickly. Quickly! Then find some ice."

As she bathed George's face and neck, she lifted his head to moisten the back and felt that the expanse of it had so swelled and pushed out that her whole hand couldn't cover it, as if his skull had been crushed and his brain were leaking out. She did not weep or hesitate at all now in what she had to do. She began telephoning, and the people she called came quickly.

In the end, one of the specialists injected something, but said that all they could really do was to keep cold compresses on it and wait. Even moving him to a hospital now might be a risk. It was impossible to tell. So Imogene settled in next to the bed and waited. In the other room, Babe kept his own vigil.

Her father came in the evening. He barely glanced at Remus.

"Imogene," he said. "You are sitting in a man's bedroom."

"Your powers of observation, Father—" she began, but allowed the comment to trail off.

"Why are you doing this to me?"

"To you? Look at him," she said. "He may be near death. Do you understand that? He was in your office, and all you managed to do was get him out of your hair."

"I'm only his lawyer."

"That says it all, doesn't it."

"You'll come with me, right now."

"I am staying here until he wakes up, or until we can move him someplace safer. If you don't like that, Father, then I'll just have all my things moved over here right now."

"Imogene!"

"S'cuse me." Marcus had come in.

"What do you want?" Ring said.

Marcus stared at him. Imogene did not think her father had ever seen this man before.

Ring opened his mouth, then closed it and cleared his throat. He looked once more at his daughter, then stalked from the room.

She said to Marcus, "I hope it was a good adventure."

"It was a setup," he said. "The Covington warehouse crew never showed up. It was wide open. I just happened to be over there and found it before it got raided. We brought out four trucks. They cut us off on the Suspension Bridge, ten of 'em. They figured we'd jump out and run. But not George Remus. He lets out this yell to curl your hair and picks one up and tries to launch him off'a the bridge, though he hit a cable."

Babe had come in to hear the story told again. He said, "N'en one brings the butt a his gun right down on Mr. Remus head. N'en they come at me. On'y he up gets behind 'em, blood all over his face, and hollers again. They like to jump out their skin."

The two of them started to laugh.

Marcus said, "They couldn't shoot, see. We all seen the two mounted deputies down at the ramp. All's they could do was get their livers kicked out 'til they managed to get one truck rolling. That's it—ten men and they get one truck out of four." He wiped at his eyes.

"Mr. Remus jumped on the runnin' board," Babe said. "They kick him off. That's what hurt him so bad. I had'a pop his shoulder back in." Babe's smile faded.

The doctors returned from time to time. For another day and night she sat wiping his face and neck, checking his temperature, adjusting his head on the compresses, feeding him sips of water, and asking Babe when she needed something. Waiting.

SHE MUST HAVE DOZED. ON SUNDAY MORNING SHE AWOKE to find him looking up at the design in the plaster ceiling.

"Is it you?" she said.

He looked at her, then back at the ceiling. He said, "When you talk to your father, have him send the contracts here."

"And good morning to you, too, Mr. Remus."

She went home that afternoon and slept through until the next morning. She came each day to see him, but it was clear that he was going to live after all. On Monday he stood up. On Wednesday, she found him sitting in the main room, in a dressing gown. When she sat next to him, he took her hand and held it for some time before he said, "It can be a dangerous business, this."

"Only if you're foolish."

"Who isn't foolish?"

She looked at him.

"I can't take you in," he said. "We don't know when that time will come. Maybe not for years."

"But you can take care of me."

"I can give you money. I can't give you a station."

"To hell with a station." She was, she realized, as trapped in her society as poor Malcolm was in his ruined body. Well, now she would be free of that.

"Are you sure?"

"I hate that life. I hate them."

"Is that what this is about? That I'm some kind of convenient protest? You'll show them."

She started to cry. "Why would you say that?"

"I don't want to be put in the middle if I'm just convenient."

"I thought you knew better."

"I think I do. I hope I do."

She slipped beneath his arm and rested her face on

his chest. "You know." Later, she said, "Do you ever think about how big this business of yours could get?"

"Only all the time. I'm not sure you can imagine it, Imogene, how much it could be. I sometimes have these flashes, when it all unfolds out in front of me—"

"And does it frighten you?"

"Maybe," he said. "A little."

"It should," she said. "Because that's the real danger, you know. Success."

SHE HAD GONE INTO ONE OF THE SUITE'S BEDROOMS TO rest that afternoon when raised voices woke her.

"It would double our revenues!" one said. "They dilute it anyway as soon as you sell it, so what's the difference?"

"It's my reputation," Remus said, "not yours. I'm not cutting my product."

"Jesus Christ! Tens of thousands you're throwing away. Our dollars. It's goofy."

"If it weren't for me, there'd be no dollars."

Another voice said, "We own half. We have a say."

"I'm *not* cutting!"

She got up and went to the bedroom door. "He's recovering," she said to the two men with him. "He needs to rest. You can have this discussion later. Please."

"Imogene," said George. "I'm sorry. This is Mr. Landau and Mr. Hess."

"Yes," she said.

Landau said, "We didn't mean to disturb you."

When they were gone, as she began to prepare tea, she said, "Those men."

"My financial partners—"

"I've met them."

He stood up.

"They're clients, George. Of my father's. They've been for some time."

"Are you sure?"

"Yes." He had the palest, coldest look on his face she'd ever seen, and it frightened her as much as anything had. "What does it mean?"

But he didn't answer. He took her downstairs and put her in her machine and told her to go home.

AUTUMNS

FROM HIS WINDOW HE SAW THE EARLY CROWDS STRETCH-
ing down the block and spilling into the street. He
wondered what they thought they were going to see—
Shook had reserved half of the courtroom seats for
the press. They came anyway, just to be here when it
started. The "Trial of the Century," the *Enquirer* had
called it.

The courtroom felt different that morning. For one
thing, it was filled not with reporters or spectators but
the pool of seventy-five veniremen from which the
jury would be drawn. They were quiet as they looked
about. A platform had been erected behind Shook's
bench for the three alienists who would oversee the
proceeding.

Remus, dressed in his typical elegance in a blue
serge suit, high-collared white silk shirt, and black tie,
sat alone at the defense table, writing in one of the
several notebooks he kept. The prosecutors entered
together. He felt them watching him, but refused to
give them the satisfaction of looking back. As the
heavy doors opened again, the sounds of the crowds
swirled in and with them came Carl Elston. A bulb

flashed in the marbled hallway before the doors closed. Elston made a point of going over first and shaking hands with each prosecutor.

Outside, autumn was passing. The wind had turned cold, and the leaves had fallen. Remus looked through the high windows at the little bit of the world he could see: barren branches shifting in stark relief against a leaden sky.

At eleven, the room was cleared of the veniremen. The press was seated first, and then the doors thrown open to the public. The floorboards shook as a swarm rushed in and scurried for seats. It was over in a minute. The bailiffs pushed the disappointed losers back into the hallway and secured the doors, which were guarded, at Shook's instruction, by armed deputies.

The clerk said, "All rise!" and announced that the case of the people of the great state of Ohio against one George Remus was now under way. Shook entered, sat, and tapped his gavel, though halfheartedly. Before he could even speak, Taft was on his feet. Remus knew what it was about: another motion to suppress the depositions. Remus leapt up and fairly shouted, "Your Honor! Before you begin to call the jury, I have a motion." He glanced sideways at Taft, who shook his head and whispered something to Walt Sibbald.

Remus asked that the court serve processes on Imogene's mother, Frank Dodge, and Laura Peterson, for any records, receipts, or other paperwork, including correspondence, that had passed between him and his wife and for any whiskey certificates she had stolen.

"Your Honor," Taft said, already sounding exasperated. "Mr. Remus can have subpoenas served. This isn't necessary."

Remus said, "These documents are important. We believe a court order will carry more weight than a subpoena."

"Judge," said Taft. "This is all a part of the broader strategy of allowing background information on the victim to be entered as a part of the defense. The same can be said of the depositions we've discussed before. The state asks that you deny this motion, and furthermore that any remaining depositions be disallowed. The only evidence that should be allowed regarding the victim is from the twenty-four-hour period preceding the murder. And as for Mr. Remus's supposed insanity, I don't think we need to look back any farther than three months before the crime. That's when he claims he was insane. That's the relevant period here. What else should he need to present?"

"Mr. Taft—" said Shook.

"Your Honor, it's clear that Mr. Remus's strategy is to have it both ways. To claim insanity, and yet to put Imogene Remus on trial. I cannot abide—"

"Mr. Taft," Shook said. "I agree with you. A court order isn't necessary. And these depositions could easily be abused. Still, I'm going to allow the motion. I will, as I've said, monitor the use of this information. If it's abused, I'll disallow it. That's all."

Remus sat down and glanced at Elston, who nodded in approval.

"Now, gentlemen," said the judge. "May we please begin?"

Jury selection would take the remainder of the week. On that first day, the crowd got to see a hot fight between Elston and Basler over how peremptory challenges to jurors were to be delivered, but Remus sat quietly through it, merely listening and nodding at Elston, who won the argument.

By day's end, six potential jurors had been seated, two women and four men. Charlie requested that these six, though they were still tentative, be immediately sequestered. Shook, without comment, and over the protestations of Elston, granted the request. The jurors looked shocked, and whispered to one another. No one, the press later declared, could remember the sequestering of a jury before it was even finalized.

THAT EVENING, REMUS LAY RUMINATING ON HIS COT AS Elston and Conners discussed the merits of the jury so far. Romola sat on the sofa reading the recent best-seller, *Trader Horn,* that Remus had asked a nearby shop to send up. A deputy knocked and carried in a red-foil heart tied with a white bow. Remus sat up, put the heart on his lap, and untied the ribbon. He smelled rich chocolate. "I am well liked," he said. He received many packages.

Romola took a chocolate-covered nut, but absently set it on the arm of the sofa and continued to read. Elston and Conners refused. Remus chose a rectangular one, surely a caramel.

"I've got a couple of peremptory challenges already," Elston was saying. "We'll save them 'til the end."

"They're all good working people," Remus said. He

held the chocolate up and gazed at it, then bit off the end. He'd been right, it was a caramel.

"Anyway," said Elston. "We've got a large pool left—" He stood up. "George!"

Remus ran, bent over, toward the bathroom. He spat the candy onto the floor and cupped water to his mouth and spit it out. "Strychnine!" he gasped.

Later, he said, "They love me. Who would try to kill me?" But it wasn't the first time someone had arranged such an attempt.

ON ANOTHER NOVEMBER EVENING, SEVEN YEARS BEFORE, Remus was cleaning out the office in the Front Street garage when Marcus brought in a young man, a drinker, Remus saw, from the ruddy countenance. The man held his hat in both hands and didn't meet Remus's gaze. Marcus prodded him in the back.

"I told Mr. Marcus," the man began. "I heard some things about you. Things you should hear."

"Do you want money? Is that what you're asking?"

"Why, no, sir. I just think you're a good man and all, a friend of the people of this city which ain't got many no more."

"What's your name?" Remus said.

"Schmidt, sir." Another poor German left without his beer.

"Tell me what you know."

"Place I go, for, you know, your product, well—"

"Come on," Marcus said.

"Someone's put the finger on you."

What surprised him most was that it had taken this long. He was huge now, and everyone knew it. Whatever semblance of anonymity he'd maintained in the beginning had fallen away to Imogene's parading him about and her reinvigoration of his quest to become the Carnegie of whiskey.

Conners had established a new depot at a farm north of the city managed by a couple named Johnny and Ida Gherum. It was unconnected to any of the warehouses, and naturally protected by a high rock wall to its immediate north and west. They called it Death Valley, and it had opened the North. Soon the lines of cars and trucks from Columbus and Dayton and Cleveland and Toledo and Detroit and even Chicago began to pour down the Lick Run Road and through the entrance hidden in a poplar grove. Marcus, meanwhile, had solidified his lock on Cincinnati and northern Kentucky. Within a month of its acquisition, ten of the thirty thousand Fleischmann cases had moved. Remus held his wholesale price to Marcus and Conners at eighty the case, giving him a gross on these shipments alone of eight hundred thousand dollars.

Conners had negotiated for another distillery as well, the Edgewood, with ten thousand cases of Old Keller in stock, and a manufacturing warehouse in the west city with its own rail spur. Marcus installed a crew in the Fleischmann plant to resume distilling and bottling. Remus created the Kentucky Drug Company in Covington, and bought an outfit called Reed Pharmaceuticals in Pittsburgh. And then, in October, Conners negotiated for the purchase of an office building at the corner of Race and Pearl, six dark and ornate stories in the warehouse district where the basin floor fell away to the river flats. Workmen immediately began tearing up a section of the lobby floor, to lay in marble the words THE REMUS BUILDING.

"Is this so?" Remus said to his German snitch.

"They're bringing in a couple'a guns. Professionals."

"Do you know when?"

"No, I—"

"Or who's behind it?"

"No, sir. I just overheard some talk."

"Who was talking?"

"I don't know their names. I could find them again. They come in this place regular."

"You don't know anything about them? Who they work for?"

"I don't, sir, I'm sorry—"

"We'll find out," Marcus said.

"I think we know, already," Remus said. The hijackings had abated for a time after the incident on the bridge. Remus hadn't revealed to his partners or to the lawyer Ring his knowledge of their liaison. He knew Ring must have abetted them in their double-crossings—anything to damage this Hun who'd corrupted his daughter and besmirched the family name, even if that meant betraying his legal obligation. The partners, the two Jews, who used that to persecute him, had now apparently decided to make a play for the whole operation.

Ring had access to corporate papers, tax documents, finances. Even if they didn't succeed in killing him, they could take over much of the business. What recourse was there, after all?

Still, after Imogene tipped him off about the partners, he'd begun spreading out his affairs—he had new lawyers here and in other cities creating corporations and shells and handling taxes and processing money. More important, neither Ring nor the partners had any idea of the true size of the operation now. They couldn't steal what they couldn't see. Still, he had allowed them the first tactical move, and now, he knew, he was dangerously exposed.

TO OPEN THE SECOND DAY, ELSTON SAID, "WE ASK FIRST that the court order that this candy be tested by the city chemist."

"Your Honor," said Taft. "The state fails to see what possible bearing this could have on the business at hand. This is a murder trial—"

"And then," Elston continued, "that the results be submitted to the alienists charged with overseeing this proceeding. Our purpose is to answer this question: whether a person who is subjected to such a trauma as being fed poisoned candy can then logically be expected to suffer mentally in such a way that would explain, let's say, certain emotional outbursts."

Taft brought his flattened hand down sharply on his table. "Judge! This is exactly the kind of nonsense—"

"Mr. Taft, please," said Shook. "Mr. Remus, I'm not sure what you expect the court to do with this. You produce some candy and say you were poisoned—"

"The guard brought it in, Your Honor, and the guard took it back out. Not two minutes passed. Are you suggesting I'd poison myself?"

"No. It's just—fine. If you were poisoned, that's

something the court and the alienists should know. The jury's another matter. We'll see about that. Do you agree, Mr. Taft?"

"I don't. And I hope the court can see where this is going. If poisoned candy can make Mr. Remus unstable, then, my goodness, imagine what a wife's betrayal could do."

"In any case," Shook said, "we can at least have it tested. That can't hurt anything."

HAND TO HAND

ON THIS DAY, THE PEOPLE GOT A LITTLE MORE OF WHAT they came for, beginning with the arguments over Carl Elston's opening motions. For the remainder of the morning, Elston conducted juror examinations for the defense, Sibbald and Basler for the prosecution, and three more potential jurors were seated. Then after lunch, in questioning a man named Trautman, Clyde Basler said, "Do you know this George Conners, Remus's lieutenant?"

Remus leapt up. "Mr. Conners is not my lieutenant! You make him sound like some cheap gangster. He's a better man than you, and you'll treat him with respect."

"Mr. Remus!" the judge said.

"Your Honor," Remus said. "I resent this implication. Mr. Conners is my secretary, nothing more."

"The clerk will strike Mr. Remus's remarks. Mr. Basler, please refer to Mr. Conners as Mr. Remus's secretary."

"If I can without choking on it," Basler said.

"The clerk will strike that remark as well."

"Mr. Trautman," Basler said. "Are you familiar

with this Mr. Conners, who was incarcerated in the Atlanta federal penitentiary at the same time as Mr. Remus?"

Now Remus and Elston were both on their feet. Shook hammered for a full minute as the deputies circulated, motioning for quiet. When the room calmed, Remus said, "If that was not meant to be prejudicial, then I don't know—"

"Withdrawn," Basler said. "I'm finished."

Remus remained standing, though up until now Elston had conducted all the interviews. He said, "Mr. Trautman, I'm interested in how you feel about the fact that I'm defending myself."

Charlie looked at Walt, then stood. "Judge," he said, "is this man who claims to be insane now going to examine veniremen?"

"I'm not insane," Remus said.

"Our claim," Elston said, "is that Mr. Remus was insane at the moment of the shooting. That's all."

"Are you claiming that he's sane now?" Shook asked.

"We're not claiming anything in that regard. Simply that he was insane on October sixth and for some time leading up to that day."

"Well then, Mr. Elston. I'm at a loss. How can I rule on this issue until I know whether your client is sane or not?"

"I'm *sane*," Remus said.

"We are *not* making that claim," said Elston. He looked sharply at Remus, then back at Shook. "And I don't think, Your Honor, that you can require us to make it. Our defense is that this man was insane at the time of the shooting. The issue of his sanity after that moment does not concern this jury."

"It's absurd," said Walt. "He claims to have been insane little more than a month ago, but now he's fully able and qualified to participate in the seating of a jury. *This* is insane."

"Bailiff, remove the jurors, please," the judge said. Already he sounded tired. He turned and spoke with the alienists seated behind him. Elston and Sibbald approached. Charlie sat back and looked at Remus, who was writing again on one of the pads spread out among the legal texts on the desk before him. What a strange and obsessive man, he thought, scribbling away, composing notes no one would ever read and that would make not one iota of difference in the end. Charlie watched the judge, then, and knew before the ruling that they'd lose it. And over Walt's furious protestations that was how it turned out—Remus was allowed to go ahead with his own voir dire.

HE MET FRANK DODGE FOR A LATE DINNER AT A HASH house called Arnold's on Eighth near Main, a couple of blocks down from the courthouse.

"It seems to be going well enough," Dodge said.

"Mmm," Charlie said. "He's one angry man."

"He deserves everything he's going to get."

"I hope it wasn't a mistake, allowing them this defense."

"Come on, Charlie. No one believes he was insane, not even him."

Charlie turned his cup in its saucer and looked out through the plate glass at the wet brick pavement and a pile of horse dung that looked yellow in the electric light. His overcoat hung from the back of his chair, dripping on the tiled floor. The Blue Plates came, pork steak and mashed potatoes and muddy green peas. The waitress was on her break, so the counter-man walked over, pot in hand, to top them off. They ate without speaking, but it was only a minute before Dodge pushed his plate away and took out a pack of Lucky Strikes. He scraped the end of a match with his thumbnail and a plume of sulphurous smoke floated across. Charlie pushed his plate away, too. He sipped at the hot coffee and stared out at the rain slanting through the cone of light.

"You do think it's going well, don't you?" said Dodge.

"Oh, it's all right. I don't care for some of Shook's rulings. He seems to be perfectly willing to give Remus whatever he asks for."

"He's looking toward the appeal. It won't matter in the end."

"Well, you helped the cause, Frank, with that lead you gave Clyde. I meant to thank you for it."

Dodge nodded and looked away. "You get any-where on it?"

"The driver more or less corroborated it. Then we found this Old Mother Hubbard."

Dodge laughed and said, "I remember her."

"Yesterday, Remus asked Shook to serve processes to recover correspondences and so forth between him and Imogene."

"I heard."

"He included you in the list, Frank."

"What's your point?"

"It just seems they're looking at you awfully closely."

"Come on, Charlie." Dodge dragged on the cigarette and exhaled, then said, "Remus hates me. He's seen me as his nemesis for years. The whole collapse of his business was my fault, you know. It had nothing to do with the fact that it was illegal." He dragged again on the cigarette then stubbed it out. "You want to know what he thinks I know, ask him. I can tell you that it's as crazy as all the other nonsense he's claimed."

"Don't get angry."

"It makes me angry."

"I had to ask. It's not really why I wanted to see you. I want to know about 1920, Frank. When they were starting out."

Dodge was quiet another moment, then said, "I don't know what I can really tell you. That was before I got involved."

"From what I gather, that's about when you got involved. With Alfred Ring, anyway."

"But I didn't know about Remus then."

"You knew about Imogene."

"In a sense I did. I didn't know her."

"What was her involvement in it?"

"In what?"

"Remus was being double-crossed by some financial partners. Did you know anything about that?"

Dodge regarded him for a moment, then said, "Much later on, I did. I can't see how it matters—"

"I want to know about her."

Dodge smoked a moment. He said, "I was in D.C. then, you know. This wasn't really my territory. But I happened to get in with a *Post* reporter here named Dolittle. The type who'd cross anyone for a lead. We traded a little information now and then."

"He knew her?"

"Yes."

"All right."

"She's under your skin, isn't she, Charlie?"

Charlie looked at him.

"It doesn't surprise me," Dodge said.

ON THE MORNING OF THE THIRD DAY, WHEN REMUS ASKED a venireman how he'd rule if he believed Remus was insane but the alienists found otherwise, Charlie objected. Shook sustained it.

Charlie said, "Can we assume Mr. Remus has enough basic legal experience to at least function in a courtroom?"

Remus scowled.

"That's enough," Shook said. "Continue, Mr. Remus."

When Remus moved after lunch to be allowed to subpoena the U.S. Secretary of Labor, Basler laughed out loud, then apologized. Again Charlie saw the blackness fall across Remus's face, the glare of rage directed at Basler. Remus explained then that his request had to do with Imogene's attempts to deport him. Behind them, Charlie heard snorting in the press corps, and saw Remus turn and glare at them as well.

Shook denied the request.

They fought several more times that day and each

time Charlie saw the dark rage come. That night, he later heard from a deputy, when Remus learned the prosecution had sent out grand jury subpoenas for Conners and his wife, he'd torn his room apart again.

Still, the next day he seemed composed, subdued, even. But Charlie felt the burn smoldering, and felt it in Basler, too. If these two had the option of deciding this contest any way they wanted, he thought, they'd be out on Court Street right now, swinging away.

"UNDERSTAND," SAID HINKY DOLITTLE, "I WAS ON THE crime beat. Not the person she wanted to see at her do. She was intent on installing Remus in high society."

"Did she succeed?"

"People knew what he was. They'd buy his product and enjoy his parties, but never think of him as one of them. The society reporters came and ate, but didn't write much about it."

"So how did a crime reporter get in with that crowd?"

"Well, that's my point, why I said she wasn't happy to see me, at least not at first. I crashed it, see? The first one she ever threw for him. A Jazz Ball, she called it."

"It still seems a little strange to me that she'd be so intent on bringing him out publicly like that when what he was doing was so illegal."

"It didn't matter. I mean they didn't *say* he was a bootlegger. He was just a new businessman in town. And she made sure to invite anyone who could give them trouble—politicians, police officials. She was very savvy that way. She knew they all drank it. But it was what lay behind it that interested me."

"Her father, you mean."

"Yes. I think she did it as much to embarrass him as anything. To publicly reject him. She thought he was betraying Remus."

"The two partners, Hess and Landau."

"You know this."

"Only a little," Charlie said.

"But my God, when she did a party—afterward, you know, that's when they gave her her name."

"Who?"

"Remus's men. They started calling her the Jazz Bird."

IT WAS HELD IN THE LOUIS XIV ROOM OF THE SINTON Hotel, the very room in which Imogene had come out when she was sixteen. It was not a terribly large gathering, eighty people accompanied by a fine jazz orchestra of ten tuxedo-clad Negroes she'd brought in: King Oliver's Dixieland Band. Joe Oliver had hit the big time in Chicago, and he'd laughed when approached by Imogene's emissary about going clear to Cincinnati for a one-night job. He laughed until he heard what she was offering.

Drums, trumpet, trombone, French horn, clarinet, sax, piano, banjo, and bass. The music was like nothing these people had ever heard:

> The monkey came in a Cabriolet
> Baboon put on a mambochet
> Tiger's legs began to mooch
> And the elephant did the hoochamacooch.

Well they really had a time
Dancing one and all
Way down in that jungle
At the animals' ball.

Imogene glided through her guests, towing an un-comfortable George Remus. She delighted in the stares, the gasps of recognition, for she had not included her name on the invitations. How was she here? What was her relationship with this mysterious man?

She accepted compliments on the excellence of it all, the superb food, the fine champagne, the amazing decor and music. When the newest wife of the head of the city's largest banking family was introduced to Imogene, the young woman said exactly that, that everything, to the last detail, was perfect. Imogene smiled. This young bride of an old man took Imogene by the elbow and steered her away from Remus. Hinky Dolittle, unobserved, followed.

"He looks delicious," she whispered.

"It's true," Imogene said, "but we're friends, nothing more. I've merely taken charge of his social calendar."

"A pity," said the woman.

Imogene introduced Remus to a reporter named Lott who edited the *Enquirer's* society page. When she was herself introduced to Dolittle, she asked how he'd gotten in. He told her he'd come as someone's guest. But he could charm when he needed to, and they ended up speaking for some time. It may have occurred to her, he thought, that a crime reporter could be a valuable friend to have.

❧ ❧ ❧

FRIDAY CAME AT LAST. THEY HAD IMPANELED TEN JURORS, and the defense had already used most of its challenges, so they would have a jury of twelve and an alternate by evening.

In questioning one of the last venireman, Remus said, "Imagine, sir, the other eleven have voted to convict, but you feel otherwise. What would you do?"

"Objection."

"Sustained."

"Sir," Remus said. "Would the fact that I represented certain labor unions and their members in Chicago prejudice you?"

"Objection." It was Basler. "I don't believe him. Mr. Remus never represented a union. A couple of factory workers, maybe. He's trying to get it through to the jury that he's some kind of champion of the working class. It's a ploy."

"Approach." They argued for twenty minutes, but the judge finally allowed the question. Remus then asked, "Will you be prejudiced by the fact that I was disbarred in Illinois because of my bootlegging convictions?"

Basler came to his feet again, almost as if he were trying to provoke something. Charlie sat still. He watched Elston put his hand on Remus's shoulder and Remus brush it off. Shook had the jury removed this time before he let the arguments continue.

Basler said, "This man was under investigation of the bar, Your Honor, before he ever left Illinois."

Charlie saw it coming on, now. Remus choked out, "I object."

"The jury's out, Mr. Remus," said Shook.

"Well," said Remus, "the press is here, and that's the point of this."

"As far as I know, this case is not being tried in the press. The jury has been sequestered. Now, Mr. Basler."

Basler said, "He was under investigation for a murder defense he conducted. A crocked-up insanity plea for another lawyer, no less! Leo Gillenbeck."

Remus lifted a sheaf of papers and flung them at the prosecution table. "You," Remus screamed at Basler, "are a drunk! I know you were one of my best customers. You drank it by the case, not the bottle!"

"Your Honor!" Charlie yelled.

"And you!" Remus said, pointing at Charlie. "Son of a great man. You're a poor excuse. It must be hard to follow that act knowing you'll never live up to it." His voice rose to a shriek and Charlie felt the rage infect him now, too, in the heat of that red, red room.

The judge pounded and the crowd roared as Remus left his table and came across the aisle, Elston chasing him.

"I'll take any two of you right now," Remus said, leaning over their table, his spittle flying. "Any two, and I'll ruin you!"

As the deputies got to Remus, one taking each of his arms, Walt held onto Basler's lapels to restrain him.

"Cowards," said Remus. And then, just like that, he came back into his head. Charlie saw it in his face. He was gone, raving, and then he was here, a lawyer. This was how he killed her, Charlie thought. Just exactly like this.

Now, speaking calmly, Remus said, "None of you has what it takes to fight a real battle, to go hand to hand. I'm not worried, now that I see what I'm up against."

Shook cleared the room of all spectators and press. When it was finally quiet, he said, "Mr. Remus, I'm in a difficult position. If you were just an attorney, you'd find yourself in jail for contempt, and your client would have to find new counsel. Since you're the defendant as well as the attorney, I can't do that. But if it continues, I swear I'll find a way to remove you as your own attorney, or at least to limit your ability to argue in this courtroom. You're not going to throw this trial by acting like an idiot. It's just not going to happen."

"That's not at all my intention, sir. I'm as anxious as anyone to have this over with."

"Then act like it," Shook said.

The last juror and the alternate were chosen quickly, and the trial was continued until Monday.

Later, as they sat smoking in Charlie's office, Basler said, "You wonder if maybe this is all scripted? Maybe the guy's a kind of genius, and he's got this whole thing planned. You want the jury to think you're a nut, act like one."

"But the jury was out," said Walt.

"And if so," Charlie said, "I think his co-counsel doesn't know it. I don't believe Elston knew what he was getting into."

"Who did?" said Walt.

Charlie nodded. "Walt," he said, "you're going to open."

"I am?"

"How do you feel about it?"

"I—great," Walt said. "Thanks, Charlie. Thank you."

"Can you get it ready over the weekend?"

"Sure," Walt said. "Sure I can."

"I'll help you," Basler said. "We'll make it a knock-out."

"There you go," said Charlie. "A knockout. That's just what we need."

WHEN HE CAME IN LATE THAT EVENING, AS HE HAD NEARLY every day for the past month, he found Eleanor sitting in the parlor.

"What are you doing up?" he said.

"I wanted to talk to you. I didn't know when to do it, other than just waiting until you came home."

"What's the matter?"

"That was going to be my question."

"Eleanor, this trial—"

"I know about the trial, Charlie. I know how hard you work, and how important this is, and that you're all putting in extra hours. I'm not begrudging you that. Have I ever? It's not like you haven't always worked this way. But lately, it seems you're never here."

"I'm just . . . preoccupied."

"With the trial."

"Yes."

"Is that all?

"Well, yes. What else would it be?"

"That was also going to be my question."

"Eleanor—"

"Are you seeing someone?"

He looked at her, dumbstruck.

"A woman," she said. "Do you have a woman?"

"No."

She nodded.

"Why would you ask me that?"

"You've just never acted this way around me before. You're not with me even when you're with me. Not that you're with me very often. How often in the last month have we—"

"I know," he said. "I mean I don't know."

"Twice," she said.

He nodded. "I'm sorry."

"I call some evenings, you're the only one in the entire office. Doing what? Other evenings I call, no one's there, Charlie. But you don't come home. Where do you go? Who do you talk to? I'd ask Sam, but lately you've been sending him home."

"I can't see making him sit there for hours."

"Well, that's decent of you," she said. "At least you're considerate of Sam. That's nice." She stood up.

"Eleanor," he said.

She regarded him and then turned toward the doorway.

He stood up. "It's her," he said.

She stopped, but did not turn around. "Who?"

"Imogene," he said. "I've been reading . . . some things she wrote. In the evenings, I see people she knew. Or I visit places she went. One night I went to a jazz club, if you can believe that, a speakeasy. Alone. I didn't like it much. I just sat there, trying to see her. I go into Eden Park. The Alms. The Sinton. Sometimes

I just walk. She wasn't, by the way. Pregnant, I mean. You . . . had asked."

"Yes. That's good," she said. "What do you read?"

"A diary. I'm nearly done with it. I'm avoiding finishing."

"Why?"

"Because I don't want to."

"Are you in love with her?"

He laughed. "She's a dead woman, Ellie."

"Are you in love with her?"

He exhaled and sat back down and shook his head. "No," he said. "It's not that. It's just that I . . . can't make sense of it."

"A man killed his wife. You've seen it before. What sense is there to make?"

"There are things we're not seeing. I feel it."

"Is that it?"

"No. It's . . . I knew her. I could have been her, had that life, I mean."

"The Jazz life."

"Yes."

"Is that what you want? Are you bored with us?"

"No. For God's sake, Ellie. I just . . . I can't figure her out. And I want to."

"It's a mystery."

"I suppose that comes as close as anything."

"But it doesn't explain why you don't want to finish her diary. Why you don't want to stop spending time with her."

He shook his head.

"She was beautiful and dangerous, Charlie. Daring. Powerful. Passionate, I'm sure. I can only imagine what sorts of descriptions you're finding in that diary."

"It's not like that."

"In its way, it must be. How could you not be captivated, when all you've got here is plain old Eleanor?"

"Ellie, stop."

"You can't deny that something's come over you."

He rested his forehead in his hands. "I know. I'm just a little . . ."

"Preoccupied, you said."

"Yes."

She watched him a moment, then said, "Good night, Charlie."

Later, he read:

December 18, 1920

It was not until after the Jazz Ball that he finally explained to me about Hess and Landau, his partners, about the true state of affairs, that I understood the significance of the relationship between these men and my father—that it could only have been my father who betrayed George's confidence and trust . . .

THE JAZZ BIRD SINGS

THE CHILL SHE FELT STARTLED HER. SHE PUSHED HIM AWAY when he tried to hold her, and stared forward through the windshield of the Marmon he'd bought her. They were to have had a simple date, a walk, dinner perhaps. But when, on this December evening, she met him in front of the Sinton, he began to explain. She drove into Eden Park, up to Breezy Point. As her anger settled into a low seething, she said, "You're so much bigger than these men."

"Things are changing quickly," he said. "I don't know what will happen, but I need you to know this—I'm in love with you."

She placed her hands on his face and drew him back to her.

"If we're to be together," he said, "truly together, the cost to us both could be great. You need to understand that. It's a great risk we'll take, in many different ways."

"I do understand," she said. "I accept it. I want you."

"Remember that," he told her. "There's something else, then. Someone has hired two men to come here, to kill me."

She moved into the rough tweed of his overcoat, and pressed her nose into his neck. She said, "Who's doing this?"

"I could only guess, but I imagine it would be a good guess." He said nothing else except that he had faith that his men would protect him. He took a cloth sack from his pocket and gave it to her. It held a small pearl-handled revolver.

"It holds five rounds," he said. "In case."

She held him as tightly as she could. And for the first time, then, she kissed him. No gentle kiss of friendship, this. No sweet thing of proper courtship. She let him lean into her, his chest hard against her breasts, his teeth scraping hers. She let him push his tongue deeply into her mouth. She opened until the tip of it touched the back of her throat. She allowed him to undo the buttons on the front of her dress and the eyelets on her corset and to open her clothing and expose her breasts to the night. She let him kiss them and roll them in his fingers until her nipples grew as hard as stones.

SHE DID NOT SEE HIM THE NEXT DAY, THOUGH SHE SPOKE to him several times briefly on the telephone, calls she placed simply to know that he was still there. The day felt like a dream, and lasted far longer than it should have. Every machine that passed in the street made her jump, and when it sounded as if one had stopped in front of the house, she felt her throat closing. It would be a man, she knew, or two. Remus's men. Or maybe detectives. They would come to tell her the terrible news . . .

She went for a walk in the chill of the late afternoon. She needed air. The sky hung low and dark and somber, and the neighborhood was unnaturally quiet. No men came.

She went to bed early. As she was falling asleep, she heard her father come in, and immediately up the stairs and down the hallway to her room. He opened her door without so much as a knock and turned on her light. His lips were white.

"I see," he said, "that you are determined to shame us all."

She didn't answer. She shielded her eyes.

He said, "I understand that you are now making love to Mr. Remus. That last night, in public, you were . . . you were . . . cavorting in the most shameful manner imaginable. In public, Imogene, with a man not your husband."

She stared at him. "What have you done?" she said. There was only one explanation. It was obvious. She said, "You've paid men to watch us."

"Never mind."

"You still don't know anything."

"I warned you to stop. You may not care if you ruin your own life, but you won't ruin your family's."

"Ruin? Because why? He's from the wrong country? You do business with him."

"Business is one thing. Social relationships are something else. Besides that, Imogene, he's a criminal."

"He's a better man than you," she said, in her fury. "And who isn't a criminal, Father? Some are just more honest than others."

He put his hands roughly on her shoulders and

pressed her into the mattress until it hurt and said, "What does that mean?"

She hadn't meant to say. She hadn't meant to crush him. But he was crushing her, and she hated him, and what he wanted her to be. "Ask your clients," she said, "Hess and Landau." Barely a whisper. "Ask them what I'm talking about."

"It will stop," he told her, "you and this Remus. I guarantee that one way or another, I will see it stopped."

She stared at him, and then her mind screamed. "It's you," she said. "My God! Of all people—"

He stepped away from her. "What are you talking about?"

"I understand now. That you—"

He looked confused.

"Please," she said, "get out."

SHE TOLD REMUS THAT MORNING, OVER BREAKFAST. "It's my father. He called in these killers."

"Imogene," he said. "I don't think—"

"I'm telling you, George. It's him."

"All right," he told her, and lifted her hand and kissed her palm. "I'll look into it." But she knew he didn't believe it. She thought about it for the rest of the morning, then placed a call to the *Post*.

"Mr. Dolittle," she said. "I don't know if you remember me or not. My name is Imogene Coffey."

"Mrs. Coffey," he said. "Could I ever forget the Jazz Bird?"

"I beg your pardon."

"Never mind."

"Mr. Dolittle," she said. "I wondered if you might be free for lunch today. I have a story that I think might interest you."

SHE WAS AT THE BREAKFAST TABLE WITH HER MOTHER when their girl, Dinty, set down the early-morning *Post*. It said: "LOCAL LAW FIRM TIED TO RACKETS—WELL-KNOWN ATTORNEY IMPLICATED IN WHISKEY BUSINESS." She'd foreseen various consequences of her betrayal, but when she saw the cold black fact of the headline, she knew suddenly, abruptly, exactly what she had done. She ran from the table and got her coat.

He was still in his chair, facing the window, when she arrived, though they had covered him with a blanket. The door was closed, but she could see because the bullet had exited the rear of his head and shattered a pane of the nubby opaque glass. The mess of blood and brain matter had already begun to dry on the desk. His gray suit coat still hung on the stand in the corner.

OPEN

THE STORY, WALT SIBBALD SAID, WAS A SIMPLE ONE. A man, enraged at his wife, plots to kill her, and then does. That is the extent of it. That is the case of the state of Ohio.

Unlike many lawyers making a statement to a jury, he spoke from his seat behind the prosecution table, from between his colleagues. It was his height. If he were to approach the panel, they'd have to lean back and crane their necks to see his face. If he were to stand and walk out into the arena formed by the tables of the prosecution and defense on one side, the judge's bench on the other, and the jury box at the end, they would think about how he looked. He wanted them only to listen, at first. He wanted them focused on his words.

"There are details, of course," he told them. "Circumstances. Background. Complications. But in the end, in its essence, this is the crime of George Remus: Rage. Plot. Kill. As perfect an example of the textbook definition of first-degree murder as one could ever hope to find in the real world." He tapped his fingertip on the tabletop as he repeated each word. "Rage.

Plot. Kill. A capital offense crying out for the death penalty. If this case is not worthy of that punishment, then no case will ever be. This is as clear and simple as it gets in a court of law."

When he had entranced them, only then did he rise up to his full height, tug on his argyle vest, and button his tweed jacket. Only then did he walk out into the arena to face them directly, to tell his story:

"George Remus goes to the federal prison in Atlanta in January of 1924 for liquor violations. Just before he leaves, he signs power of attorney over to his wife, Imogene, and trusts her to run a business—an illegal business—that is so complicated, so byzantine in its structure, and so dependent upon personal connections and the knowledge of who has been bribed and for how much, that no one but the man who created it could ever possibly hope to manage it. Even his closest associates, George Conners, John Marcus, Harry Stratton, only understand parts of it. Remus has kept it partitioned, closeted, fragmented. Only Remus knows how all the pieces fit together. Besides, Conners is going to prison, too, and Marcus is gone from Cincinnati, and Stratton has been humiliated and ruined. So Remus leaves it all on the shoulders of this woman who has supported him blindly almost from the moment they met, in the early months of 1920. In the early months of Prohibition.

"In prison, Remus and his gang are, for a time, for the payment of certain fees, very comfortable. Remus has a huge cell to himself. A full wardrobe. Conjugal visits. Dinner with the warden. For a time, it is not such a bad place to be. Then the Justice Department, which has put Remus there, gets wind of what's going on, and stops it. Now Remus and his gang find themselves in a real prison. It's not so pleasant anymore. So Remus turns to the one person he has always been able to turn to, the strength behind him: Imogene. Find a way out, he tells her. I will tell them anything. Go, tell them that.

"Them," Walt Sibbald told the jury. "Who was 'them'? Remus meant the authorities of the Justice Department. And one man in particular, who had hounded him and brought him down. One man who would not take a bribe. One man whom Remus hated and yet perhaps respected above all others: an agent named Franklin Dodge. 'Go to him,' Remus told his wife. She was frantic and emotional and beside herself under the strain of trying to manage all of this man's affairs and trying to free him as well. Though he couldn't see it, because he was so preoccupied with his own fate, this good woman was beginning to crack. But she went, as she'd been told.

"What happened? She met Frank Dodge, a stalwart, honorable man. A decent man. An untouchable. And a man who understood that this woman had been drawn into a world where she did not belong, and that it was killing her. He offered her what Remus never could: decency, absolution, deliverance. Come over to us, he told her. Tell us what you know. Help us. Leave the world of crime behind you. This of course didn't take place in one conversation. Her conversion happened over a period of months, a year. But in the end, she did what was right.

"She began to pull away from the dark world of

George Remus. By the time of his release, the anger that had been directed before at Frank Dodge, the man he saw as his enemy, was now also directed at his wife.

"Though he's released in September of 1925, Remus will find that he's not done with prison. He'll end up spending most of the next year and a half in jails, time he bitterly resents and protests, but which he's required to serve for other whiskey-related crimes. He finally gets out in April of this year, a very angry man.

"Now his fortune is decimated. But how could a fortune built on the sandy foundations of bald crimes and massive bribes ever be sustained and nurtured for three years without the hand of the man who built it? What did he expect to happen to it? Of course it was gone. It was never really a fortune to begin with, but a massive flow of illegal cash that came in and went right back out to criminals and the crooked authorities who protected it. And though it had stopped coming in, that didn't stop it from going out. So it went. It was almost all gone by the time he got back to it. Perfectly understandable. Perfectly predictable.

"But not to George Remus. He had to blame someone. And so he blamed the obvious person: Imogene. At that moment, George Remus swore vengeance. He did not go insane. He did not lose his mind. He knew exactly what he wanted to do, and focused on it in the determined way he had once focused on his career.

"Still, he was not pushed to it, in the end, until he learned, shortly before the divorce, that his wife was prepared to tell a story of her own, of the murder of a

Kentucky lawman. A murder ordered by her husband, and carried out by one of his lieutenants. Now Remus had no choice. On top of the fury he felt at losing his wife and his fortune and his place in the world, now this woman was going to send him back to prison, this time forever. He could not allow it. Nor could his associates. Mr. Conners was likely involved in the killing, as was Russell 'Babe' Klegg, Remus's driver and strong arm. They, like Remus, could not allow Imogene to tell her story. And so, as you will see, they plotted.

"It was a simple plan they devised. Remus, the lawyer, Remus, the showman, Remus, the aggrieved husband, Remus, the maker and loser of a vast empire, would just kill her. He had every excuse, every reason, to do it. And every hope of a legal escape, afterward. He knew exactly how these things worked.

"My fellow citizens, this is what we're doing here today. George Remus is now trying to execute that escape. It has come down to this. This is how he planned it from the first. This is what he relied upon. But what we will show you in the course of this trial will expose his plan. You will see how his fury built. You will see how he constructed the murder plot. You will hear testimony from those who were there. You will hear eyewitness accounts of Remus stalking his wife, and of the horrible moment of the murder. You will hear testimony demonstrating that Remus knew well before the killing that he would never have a need to divorce his wife. You will hear what he said to the policemen he surrendered to in the moments after the murder, what he felt at that time, and what he told the press.

"Then it will be up to you, the twelve of you, to stop his escape."

Charlie looked across the aisle. Remus's face had turned red. He clenched his fists on the table. He had sweated clear through his suit coat—the armpits were soaked, and a line ran down the middle of the back.

CHARLIE ATE LUNCH ALONE IN HIS OFFICE. ALONE WITH AN envelope that had come in that morning from the office of the Prosecutor of the Bronx, New York City. His office had, at Charlie's request, collected a jail-house deposition from a convicted racketeer named Hess.

ON THE SAME AFTERNOON OF THE SUICIDE OF ALFRED Ring, Marcus and Conners met two Cleveland gunmen at the Dixie Terminal. Marcus did not kill them. Remus must have been explicit in his instructions. Instead, Conners gave them five thousand dollars, instructed them to get back on the train, and to remember who had saved their lives. Word spread quickly. It was later rumored that neither of these gunmen ever took another job.

That night, Remus invited the two partners to his office on the top floor of the Remus Building at the corner of Race and Pearl, with a good long view out over the Ohio River and beyond it to the cities of Newport and Covington, Kentucky. When they were seated, Marcus stepped from a shadowed corner and pressed a gun against Izzy Landau's head. Landau urinated in his trousers. But Remus assured them he had no desire for blood. He wanted just to be fair, and the time had come for him to consolidate his interests. He offered them a million dollars for their share in the business. They were incredulous. Landau wept, Hess said.

They were not allowed to go to their houses, to collect anything. Babe drove them directly to the train station, and waited there until they were gone.

CHARLIE WAS DUE BACK IN COURT IN MINUTES FOR Remus's opening, but he rang Laura at the Alms.

"Tell me something," he said. "What happened between the two of them after the suicide?"

"She left with her mother immediately after the funeral," Laura said. "She never saw him."

"She didn't even speak to him?"

"She was consumed with guilt. And shame. She'd wanted to hurt her father, to threaten him, make him leave Remus alone. But not to ruin him, certainly not to kill him. And on top of her having caused his death, the family was disgraced by the revelations of what he'd been involved in. Her mother, her brother, were badly damaged. She'd even cost me my own job, remember. In her mind, everything was finished. That included Remus. I honestly believe she was relieved by that fact. She loved him, but it had been wrong, and so destructive, and now it was over. Now she could begin her penance. Begin some kind of new life of contrition that she didn't understand yet."

"You spoke with Remus?"

"Oh, he called me time and again. He was desperate. But I'd sworn not to tell him where they'd gone. I told him truthfully that I didn't know when they'd be back, if ever. He did ask me to remove his files from Mr. Ring's offices, which I did for him. But he told me later it didn't matter anymore, without her. The business, he meant. The money. He owned the whole world now, and didn't want it."

ELSTON ROSE. HE LOOKED IMPOSING IN A NEW DOUBLE-breasted navy suit, white silk shirt, and kelly green tie. A page from the Remus fashion book, the press would declare. Elston stepped forward, but not just into the arena. He was not tall and magnificent at all, but rounded and beefy and ill-defined. Except for his eyes. He wanted them to see his eyes, Charlie thought. And so, unlike Walt, before he ever spoke a word, he walked across and stood in front of those thirteen, placed his hands on the banister, and smiled.

"Mr. Remus was going to talk to you today," he said. "But his voice is gone. The stress of all of this . . ." He allowed the thought to trail off.

"So I will say what Mr. Remus wanted to say, though certainly with less eloquence. I will tell you the truth of this case. I will explain how we are going to demonstrate it in this trial. But I am not going to go on as long as Mr. Sibbald. I have no entertaining narrative to spin for you. I have no simple story, no easy answer. That's because what I want to talk to you about is real life, not fiction. Stories are lovely things. They have beginnings and middles and ends. They build as we expect them to, and then resolve themselves. Mr. Sibbald is a good storyteller. I'll bet he has wonderful little children who love to have him come in at night and sit on their beds and spin his tales. But the reason stories are so lovely, ladies and gentlemen, is that they are not life. Life, that messy, ill-defined, confusing, unknowable business we wake up into every day. The only beginning is birth, the only end is death, and everything in the middle is just us blindly putting one foot in front of the other.

"Mr. Sibbald and Mr. Taft and Mr. Basler will not demonstrate to you a murder conspiracy, because there was no conspiracy. There were never any plans to murder Mrs. Remus. None. We will prove that fact.

"They will not demonstrate to you the veracity of the story Mrs. Remus was supposedly going to tell the authorities. Of Remus and Conners ordering the murder of a deputy sheriff. I do not know if Mrs. Remus was going to tell this story at all. But I know this: it's nonsense. Neither Remus nor Conners condoned killing anyone, let alone a lawman. Neither had any reason whatever to want that man dead. They had nothing to do with him.

"The prosecutors will not show you that Remus's rage built to the point of a boil, and that he then succumbed to it, because that is not what happened. Did Mr. Remus feel rage? Absolutely, at times, and you will see why, and you will feel it, too. But what else did he feel in those horrible, dark days in which his life itself was deconstructing? He felt many things, and chief among them, I believe, was grief. He felt blinding confusion. He felt despair. He felt, frankly, his life coming apart at the seams, and at times, ladies and gentlemen, he felt himself going crazy. Though I am not

sure he knew that that was what was happening, he
felt it nonetheless. It's messy, as I said. Complicated,
gray, disturbing. Not a pretty story at all.

"Where this man came from, this immigrant who
went to work when he was fourteen to support his
family, matters, too. How he drove himself his entire
life to succeed, and what the failure of it all did to
him, this you must see, as well.

"There's something else we will show you that the
prosecution would love to suppress: that Mr. Remus
had real cause to fear, first, for the privilege of being
allowed to stay in this country, and then, later, for his
own life. Why? At whose hand? We will show you how
this involved the victim, Imogene Remus—"

"Objection!" Clyde Basler said.

"—and how this contributed directly and undeni-
ably to the final slide into madness that caused
George Remus to snap."

"Denied," Shook said.

"We will show you, ladies and gentlemen, what
really happened to the money. It's simple and nice to
think that because it was illegal, had been made from
criminal activity, that that somehow led to its disappearance. Wouldn't we like to believe that? That dirty
money just fritters itself away simply because it's bad.
We all know that that's not how the world works. This
money was not stuffed into bed mattresses and holes
in walls. It was largely in the good solid banks of this
city. And when Remus came out, it was gone. We'll follow the money, show you where it went, and how this
contributed to Mr. Remus's breakdown.

"Mr. Sibbald asked what happened when Imogene

Remus met Frank Dodge. His answer was some mystical conversion from evil to good. A fairy tale. The truth is not a fairy tale, though. We'll show you that to call Frank Dodge an honest and good and legal man is laughable. This will go a long way toward explaining what really happened on the fateful day of October sixth.

"I simply ask you now not to be seduced by creative storytelling, nice as it is. Be open to the possibility that things are not as simple and neat as the prosecutors will make them out to be. Think about your own lives, how accidental they sometimes seem. And ask yourself, then, which of the two versions you will hear of Mr. Remus's life is really the more believable.

"On behalf of George Remus, I thank you."

The stress must be affecting him, Charlie thought, as he watched Remus. For as Elston came back to the table, Remus wiped tears from his face.

PROSECUTION

SCENES FROM A KILLING

"MRS. ETHEL BACHMANN."

"How well did you know the deceased?"

"Very well, I'd say. I was her personal secretary for over two years. At the mansion, you know."

"This was during the time of Mr. Remus's previous incarceration."

"That's right. And then after, from time to time."

"You worked for her occasionally after that."

"Yes, that's right."

"When was the last time you saw her?"

"The night before she died, October fifth."

"Where?"

"In the Alms Hotel. In her room."

"And how did it happen that you were with her then?"

"I'd spent the past several nights with her. She was upset. The divorce, you know. I'd been assisting her with various things: bookkeeping, accounting. It needed to be finished."

"So she was working."

"Yes. Well, no. Not that night."

"Not the night before she died."

"That's right. You see, she had a whole list for us to do. But once I'd started on it, she left."

"This was at what time?"

"Oh, about eight o'clock, I suppose."

"What did she tell you?"

"Nothing. Just that she had to go out, and she'd be back in a little while."

"So you worked alone after that."

"Yes."

"Did she return?"

"Not until about midnight."

"And how did she seem?"

HIGH. SHE SEEMED HIGH. ETHEL HEARD THE KEY IN THE lock, but the door didn't open. The key scraped again. She opened it. Imogene, weaving a little, thanked her and came in. As she did, her shoulder hit the door and knocked it into the wall. She threw her coat off her shoulders and fell onto a couch. She pushed her shoes off. The smell of liquor and smoke wafted off her.

"To hell with all that," she said. "To hell with the lawyers."

"Are you all right?"

"I'm happy, Ethel. For the first time in a long time, I'm happy."

"I hope you are, Mrs. Remus."

"Imogene."

"Imogene."

"Would you have a drink with me, Ethel?"

"No, well, I—"

"Remus's best." She smiled.

"Well—"

"Have a little sip. Here." She lifted her skirt and spread her legs and removed a slender silver flask from her garter belt.

Ethel sipped.

"Thank you, Imogene."

"You've been good to me, Ethel."

"Thank you, ma'am. Well, I got through most of this."

"It's perfect, Ethel. Don't worry about the rest of it. That's what these damned lawyers are for, anyway. Thank you, dear. For everything."

"You're welcome."

Ethel put on her coat. "So, Laura will be here in the morning?"

"Yes," Imogene said. "You just stop worrying."

She helped Imogene up, and Imogene walked her to the door. They embraced. Imogene did not let her go for a long time. She held her there, tightly, and it sounded to Ethel like she was crying a little. Then she let her go.

"Good night, Imogene."

"Good-bye, Ethel."

"WELL, SIR, I HAD DRIVEN HER PRETTY REGULAR."

"You were her chauffeur."

"Well, I—I guess so. I'm a taxi driver, see. But she kept an account and used me regular. Almost exclusive. She'd call in ahead and say when she'd be needin' took somewhere, and I'd go and get her. Sometimes though, she'd call and need a ride right now. Well, I might be on a run. She often said she'd wait. So, I was her driver, I guess you could call it."

"Do you remember the events of October sixth of this year?"

"By God I bet I do. I will never forget that day as long as I draw breath."

"Can you describe them for us?"

"I can sure try. Well, the pickup had been scheduled for eight-thirty. She had to be at the offices of Judge Dixon, her lawyer, at nine A.M. She was getting divorced that day. The courtroom part was a little later—"

"Objection."

"Go on, Mr. Stevens. Just tell us the facts of what you actually saw yourself."

"I understand. Anyway, the judge's offices were just across the street from the courthouse, so she wouldn't be needin' me most of the day. I pulled up to the Alms, there up in Walnut Hills, you know, like I always done. I was a little early, a few minutes, but she and her friend were waiting already, just inside the doors. The doorman held them open, then opened the cab. The other lady got in first."

"This was her friend, Laura Peterson?"

"I believe that was her name."

"Go on."

"Well, we started to drive, like any normal day. I turned around on the parkway, made a left on Locust, and headed toward Gilbert. But then, not a block away, I knew something was wrong."

THE BIG CAR KEPT RUSHING. IT CAME UP FROM BEHIND SO hard on him he thought sure they'd hit, and then backed off. He saw it was an older Cadillac. Big heavy thing. A brougham. It ran right on him again, then slowed. What the hell. He pressed the accelerator, opened up a little space.

"What is it, Mr. Stevens?"

Her friend knew right away, as soon as he hit the gas. But Mrs. Remus didn't know. She leaned forward to speak with him. She was so pretty. He'd always thought how pretty she was.

"Some impatient nut, ma'am. Hurrying to work—" He pulled a right onto a side street, but it followed him.

Her friend turned to look. She said, "It's him."

The big Caddy came up around, alongside, only inches away. He thought sure they'd scrape. He could see the driver, big, like the car. Another man in the back, leaned forward, pointing at them. They tried to get around, but Mrs. Remus screamed and he gassed it again and kept it even. The hell he'd let them get around on him, scaring her like that.

"Don't stop!" she screamed.

He turned again and really gassed it now. Let a copper chase him. That'd be fine. He waited until the last second, then yanked it hard back onto the Victory Parkway, his tires squealing on the brick. But the Caddy made the turn and then they were headed toward the park and the big car with its big juice pulled alongside, and then ahead. So he braked.

"Don't stop!" she screamed.

The Cadillac shot out ahead of them. It shrieked and stopped. He gassed it again and pulled into the oncoming traffic, nearly catching a head-on, and got around the brougham again and pressed it. The bridge was in front of them, and just beyond that the park. He knew those roads that curved all around and climbed and fell so you didn't know after a while which direction you were headed. He figured he could lose it in there or at least get down into town. The Second Precinct was right there on Broadway. He could get there.

But the Caddy was too much. The only way to go here was down the Eden Park Drive itself. The road dropped past Waterworks, but he couldn't make the turn at this speed, and then he was into that long hard curve, the tires screeching and trying to slide and even here, blind, the brougham pulled into the other lane. A machine blared and slid off the road to avoid it. They were going to kill someone. Besides, now, Stevens was pinned in. Traffic was heavy at the intersection with the morning rush, and he saw slow machines ahead as he came off the curve, but still the Cadillac stayed alongside. He had nowhere to go. Then, as they approached the triangle, where he needed to pull left to stay on the drive, the big car veered in on him. He yanked the wheel and braked, and they slid along the pebbly berm and onto the grass. The Caddy stopped across the road, blocking traffic.

It all happened so quickly. The rear driver's side door of the cab opened and a man leaned in, cursing, trying to get to her. But Laura was between them. She screamed at him.

Then Mrs. Remus opened the other door and got out. He didn't see after that. He heard another scream, down the road, and then a single flat pop. It wasn't much there in the trees and grass, but it was a sound that went through him when he heard it. He knew what it was. It froze him there, behind the wheel. He remembered how his head tingled. Laura was crying. She got out.

And then Mrs. Remus was back, the man chasing her. She came in the rear door that Laura had just got out of, but the man came in after her. She crawled across the backseat and out the other side again, and he chased her back up the street.

When Stevens looked back, he saw blood all over the seat, as if something had been slaughtered, and he knew.

He didn't see her after that.

"The traffic had stopped. We didn't know why, 'course. Lewis pulled up and waited. There were maybe four cars in front of us, and up ahead we could see another car, a taxi, pulled off the side, kind of strangely."

"Strangely?"

"Well, you could tell something was wrong, how it was pulled over. A wreck, I assumed. Like it'd been knocked over there."

"Now, you were on your way to work."

"Yes."

"You and another young woman were riding with—"

"Lewis. My brother. He often rides us in."

"And what do you do, Miss Schultz?"

"I work at the public library."

"You're a clerk there."

"Yes."

"And you stated that you were sitting on the passenger side of the motorcar."

"That's right, and Audrey, she was in the middle, and Lewis was driving."

"So from where you were sitting . . ."

"Well, I couldn't see anything at first. 'Course, Lewis and Audrey had the better view 'cause I heard Lewis say, 'Oh,' then Audrey said, 'My God,' and I said 'What?' And then I saw her."

SHE CAME RUNNING UP THE MIDDLE OF THE ROAD, ARMS held out away from her body, as if they burned her. They were smeared with blood. Her mouth was round and open and her eyes were wide. Blood ran down her legs. Her dress was bloody, too, but it was black so you couldn't see the red, just that it was soaked and matted, but you could see the blood running off it. She ran toward them, and then you saw a man coming after her. He held something in his hand and he chased her. They ran past the car, right past Lewis's window. You could see everything. There was blood smeared on her neck, too, and on her face. Up along the side of her cheek, toward her ear. She was so close. She was crying, but not crying. She looked like she was sobbing, but she wasn't making any sound. It looked as if she wasn't even breathing, but she ran and sobbed, and the man came after her.

"MISS AUDREY STEWART."

"You were the one in the middle."

"Yessir."

"Miss Schultz is a friend of yours?"

"Oh, yessir. But, also, I let a room in her house. Her parents' house—"

"All right, Miss Stewart. Tell us what you saw when the car stopped."

"Well, up ahead in the roadway, I saw a woman on the ground."

"Lying on the ground."

"No sir. She was kneeling, in a way. No, not kneeling. Crouching, I suppose."

"Crouching."

"Yessir. Like that. And a man was standing over her."

"Can you identify the man now?"

"He's sitting right there."

"Let the record indicate that Miss Stewart has pointed at the defendant, George Remus. He was standing over her. Had you seen anything before that?"

"The shot, you mean?"

"Objection."

"Sustained."

"Just what you saw, Miss Stewart."

"Well, that's the first thing I saw, was her crouched there, and him over her. And then she stood up and ran forward."

"Forward."

"Away from us. I couldn't see where she went. But then, a moment later, I saw her back in the road, running."

"Toward you."

"Yes. Now she came past us. She was in pain."

"Objection."

"Sustained."

"She looked like she was in pain. Her face."

"Objection. These are conclusions—"

"Overruled."

"Go on, Miss Stewart. Tell us about the man."

"He looked so calm."

"Objection."

"Overruled."

AS IF THERE WERE NO EMOTION IN HIM. AS IF HE WERE IN A trance or something. His face just blank. He did not look angry or anything like that. He looked like these zombies you hear about, the walking dead. She ran past and he came past after her, just walking, not chasing her. Just following.

And then another woman came running past. She was crying and yelling for help. And then, a few seconds or a minute later a machine came out of the line and went past. A man was driving, not the man with the gun. A different man. The two women were in there. The first one, who'd been bleeding, had her head on the shoulder of the other one.

"LEWIS SCHULTZ. I'M IN REAL ESTATE."

"Go ahead."

"Well, I saw her get back into the cab. She went into one side of it, and that man went right in after her. I didn't see, and then she was running toward us."

"How about before that, when you first arrived?"

"I saw these motorcars stopped. I started to pull around, and then saw this woman in the road, and stopped. I saw the man over her. I saw him point at her. Or point something at her."

"He pointed something?"

"Yes."

HE LEANED OVER HER. HE POINTED AT HER. HE JABBED. HE pointed, and then she tried to stand up. He actually helped her, then. He reached out and grabbed her arm, and lifted her up. Like they were taking a break in his killing her. Then she broke away and ran toward the cab.

"JOHN W. MATTHEWS, ATTORNEY-AT-LAW."

"Thank you for giving us your time."

"Of course. Of course."

"Go on, sir."

"Well, as I said, I had just pulled up. It was all right there in front of me. There was I think one machine between mine and the taxi. I did not hear the shot, but I saw her fall. I thought at first that maybe he'd struck her. She fell into his arms, you know. He held her, and then lowered her to the ground, to her knees. I saw the gun in his left hand."

"You saw the gun?"

"Oh, yes. Very clearly. She fell into him and he held her like that, in his arms, but with the gun sticking out. Then he lowered her. He aimed it at her again, at her head. I thought, my God, I'm going to witness an execution. I didn't realize I already had . . ."

THAT STRANGE FEELING WHEN YOUR MOUTH GOES DRY and your head tingles and the hairs stand up. You don't want to look but you can't not look. A part of you says to run, run, get away from this, or lie down on the floor and hide, but another part keeps you there, watching. He aimed it at her, but he didn't fire again. Twice he did that, aimed, like he wanted to shoot again, but could not. Then she stood up. He seemed to grab at her. She ran into the taxi, and came out of it again and ran up the road. He followed her, and again, when he was right there on the other side of the window glass, he aimed the gun. Matthews braced himself for the shot. It never came.

"No, SIR. I WAS THERE, IN THE PARK, WALKING. JUS' WALKING and I seen him grab her to him and I hear this bang and jus' stop right cold. She went down. He held her up, but she went down. Then he pulled her up again. These cars was all stopping and I stopped, too, seen her struggling with him. Then she gets away and goes to the machine, then comes up the road and I seen that gun still in his hand. I wanted to move but I didn't. I just stood there froze up like a statue. I din' even breathe. I sure wasn't gonna move 'til that man was long gone."

"Order."

"I din' think it was so funny then."

WHEN SHE AND THE OTHER LADY GOT IN THE CAR, THE man walked off. He just went slowly into the park, like he was taking a morning stroll. He put the gun in his pocket. He walked up the grass, toward the crest of the hill, and over the top of it, and out of sight. Then it was OK to move again.

"WELL, THEY TRIED TO GET INTO THE MACHINE IN FRONT of me. I could see it clearly. The driver shook his head.

He waved at them, to say, 'No.' Can you imagine? They came to me, and of course I let them in. I could see she was hurt. I didn't know what had happened, but I had heard a noise—"

SHE TALKED. THE OTHER ONE WEPT. THE OTHER ONE KEPT her arms around her and held her head on her chest and whispered to her. The shot woman kept talking about her child. "My baby," she said. "Sweet baby. Why, baby? Why?"

Later, she got on her knees on the floor and leaned on the seat. It seemed to make her feel better, though she was in agony the whole time.

Afterward, the seat and the floor were soaked with blood. It ruined the fabric. They tried to clean it at the garage. They used soaps and solvents, and they scrubbed. But if you kept the machine closed up, and it was the least bit warm outside, when you opened it, you could still smell it, and always would.

"IT ENTERED ON HER LEFT SIDE, ABOUT THREE INCHES below the bottom rib. About here. It passed through the spleen and the stomach, first, and the pleura. It was moving upwards, and across. Like this. It hit the liver, and the lower lobe of the right lung, and then lodged in her back, just beneath the skin. I felt it there. You could have taken it out with a pen knife."

"And these wounds in combination would surely be fatal."

"Any one of these wounds could be fatal. Together, there was simply no hope. No possibility of our stopping that much bleeding in time to save her. She was nearly dead when she got to us, but she was strong, and we did manage to get in and tie off some of the major arteries. Her blood pressure came up a little, then, and I had some small hope, but she had nearly bled out. Her blood volume was terribly low. And she was still bleeding heavily all over. It just poured out of her—"

"Objection."

"To what?

"It's sensationalizing."

"Your Honor, this is a purely clinical description . . ."

"It's not necessary."

"Overruled. Continue."

"She never regained consciousness, Dr. Farley?"

"No. That's correct. Dr. Myerson pronounced her."

"THE SPLEEN," MYERSON SAID. HE HAD BLOOD ALL OVER himself already, up the front of his gown. "Liver fracture," said Farley. There was a long pause as they worked. You could hear the sliding, the seeping. "Lower lobe over here, too. Get it there. *Quickly.*" You could hear the spattering, then, like water running onto the floor, and Myerson said, "Jesus Christ."

She just opened up and bled out right there on the goddamn floor. Later, Farley let Myerson call her. He was young. "Time of death, ten forty-five," he said. His voice quavered just a little. He'd never called one before.

CHARLIE HAD COME TO THE LAST SECTION OF THE DIARY. His melancholy surprised him. He'd miss her in the way he missed old comrades, soldiers. He'd saved this

section until now, to read in the aftermath of what
he'd revealed in court. This was not about bootlegging
or her father or even Remus, really, but simply her.
That is what he wanted to read. He poured himself a
scotch and turned out all the lights but one, and settled in:

January 1921

We left the day after the funeral, Mother and
I. The train ride was terribly long and tedious,
but this was because I did not want to make this
trip. For the first time I was traveling against my
will, to a place I did not want to go. It grew hotter as we came nearer, until, by the end, all we
could do was sit and perspire. The natives met us
there, at the little excuse for a station, and took
us the rest of the way . . .

A DRY HEAT

SHE OFTEN SAT IN A LONG-SLEEVED, HIGH-COLLARED DRESS of good linen and plain design with white gloves and broad-brimmed hat and tinted glasses. She sat beneath a sun she had never before experienced in all her travels. There was nothing to stop it here, not trees or buildings or clouds or even atmosphere, it seemed. It was a simple naked relationship these settlers and natives had with the perfect 180-degree dome of the sky and its light, a direct linking without intermediaries, a constant exposure. She sat at the edge of the desert upon a wicker chaise beneath a wide umbrella, and the co-opted natives brought her bitter healthful drinks in slender frosted glasses. She sat in the sun of the days in her dresses or skirts and blouses, sweltering, sweating, sizzling, swooning, but not ever letting its rays touch her skin directly in any spot, another tiny battle won. This was her strategy. Every day she felt the need to invent a battle and fight it, no matter how small: an ill-prepared dish returned to the kitchen, a new exercise mastered, a pound shed, the sun denied its piece of flesh. They carried her onward, these minor meaningless victories.

She and her mother had been here now in this famous spa since the new year, since the effect of her father's death had renewed, almost overnight, her mother's suffocating attacks of asthma. Although Imogene herself was not unhealthy, there was so little else to do, one could only read so much, that out of simple boredom she partook of certain of the treatments. The massages were painful (she had come to prefer Paul, the Swiss masseur) but invigorating. She felt new circulation, the hot blood beneath her skin. The steam baths made her head feel light and her body hollow but that was interesting sometimes. The dry saunas simply drained her of everything but then she always slept well afterward. Some of the other more bizarre treatments, enemas, irrigations, fasts, strange ascetic diets, weakened her and made her nauseous. But afterward, after being made hollow or drained or nauseated, there was always the sun and nothing else to do but lay beneath it and sip the cold nourishing drinks and gather her strength again. This process, they were taught, of being weakened then allowed to heal, was the source of true power.

It was especially during these moments, these states of near-illness, that she considered her future: a flat, stable place, as she saw it, wholesome and constructive. Teaching, perhaps. Nursing. Charity work. She did not know, yet, but it didn't matter. Good works were good works. It would be the sort of jazzless life she would never have considered before, without romance, without spice or danger. But when she lay listless and queasy from the treatments, or sickened in her soul by what she had done, she rested her head upon the very dimness and conventionality of her future, and it comforted her.

Sometimes the natives drove them in a motorbus to the mountains many miles to the north. These mountains were often barely visible beyond the dancing rolling waves of energy or the early morning mists or the afternoon hazes, nothing more than hulking suggestions of some presence butted against the northern horizon. But then sometimes the air would clear and the light would fall at a certain angle and she could see them there in their stark splendor, clear and knife-edged and violent and at the same time deep and mysterious under layers of violets and blues and blacks and greens. It startled her, this abrupt shattering of the smooth monotony of the desert floor. When they drove northward though it always changed, proximity lessening the mystery, or rather changing it. What had been horizontal and violent and hazy became vertical and beautiful and detailed, and even that changed as they entered. It was just climbing then, the gears of the motorbus singing high under the tension, through pastures of boulders, along sparse coniferous forests, the smooth dirt road turning gradually to a rutted trail that tossed them out of their seats, the natives laughing up in front. Finally they would stop, and hike in along a narrow shaded trail carpeted with pine needles and a light dusting of snow that followed the canyon of a small but churning river. Up they would climb to a spot where the earth leaked steam. She smelled it first, or tasted it, a metallic tang on the air, the flavor of minerals. This steam and the hot springs that came with it had formed a series of naturally heated pools along the banks of the frigid creek. The natives set up black-and-white striped canvas changing tents in which the clients would don their bathing costumes before lowering themselves into the misty baths, the temperature of which increased in direct relation to their distance from the river. She began with the more tepid, those in the rocks forming the immediate border of the river where its water poured over and into the pool, then worked her way along the gradient until finally she entered the hottest, farthest baths that even the natives did not use, and no other client came near. She would step in and bite her lips to keep from crying out, knowing she could only stay a few moments, that she would blister otherwise, that even so she would emerge lobsterlike, her white skin boiled red. But she sank herself down. She sat and wept knowing fully that it wasn't the minerals or the heat or the health she craved in the end. It was the pain.

IN THE FIFTH WEEK, A LETTER CAME INSIDE ONE OF LAURA'S letters. It was a simple note, on the fine creamy linen stationery she had had designed and printed for George, with his name in script at the top, and the address of the Sinton Hotel at the bottom.

"My Dearest Imogene," it began.

"In my life I've counted many people as friends, and known some women, and been married. But it wasn't until you that I understood the meaning of true friendship, and love. Now, having known it, I miss it terribly. And I want it back. I want you.

"The business goes better than you can imagine. I

do little with the money but pour it back in. There's always new stock to buy or trucks to lease or men to hire, and Conners is looking at some new plants. I still live in the Sinton, though I work now in the Remus Building. You'd like it. I hope one day you'll see it.

"I just want to say this: that I'm as guilty, no, guiltier, than you could ever be for what happened. I killed your father, and drove you away, and in the process ruined your family and your life. For that, I will probably burn in hell. But now, Imogene, all I want, though I do not deserve it, is to have you back here in this city, as my friend.

"Yours as ever, George."

She kept it for an entire day, and read it many times. And then she tore it into small pieces and gave it to one of the natives and instructed him to burn it.

THE NOVELTY OF THE TREATMENTS FADED; THEIR EFFECTS grew tiresome except for Paul's massages, so that she mostly just sat at the edge of the expanse of the nothingness surrounding them, covered and shielded, and contemplated the sun. Its never-ceasing presence, light, glare, heat, had disturbed her at first, then angered her, then nearly driven her mad. But as her time here approached ten weeks she began to feel herself enter into a kind of relationship with it, something akin to what the natives and settlers must have enjoyed. It had begun to impress her. The sun. It never left, not really, not even in the night.

The nights grew so dark that what little had remained of the earth seemed to fall away altogether. There was nothing but this infinite blackness overhead dotted with more thousands of stars than Imogene could ever have imagined existed. And yet even then the earth still lay pinned beneath its obedience to the sun. Imogene knew this because she had felt it.

She had an unflagging need to ponder what had happened, what she had done, to turn it so she could examine it from various angles. It was almost as if she were trying to make something from it, to find something in it that could carry her forward. She spent many hours at this. She also had no reason to sleep, for nothing drew her energies during the day but the exposure to more sunlight. And so at some point she did not exactly remember, she began staying up on certain nights until two or three in the morning, usually just thinking, though sometimes she read or wrote or walked through the compound.

Then one night, when everyone was asleep, staff and clientele, she slipped from the compound and walked away from the low buildings into the desert, where, she had been warned, dangers awaited: scorpions and thick rattlers and coyotes and poisonous spined plants and vultures. The first time she didn't walk far or stay long. The air felt marvelously brisk, and it was enough on this night to breathe it. The next night she went again. She walked farther this time under a half moon and circled through the desert, coming back to the compound from a different direction than she had left it.

Until finally one night when the moon was all but full, she just kept walking. She could not have guessed how far she went. She walked until the compound was reduced to a single fused beacon of light on the invisible horizon, enough so that she could see it to get back, so she would not become disoriented. She turned her face up to the stars and the shining moon. She shivered in the cold but she was tired, so tired, of heat. She unbuttoned her blouse and held it open to the air and the light. She pulled her arms from the sleeves and let it fall below her waist. Then she unbuckled the brassiere she wore beneath it (and that is all she would deign to wear here, no shifts, no corsets, her mother's protests notwithstanding), and slipped it from her arms. Oh, the air. She cupped her hands beneath her breasts and lifted their weight toward the sky and bathed them in the moonlight. She looked down at them. They were blue, and the nipples, contracted and stiffened by the chill of the air, looked black.

She sat on the hard baked earth. She crossed her legs and braced her arms behind her and leaned back against them. She shut her eyes. She allowed her hands to slide away. She lowered herself until she was lying on the cutting grit of the desert floor.

She felt it then on the tender skin of her back—the sun. The sun in the earth. She felt its heat, its energy, still radiating, as if the earth held within itself its memory of hot light. As if it could not bear to let it go until the rising came again.

She understood this. Imogene understood how long the night could be.

HIS NEXT LETTER CAME LATER THAT WEEK.

"Dear Imogene, Even in matters of the heart, I'm not above bribery. So I'll tell you straightaway, I have bought you something. Something marvelous. Something you will love. You must come back here, though, to see it, and to claim it. Is this petty of me? Cajoling? I don't care. I'll try anything.

"I am empty. My days are filled with the lives of my men. I travel too often, from Kansas City to New York, Detroit to Atlanta. The business is becoming what we imagined it might. But if, in the process, I have lost you, then it is for nothing. If you tell me truly that you will never return, I will give up the business the following morning and never look back to it. So, I ask— are you gone forever? Please, tell me. I need to know.

"If you are not, then I will double and triple my efforts here, and await your return, though it may not be for years.

"I remain yours faithfully, George."

She took it into the desert that night. She had also taken some of the matches the natives used to light the candles on the dinner tables. She read it once more, as best she could in the moonlight, and then folded it, kissed it, and set it upon the sand. The wind was still, so the first match lit it. She sat very near as it burned, so that she could feel its small heat.

THE DISTANCE, THE ALONENESS, THE DANGER OF HER nights in the desert were not only perfect for her contemplations, they exhilarated her. For the first time since she had come to this place she felt something approximating joy, or at least a momentary break in the unending asceticism of it all that would have to pass for joy until the real thing came back to her. If it ever did. She found herself waiting for them, these moments with herself, with the stars and moon (for she only ventured into the desert when there was enough moonlight to see), as she had waited in Cincinnati to see George at night. Those nights had belonged to them, and now these belonged to her.

And she began to feel something else, too—a kind of power. She controlled these moments. She could live or die, as she chose. The desert became hers alone for these few hours. She ruled over it. She was growing strong again. And yet this degree of control she had carved out also illuminated for her how deluded she had been in her previous life, believing as she had in her abilities to make happen what she wanted. She had been, she saw now, flotsam bouncing on the whims of fate and circumstance, guided by nothing but a false and deadly pride.

Perhaps this knowledge then was what she had sought from the tragedy. Perhaps this was all she would get from it. Perhaps that would be enough.

In early May, as the days grew long and the sun hotter and higher than ever, when most clients had already left, an envelope was delivered to her by a native waiter on a silver tray along with a glass of the iced herbal potions she consumed in such quantity.

"Dear Imogene," it said. "I am still here, still waiting. I work, nothing more. Despite your failure to answer my letters, I feel no differently. Can't you at least cut me free, though, if that's how it's to be? Didn't you love me enough once to at least do that?

"George."

ONE DAY, AS SHE LAY IN A TREATMENT ROOM UNDER THE kneading hands of Swiss Paul, Imogene heard voices approaching in the hallway. She lay listening, expecting them to grow louder and then dimmer as they passed, but instead the door opened suddenly. Another member of the staff, an exercise leader, had come in for some supplies. He apologized. He had not realized the room was in use. He took what he needed and left again. As he left, he said to the person waiting for him in the hallway, "Well, at least your asthma seems to have cleared up nicely."

The woman with him said, "I don't have asthma, young man. Haven't had in years. We came here for other reasons entirely."

Imogene of course recognized the voice of her mother, and understood.

That night she went farther into the desert than she had ever gone, to the very limit of her circumference of safety, to a point where the light of the compound was so tiny and distant that it became merely a suggestion of light. She was on the border. A single additional step and the light would blink out and she would be lost out here. For without the tiny beacon, she would be as adrift as one in a dinghy at sea, disoriented, directionless. The natives would find her a day or two later, swollen and white-lipped, golden dust swirling in and out of her mouth.

One step. She dared go no farther, but this was far enough.

As if a voice had told her, she knew that George Remus was her only escape. Her access to real power. She'd never been meant to teach or heal.

She had killed her father. There was no rectifying it. She had ruined her family, as well, but that might not be such a final thing. She couldn't know from here what might happen back there, in society. How she might be seen. It would be a huge risk to go back. But did a mistake require her to stay ruined forever? Was it better to accept being destroyed by it, or to try to make something of it, to resurrect her life? To live again.

Her father hadn't really understood George, and he was under the influence of those other men, George's enemies. But surely he would have wanted her to be her own self, as fully as she could.

She stripped to the waist as she had done many times, and then feeling a sudden dizzying surge of erotic inspiration, of itching need, she removed her dress completely and her shoes and stockings and knickers and even the comb she wore in her hair so that she was entirely naked. She felt something new, a sensation, a titillation, the deep bite of a desire she had not ever felt before, a wild thing of abandon. It frightened her, what she felt capable of at that moment. She spread her dress on the sand and lay upon it beneath the moon that bathed all of her now finally in its pale bluish light. She turned so it could reach her back, and turned again so that she lay belly up, and finally she pulled her knees toward her and spread them. She arched her back and tilted her hips so that the light could come into her. She moved beneath it and felt it shoot up inside clear through to her belly and chest and head. She felt a series of contractions as a final breathless surging warmth and release she had never known spread through her in this, their simultaneous consummation and farewell.

A VISION OF A LADY

ROMOLA CAME TO COURT EVERY DAY, AND THEN TO THE jail suite. Often she just read, but Remus loved having her there, to watch, to touch. When Conners and Elston came to discuss the case, she excused herself. She needn't have, he told her, but she always did. Such a sensitive and courteous girl.

"Well, the worst is over," Elston said, in the evening. "This re-creation of the death scene was their strongest card, and they've played it. But judging from the witness list, I'd say they're going ahead with this conspiracy notion—that Imogene was going to reveal Remus's and your role in some past murder, and that he killed her to shut her up."

"It's nuts," Conners said.

"Let them stick their necks well out," said Elston. "Then we'll chop-chop." He paused and thought and nodded. "This man of yours, this Babe, is on their list." Though Remus clenched his jaw and grew red and paced the room, Conners merely smiled.

THE RAGES GRIPPED HIM AS DEEPLY AS THEY EVER HAD, BUT like a child who sees himself in the mirror while bawling, and stops for a moment to look, Remus had begun to be aware of himself during the darkness of the outbursts in a way he hadn't before. This seemed strange to him, and he didn't like it, but not liking it only made him more aware.

With this came the thought that if he was aware of them now, he must not have been before. It occurred to him abstractly what this might mean, his having been so dimly conscious of his actions. There was a word for people who acted this way. He didn't believe it. He rejected the notion out of hand. And yet he was in the absurd position of having to proclaim it: his life depended on his proving his own insanity.

What did not strike him as strange at all was the fact that this bifurcation came perfectly easily to him: to deny any possibility of truth in it, yet to speak persuasively of it, to view it as a purely legal exercise, standing in court and arguing the nuances of a thing he found laughable.

But at certain moments, usually at night, he came face-to-face with the possibility that it was real. During the days in court or in the cell-suite with Conners, he was lucid, clear-headed, resolved. Though he didn't remember killing her, he knew he had, and knew what was necessary now. In the days, it was enough to think and plot for his life. At night, though, when he was alone, it changed. He had begun to miss her. He longed for her so terribly sometimes, in fact, that it made him nauseous. So much that sometimes he couldn't even rise from his bed. He sobbed like a child at the emptiness his arms embraced.

She had said to him, once: "Even the moon is jealous of us."

One morning, in June of 1921, he stood in the kitchen of the Lackland mansion in Price Hill, which he had bought. This was the surprise he'd written her about.

She'd been away six months in her exile without so much as sending him a word. He wasn't good enough for her. That was it, really. He knew it. She needed someone from her own place, her world, someone sophisticated, able to move as she moved. It was truly over. As he looked out the rear window, contemplating this, the hope he had so stubbornly held on to for these months flickered and guttered.

Then he heard a noise, and turned, and she came in as if she had always just been there. She wore a black silk frock and she was beautiful. He opened his mouth to cry out, to greet her, but she covered it with her hand. She held him, tightly, without speaking, and led him upstairs to the bedroom he had furnished for her.

HE FILLED THE LEGAL PADS CONNERS BROUGHT HIM. BUT now, instead of thoughts regarding the trial, he found himself writing memories. He wrote of his parents, of the siblings who'd died before and after him. Of his uncle, who taught him the pharmacy business, and then sold him the stores when George forced him into retirement. Of the murderers and gangsters he'd freed in the courtrooms of Chicago. Of his wife and child, whom he abandoned to come here. Of the business he built on contraband and maneuvers that were, in spite of his protestations otherwise, illegal. And of Imogene.

Later, when he read over these notes, he'd laugh at the folly, at his sentimentality, the self-doubt he indulged himself in, that he knew would be his ruin if he let it take hold. He'd tear up the pages and spend days focused only on the trial, on the nuances of Charlie Taft's case against him, and of Elston's defense. Then, one late sleepless night, pieces would again begin to come back, and he'd feel compelled to write . . .

AS THE SUMMER OF 1921 WORE ON, THE HOUSE BECAME habitable, but Imogene did not move out of the Alms, where Remus had put her up. She spent her days at the mansion, supervising, deciding, instructing, but she would not sleep there. Not yet.

And then at the end of that August, Second Lieutenant Malcolm Coffey was discovered in his bed by an attendant, dead at least six hours. They had thought he was getting over his most recent lung congestion, but he'd apparently just stopped breathing in the night. Imogene saw him buried with military honors in the famous Spring Grove Cemetery, three months shy of three years since his injury near the Meuse-Argonne.

In September, Remus and Imogene were married in a private ceremony in the courthouse. In lieu of a honeymoon, they moved that afternoon into Price Hill. Although the papers were notified of the happy event, none carried any mention of it.

Despite the work still going on, especially on the east wing where ground had just been broken for the pool room Imogene was giving George as his wedding gift, she declared the house ready. Or a part of it, at least: the great sapphire dining hall; the rose morning room; the music room with the gold-plated grand piano (her wedding gift from Remus); three of the larger bedrooms. Enough, she said, so they could entertain a few well-chosen guests, no more than fifty at this christening. It would be a harvest moon party, she decided, the second week in October.

The guests arrived almost simultaneously in their fine motorcars, as if they had driven in parade. They entered past the two huge carved stone lions at the end of the long drive that was lit with gas torches instead of common electric lights. The rich flames shone in the chrome and paint of those passing cars. Deep burgundies. Burnished greens. Polished blacks. They came past the dozens of species of flowers and trees and shrubs Remus had had planted, many rare and unknown to this area, and came past the hundred thousand dollars' worth of carved Italian Renaissance statuary that resided now among the plant life.

These guests, most of whom were no more to Remus than names on a page, streamed in through the high oak doors that had been thrown open to the mild evening, past Remus and Imogene, then past the white-gloved staff that formed a welcoming queue behind them. Remus found himself wishing, even as he greeted couple after couple, that some of his men could have come. Instead, he welcomed strangers: judges, politicians, merchants, heirs.

In the west parlor, as the guests sipped their first drinks, they were instructed that tobacco must be limited either to the grounds or the new specially venti-

lated smoking room. Mr. Remus could not abide the
smell of it. This raised some eyebrows, but no one
seemed particularly taken aback. Remus mingled, sipping a glass of apple juice on ice, which looked
enough like whiskey. A jazz quintet played in the
music room.

For dinner, all the guests were seated at two
tremendous parallel tables in the dining hall. As they
ate, a woman happened to shift her plate. "Oh!" she
exclaimed, and pulled a hundred dollar bill from
beneath it and waved it in the air. They all looked
then. Each discovered the same prize. Laughter, language, the scent of it all, floated up toward the high
pressed-tin ceiling. Remus smiled at how simple it was
to please people.

After the meal, the party moved back into the par-
lors and out onto the lawn. Remus and Imogene were
standing together on the porch when a woman waved
and came toward them.

"Ruth Higgins," Imogene told Remus. "We came
out together. The Higginses have been in real estate
here since the Civil War."

"Imogene," the woman said. "What a lovely
evening."

"I'm so glad you're enjoying it."

"Mmm," she said.

"And how do you find our little shack?" Remus
asked her.

"Oh, everything's so . . . obviously expensive."

Remus looked at her hand-beaded gown and her
velvet hat and her little nose. "Well," he said. "Hard
work. You understand that."

She regarded him, then smiled and turned and wandered away.

"George, dear," Imogene said. "Don't be defensive."

"She—"

"She was being impolite. Let her. Don't join her." She put her arm through his and squeezed.

Later, Imogene gave a short recital on the 14-karat piano, playing Mozart's "Alla Turca," "Le Petit Negre" by the strange and modern Debussy, and the "Pine Apple Rag" by Scott Joplin. Remus stood in the foyer outside the opened parlor doors to listen. A woman in front of him, unaware of his presence, leaned toward the man with her and said, "Can you imagine her coming back at all, let alone flaunting herself like this?"

The man said, "They say it was for his money. Dirty or not, she'll need it now."

Remus slipped away, then, and climbed up to the cupola above the attic, where he could look out across the grounds and Price Hill. He could just make out the top of the Water Tower clear across the basin on Mount Adams. She found him after midnight. "Won't you join us again?" she asked.

"They despise me, you know."

"They don't. Everyone's having a grand time."

"Of course they are. But they still resent me. And they look at you with contempt."

"George," she said. "They'll see this as the event of the season. You watch."

He remained here, watching, contemplating, until the time hours hence when it was his responsibility to bid his guests farewell. As it turned out, none of the society reporters Imogene had invited chose to so much as mention the event in their papers.

ONE NIGHT REMUS GOT UP FROM HIS SWEATY COT TO GET some water. He stood at the gated window as he drank and looked over the city's skyline, dark against the river and dominated by the white peak of the Union Central Life Insurance Building at Fourth and Vine. The streets were empty, it being after 3:00 A.M., but for a figure moving up Court Street. As it approached, he saw that it was a woman in a flowing dress, a dress so white that it seemed almost luminous in the moonlight. She came to the intersection below him, and stopped. Remus pressed his face closer to the bars. The figure looked up at him.

It was Imogene. Even from this distance, he had no doubt. He knew her face as well as his own, her body, the way she moved.

He cried out in his terror. His stumbled away from the window, from the vision, and began to tremble so hard he fell to his knees. He couldn't breathe. He pounded on the door, then, until a deputy came. Later, he called Conners and woke him, and asked him to please come over, in spite of the hour, and sit with him, which Conners did, until he had fallen asleep again.

CONSPIRACY

IT HAD BEEN TOO GOOD. THE LAW OF AVERAGES HELD that something had to let go. Charlie was reading in his favorite chair in the study in the back of the house, listening with one ear to the children playing in the hallway, when the phone rang.

"Mary Hubbard," Walt said. "She's not sure all of a sudden. She can't remember. She feels funny talking about it."

"Did someone get to her?"

"Hard to say. We're bringing her in now, for one last try. See if we can turn her again. We'll wait for you."

"No. Go ahead."

"I don't hold much hope."

"It felt shaky all along. I never believed in it, I guess."

"It was worth a try."

"Sure."

"It only goes to motive, Charlie. Nothing really turns on it. It made a nice package, but it's not as if he didn't have a dozen other motives."

"That's right," Charlie said. "We've got him, anyway." But when he hung up, he whispered "Damn" to his teacup.

"THE PROSECUTION CALLS JUDGE EDWARD T. DIXON." Dixon, rotund, wearing a long, old-fashioned great-coat and vest, was sworn in. When he sat, Judge Shook said, "How are you, Ed?"

"Just fine, Chester. Thank you."

Charlie stood and said, "Judge."

"Charlie," Dixon said. "How's the old man?"

"Same as ever, I hear."

Dixon laughed.

Remus said, "Shall I order coffee and cakes for everyone, Your Honor? While we're waiting."

The crowd laughed. Shook pounded angrily, then said, "That's enough, Mr. Remus. Mr. Taft—"

"Judge Dixon, state your occupation, please."

"I'm an attorney-at-law in private practice."

"And you were once on the bench here."

"In this very courtroom, Mr. Taft, among others."

"Imogene Ring was a recent client of yours?"

"She was."

"In what matter?

"Several matters, all pertaining to lawsuits she had pending against her husband, George Remus, or that he had pending against her. The immediate issue was that of their divorce."

"When was the last time you saw Mrs. Remus?"

"At Bethesda Hospital, on that morning, October sixth. I was summoned shortly after the shooting. I was there when she was pronounced dead."

"Was the divorce case prepared, Judge?"

"Oh, yes, fully. We worked on it for some months."

"Now tell me this—had she prepared anything unusual, that is to say, outside the bounds of the normal revelations in a divorce proceeding?"

"Well, actually, yes. I was never sure exactly what, but I know that in the meeting we were to have had on the morning she died, she planned to reveal something she called 'startling.'"

"Judge, had she told you anything about an earlier case of murder involving her husband—"

"Objection," said Carl Elston. "This is hearsay. It's meant only to prejudice the jury, Your Honor."

Shook motioned for Charlie and Elston to approach.

"Charlie," he said. "Where are you going with this?"

"It all goes to demonstrating the conspiracy, and motive."

"They can't offer a shred of hard proof," said Elston.

"What else do you have?" Shook asked.

Charlie shook his head.

"Any other testimony?"

"Hearsay."

Shook waved them back and announced, "The objection is sustained." A buzz passed through the crowd.

"So, sir," Charlie said, "one would assume George Remus's divorce case was prepared as well."

"Well," said Judge Dixon, "from what I saw, Mr. Taft, that was not the case—"

HE HAD SENT ONE OF THE NEW JUNIORS TO THE COURT-house to pull the records of any subpoenas Remus had filed to have served in the case against his wife. Standard procedure. But the junior came back shortly and said there was nothing there. Dixon himself went over later that afternoon, assuming the junior had made a mistake. But it wasn't a mistake. Remus had filed no subpoenas.

Dixon remembered that feeling of discovery, of the tantalizing bite of something significant but not yet understood. He had always loved that feeling. He called Imogene that night.

"Well, I don't know," she said. "He must have something planned. I know him. He won't accept this without a fight."

It was only later, as Dixon stood in the surgical ward over her dead body, that it occurred to him: Remus had prepared no divorce case because he had known he wouldn't need to.

"YOUR HONOR," ELSTON SAID. "THIS IS REALLY UNPRECE-dented. We're to take the word of opposing counsel as proof that Mr. Remus hadn't prepared a case in his divorce? And to leap from there to the assumption that this proves some conspiracy or premeditation?"

"You can cross, Mr. Elston."

"I don't want to cross. I think the entire testimony should be disregarded. I so move. If the jury needs to see what Mr. Remus did or did not do in regard to his divorce case, let us simply submit the file for their examination. We're prepared to do that."

"I'll let the testimony stand, but I'll also accept the file as an exhibit."

"Your Honor," Remus said, standing. "Allow me to

say that I did prepare fully and that the file will bear that out. I put in hours and hours of work, as did my attorneys."

"Very well, Mr. Remus. We shall see."

"You shall. Yes. We collected scores of depositions."

"That's fine, Mr. Remus."

"It's all there in the file."

"Mr. Remus," said the judge. "I've ruled."

"Yessir," Remus said, and sat down.

BABE SAT SQUEEZED INTO THE LITTLE BOX, HIS BACK AND knees pressed against the railings. His huge hands hung over.

"Mr. Klegg," said Clyde Basler. "How are you today?"

Babe nodded.

"Speak up," the judge said.

"It's fine," Clyde said. "I'm sure Mr. Klegg will speak so that we all can hear. Isn't that right?"

"Yessir," the Babe said, a little too loudly.

Basler stood in the middle of the arena and put his hands in his pockets. He leaned back on his heels and looked up at the high ceiling, and held the pose for several moments. He began by establishing the parameters of Babe's life—that he lived alone and worked as a professional driver, that he had lived in this city for seven years now, and knew it very well, that he had known George Remus for a longer time than that, since Chicago.

Basler said, "Let's work backwards, Mr. Klegg. Tell us about the morning of the shooting. October sixth. Where were you?"

"Been work'n' a club all night."

"Until what time?"

"Six."

"Then?"

"Had breakfast."

"Then?"

"Went to the Sinton."

"The Sinton Hotel? Why?"

"Pick up Mr. Remus."

"That's pretty early. He'd arranged for you to pick him up?"

"He tol' me."

"He'd told you the night before, didn't he?"

"Objection."

"When did he tell you to pick him up, Mr. Klegg?"

"I dunno."

"You don't know? Well, did he call you that morning?"

"I dunno. He might'a. Yeah."

Charlie felt a sinking in his stomach. Basler stared at Klegg. "Do you remember getting a call at the club that morning?"

"Maybe."

"If not, then you must have been told before that. No?"

"I guess. I dunno."

"All right. We'll come back to that morning. Where were you the night before, before you went to the club?"

"At the hotel."

"The Sinton."

"Yessir."

"In Mr. Remus's room."

"Yessir."

"Who else was there?"

"Mr. Conners."

"Just the three of you?"

"Yeah."

"But Mr. Remus ordered four dinners."

"Two for me," Babe said.

"Ah. So what was discussed that evening?"

"I wasn't there long."

"What was discussed while you were there?"

"Mr. Remus and Mr. Conners din' talk ta me, much."

"Mr. Klegg!" Clyde said. "Do you remember telling me, in a statement, that you discussed Mrs. Remus that night?"

"Your Honor," Elston said. "He's cross-examining his own witness."

"Judge," said Basler. "This witness has turned hostile. I ask the court's permission to cross-examine him."

"You have it."

"Mr. Klegg, I have a document here that you signed. Do you remember this?"

"I dunno."

"Is this your mark at the bottom?"

"It's a X," Babe said.

"Is it your X?"

"I dunno. It's jus' a X."

Clyde walked across and threw the tablet down on the prosecution table. He took a moment to gather himself, then said, "On that evening, what happened when you left Mr. Remus's room?"

"Drove ta the Alms."

"You drove Mr. Remus to the Alms Hotel."

"Yeah."

"Fine. Good. What car did you drive?"

"Cadillac."

"And why did he tell you he wanted to go there?"

"Talk ta her."

"To Mrs. Remus?"

"Yeah."

"That's all? Wasn't he going to kill her that night?"

"I dunno. No. He said he needed'a see her, talk."

"Did he have a gun?"

"Din't see one."

"Do you remember telling me he told you he was going to do her once and for all?"

"I dunno."

"You don't know?"

"No, sir."

Clyde closed his eyes. He said, "What happened that night?"

"We waited a little, then he said leave. He change his mind."

"You took him back to the Sinton."

"Yessir."

"Then you picked him up there the next morning."

"Yessir."

"In the Cadillac."

"Yessir."

"And took him to the mansion."

"Yeah."

"Your Honor," Elston said. "Does Mr. Basler really need this witness? He's having a perfectly fine conversation with himself."

Shook nodded and said, "Mr. Basler, please."

"Tell us again where you took Mr. Remus, then," Basler said, "in the morning after you picked him up."

"To the house."

"What happened there?"

"Nothing. He got some stuff."

"What stuff?"

"I dunno. I didn't see. Papers, I guess."

"That's all? Just papers?"

"I dunno."

"You saw him get something else, maybe?"

"Not really."

"Well, what did you see?"

"He put something in his pocket."

"So you did see him get something."

"I guess."

"What was it?"

"It looked like papers."

"Maybe something wrapped in paper?"

"Objection," Elston said.

"Never mind," said Basler. "Then what?"

"He said go ta the Alms."

"And what happened there?"

"We waited."

"For her to come out?"

"Yeah."

"And then?"

"He said'a follow. We went in'a park. He said he had'a talk ta her now, so catch up with 'em."

"And you forced their car off the road."

"No, sir."

"Objection!" Remus said.

"Sit down, Mr. Remus!"

"He didn't force them over. They just stopped—"

"Bailiffs! Mr. Remus, you keep your mouth shut, or I swear I will have you removed."

"What then, Mr. Klegg?"

"Mr. Remus got out."

"Did you see him shoot Mrs. Remus?"

"No, sir."

Basler shook his head. "The state reserves the right to redirect, Your Honor. I have nothing more right now."

"Mr. Elston," said the judge.

Elston came over to the prosecution table and picked up the tablet that Babe had signed in the jail with his X.

"May I?" he asked. Basler shrugged.

"Mr. Klegg." Elston said. "Does anyone call you that? Mr. Klegg?"

"No, sir.

"What do you like to be called?"

"Babe."

"May I call you that?"

"Yessir."

"On the morning of the shooting, Babe, did you have any idea Mr. Remus was going to kill his wife?"

"No, sir."

"Did you know he had a gun?"

"No, sir."

"Did you chase Mrs. Remus's car?"

"Yessir."

"Did you run it off the road?"

"Well—no, sir."

"But you were driving the machine, no?"

"Yessir, but then th'other car stopped."

"And so you stopped near it?"

"Yessir."

Elston held up the tablet and said, "Babe, this is a record of a statement you supposedly made to Mr. Basler and Mr. Taft several weeks ago. Do you recognize it?"

"Yessir."

"Did you write any of this yourself?"

"No, sir."

"Who wrote it?"

"A copper."

"A detective, in fact. And why was that?"

"I don' write so well."

"Did you give these answers to Mr. Basler, and then the detective wrote them down?"

"I dunno. Kinda."

"Or did Mr. Basler ask you the questions, and then suggest answers himself, much as he's done here today?"

"Yessir."

"In fact, Babe, you've never read any of this, have you?"

"No, sir."

"You were never given the opportunity to read any of it, were you?"

"I don' read so well."

"Do you read a little?"

"Yessir."

"Now, there's an X at the end of this. Did you make it?"

"I guess. They tol' me. They was gonna hit me again."

"They beat you?"

"Some. They said I had five minutes ta talk. I din'. Then they set in to punchin' me."

"And you were kept thirsty."

"Yeah."

"And hungry.

"Oh, yeah."

"You'd have signed about anything, wouldn't you?"

"Yessir."

Elston turned to a blank page in the tablet, and removed a fountain pen from his pocket.

"Mr. Klegg," he said. "I'd like you to sign your name. Would you do that for me?"

Babe balanced the tablet on his lap. He concentrated. After some time, he handed the tablet back. The crude printing looked like it had been made by a small child, but it clearly said Babe. Elston showed it to the judge, and then took his time making sure that each member of the jury had a good look as well.

ON A MOTION FROM THE DEFENSE, SHOOK RULED THAT NO conspiracy had been demonstrated, and informed the jury that that particular charge against Remus was being dropped. It would be up to them to decide what impact, if any, this had on the question of the murder itself.

Remus then said, "We move that charges be filed against the district attorney and his lieutenants for intimidating witnesses."

"Denied," said Judge Shook. "You've had a good day, Mr. Remus. Let's leave it at that."

THE WHISKEY
MONOPOLY

THAT NIGHT, WHEN ELSTON AND CONNERS AND ROMOLA came to Remus's suite, Babe shuffled sheepishly in behind them. Remus held out his hand to grasp Babe's, then pulled against it and flung his arms around the bigger man's shoulders. "You were magnificent," he said. Babe grinned.

"I swear," said Elston, "you couldn't have been any better."

"They deserved every bit of it," Conners said.

"After what they did to this man, they ought to be on trial," said Remus.

Babe shook his head, too overcome to speak. He sat on the couch. Remus pushed a tray of cookies and biscuits and coffee toward him, and urged him to eat.

THE FOOD HAD ALWAYS SEEMED TO BE BABE'S FAVORITE part of it. In the mansion, Remus woke early, but often he found Babe already in the kitchen in his shirtsleeves, a holster strapped around his chest, attacking a plateful of the cook's eggs and sausages or waffles or a bowl of porridge and fruit.

The pool was finished in November, though the room around it would not be until the spring. Remus dragged a broomstick along the surface to break the skin of ice that had formed during the night. When he'd cleared a lane, he would perch at one end and breathe before diving. He liked to do fifty laps, a half mile. This was not so much, but he had many people waiting for him. Half a mile was enough to get the blood up.

Fowler, his new English manservant, waited inside the house, watching and counting. As Remus began the fiftieth lap, Fowler hurried out to wait at the end with towels and robe and slippers. He would have Remus's suit for the day laid out on the bed in the master suite. These were invariably black or gray flannels at this time of year. He stood nearby as Remus dressed, ready to help in any task. He brushed the suit, front and back, top to bottom, and gave the shoes a final polish.

When they came down, Babe would just be finishing his meal.

First was always the Lincoln National. Later, they'd make deposits to pseudonymous accounts in other institutions. Babe got out of the new Cadillac first, and waited, hand in coat, as Remus carried his valise from the curb. A security guard held the door. Often the president or another officer came out to take the deposit personally. They watched raptly as Remus opened the case and lifted out the banded stacks of bills. Some days, especially Mondays, it was more than a hundred thousand.

❧ ❧ ❧

As Babe ate his cookies, Conners began to coerce him into talking. "Tell us what they did, old Babe," he'd say. "What'd those coppers do to you?" Babe shook his head and pinkened and stuffed another cookie into his mouth. Conners knew he loved to talk about it, but was reticent because Romola was there.

"I'll bet it wasn't that bad," Conners said, looking at her. "They pushed him around a little, not much more than that."

Romola sat on her father's bed and watched, wide-eyed, giggling at Conners's teasing. Until finally, the Babe, unable to stand it, pointed his finger at Conners and said, "You couldn'a took it."

"I don't doubt that."

"They cuff me up and I got so hungry."

"Really, really hungry," Conners said. "They didn't feed him, you know, for a whole day."

"Yeah. An'ay beat me."

"They really beat you?" Romola said.

" 'You gotta tell us,' the copper said, and when I din', he hit me in'a head with a big book."

"Oh, my," Romola said.

"Oh, yeah," said the Babe, "right in the back'a the head." He pointed.

She looked at her father.

He said, "Do you see why I've always fought them? Why good defense lawyers are so important?"

"Yeah," Babe said. "My hand turn blue."

Remus put his hands on Babe's shoulders. "To-night," he said, "you're the hero."

"Here, here," Conners said.

Elston held up his water glass.

Later, when Babe had gone and Romola dozed off, Elston sat close beside him. "They're not far from the end," he said. "I think we've done well. We'll come into the defense without them having damaged us nearly as badly as they thought they could."

Remus nodded.

"One other thing," Elston said. "I hear that your petition to open the bank box at the Third National is going to be granted."

"It's about time," said Conners.

"Yes," Remus said. "Who knows what we'll find."

"What do you think?" Elston asked.

"Money, I hope. There's quite a bit missing, you know."

"Or maybe something to help the case," Elston said.

"Certificates," said Conners. "She may have sold most of the distilleries, but she held on to the withdrawal certificates. She knew what they were worth."

THEY HAD FOUGHT OVER THE CERTIFICATES. THE PROBLEM, Conners kept saying, was that they couldn't withdraw quickly enough. By early 1922 they were moving thirty thousand cases a month, but it wasn't enough. People wanted more. The dozen plants they owned were producing more, or Conners was buying it, but Remus couldn't get enough certificates to withdraw it.

One afternoon Marcus and Conners came out to the mansion to discuss the situation. They sat with Remus in his study. Imogene had come in to listen, as well. He never minded letting her in when she wanted.

A pile of certificates, each good for the withdrawal of five hundred cases, lay on the desk. She picked one up and read it as they argued.

"Why not just change it?" she asked.

The three of them stopped and looked at her. She unscrewed the cap from a fountain pen and wrote on the certificate. So 500 became 5000.

Marcus looked at it and laughed.

Remus shook his head. This was illegal. It was forgery.

Conners took it from her, considered it a moment, then said to Remus, "It'll work. You can take care of it, can't you?"

They all watched him.

He looked only at Conners, and said, finally, "Yes. Of course."

It had already occurred to him that, with Warren Harding and his band of Ohio thieves and racketeers now settled in Washington, a world of new possibility had opened. That afternoon he placed a call to a New York lawyer named Elijah Zoline, a specialist in federal law who'd helped them gain access to the East Coast markets and set up protection there.

A week later, Remus disembarked at Grand Central, apparently unaccompanied (though he was in fact shadowed by two of Marcus's men), and passed through the arched antechambers and the great domed hall and out into the din and bustle of Forty-second Street. He checked into a suite at the Ansonia, called Zoline's offices, checked his watch, then stood at the window. A little later, he descended to the bar, where Zoline waited for him. They shook hands.

Zoline tilted his head. At a booth in a dim corner, another man stood. Zoline nodded to him, then to Remus, then excused himself without having made an introduction.

"Mr. Remus," the man said. He was tall, and he carried himself with a pretense of elegance, or delicateness. He wore small round tortoise-shell eyeglasses. Though he was not particularly heavy, he carried a bag of flesh beneath his weak receding chin.

"Mr. Smith," said Remus. Jesse Smith had grown up in the Ohio town of Washington Court House, with his friend Harry Daugherty, who was now the attorney general of the United States. Smith had twisted as many arms as anyone on the road to Warren Harding's election, but he had no official position in the Justice Department or the Cabinet. He functioned, instead, as the sentinel. His Justice Department office was across the hall from Daugherty's. It was common knowledge that to get into the latter, you had to pass first through the former. It was also known that Daugherty, who was as corrupt and self-serving as any man Washington had ever seen, touched nothing directly. It all went to Jess Smith. He was, in short, the bag man for the head of all law enforcement in the country.

"It's a simple thing," Remus said. "We have the product. We own it, Mr. Smith. We just simply cannot withdraw it as quickly as we can acquire or manufacture it. And that, you must agree, is a frustrating position for any businessman."

"What do you propose?"

They spoke for several minutes before Remus lifted

a heavy valise onto his lap and counted out, there in the bar of the Ansonia Hotel, fifty thousand dollars in cash.

"That is a start," Smith said.

"We won't be bothered, then?"

"I can't control every man in the country, Mr. Remus. You realize that. What I can assure you is this: if something should happen, even if it should go to trial and a jury should convict you, nothing will come of it. It will die in the appellate process. In the end, you'll do no time."

Remus slid the stack of bills across the table.

At home, Conners had begun negotiations for the purchase of five more distilleries. When they were secured, they would give Remus control of a third of all bonded whiskey production in the nation, which constituted a technical monopoly. Imogene took him to speakeasy jazz clubs, Negro west-end blues clubs, society dance clubs. He bought her radios and phonographs, and she brought music home. One was a new recording of an Irving Berlin song that stuck in his head:

> Stocks are going up, going up, going up
> Stocks are going up, going up, going up
> So come on, let's dance that society bear.

In the very early mornings he would come to the new pool room and open all the doors and windows. When the air inside had cooled, he would dive. At the end, Fowler waited with the warm, good towels.

❧ ❧ ❧

ABOVE THE COUNTY JAIL, IN HIS BED, IN HIS SUITE, AT
night, Remus sometimes listened to the city and dia-
grammed in his mind the layout of the streets he had
once commanded, as she had commanded him. Oh
God, he thought. This woman! He hadn't believed he
had it in him to love like that. It was a thing he knew
he would never know again, and never understand.

On another night he again stood at the window,
and again saw her walking toward the courthouse,
from the south this time, from the river. The white
dress rippled in the breeze and shined like an aureole.
He began to tremble. Again she came to the intersection. Again she stopped and looked up. He forced
himself to watch this time, to hold the moment. He
owed her that, at least, didn't he?

But then, when her feet left the pavement, when
she rose into the air and came toward his seventh-
story window, he began to scream. Small little pips at
first, then deeper louder longer shrieks, until finally,
when they opened the door, he was bellowing and
running into the wall like some common madman.

In the hospital, Bethesda, where Imogene had died,
Conners sat by Remus's bed. Romola came, and so of
course, in the morning, did Elston. The alienists came
as well, and questioned, and prodded, and wrote volu-
minous notes. But by that afternoon Remus was back
in his jail suite. He implored Elston, and Elston reluc-
tantly agreed, not to mention the incident in court.
The prosecutors, of course, never brought it up.

THE UNTOUCHABLES

CHARLIE HAD HELD BACK HIS BOMBSHELL. FRANK DODGE would put it all into context, illuminate the entire affair. If they'd been able to continue building the conspiracy theory, he could have embellished that, too. But he had no direct knowledge of that situation, anyway. What mattered was that he had watched Imogene and Remus for years, hunted them, come to know them intimately, and could describe the crescendo of rage that led Remus to murder.

This was their last chance to add something to the case besides a re-creation of the crime. Charlie wanted no missteps. So he assembled them in his office on the Saturday before Dodge was to testify. Dodge and Basler sat in the leather chairs. Walt stood by the window, his arms folded. He said, "I want to start at the beginning. Come up through the whole history. You think?"

"Well," Charlie said, "as much as Shook'll let us, yes."

"Look," Basler said. "He's allowed them to gather these silly depositions about everyone, including our friend Mr. Dodge here. They've argued that this is as much about history as anything. Well, then, fine. We can do history, too."

"Anyway," Charlie said, "let's go through it."

"Mr. Dodge," Walt said, "when did you first meet George and Imogene Remus?"

"Meet?" Dodge said. "Or hear about?"

"Well—"

"Because I heard about them long before we ever met."

"All right, then," Walt said. "Let's talk about that. In 1920, you were tipped off by a reporter named Dolittle about a crooked lawyer here named Ring."

"That's right."

"Did you know who Dolittle's source was?"

"Not at first. But after Ring suicided, I wanted to talk to the family. Dolittle put me off it. He said the daughter was the only one who knew anything, and that I already had what she knew. I got it, then."

"And that daughter was Imogene."

"Yes."

BY EARLY 1922, FRANK HAD BEGUN HEARING ABOUT Cincinnati again. An inordinate volume of hooch was moving through there. That much everyone knew. In February, he took a trip to dig around a little. He stayed in the Palace Hotel, on Vine Street. One morning he was lying on the bed, reading the paper, when he saw a society picture of several women, one of whom was identified as Mrs. George Remus. The name Remus had floated across to Dodge a few times since he'd been here. Nothing remarkable. Another small-time bootlegger, he'd figured. But now here was the man's wife at some annual ball held at the Sinton Hotel. And this wife, the text said, was the former Imogene Ring.

Dodge called Dolittle. "This is not a coincidence," he said. "The same woman who puts you in the know about her father's dealings is now married into it."

"She's a source, Mr. Dodge," Dolittle said. "And a friend. I'm not discussing her. I'll just say that you'd undoubtedly find her husband a very interesting fellow." Still, Dodge turned up little else on that trip. Back in D.C., he put out word that he was looking for information on this Remus.

A month passed. Then one day a Treasury agent named Will Mellin walked in off the street. Mellin was a surveillance specialist from New York. "Agent Dodge," he said. "I hear you're interested in George Remus. And that you're an honest man."

Dodge looked at him, not-too-tallish, average weight, sandy hair, a face you'd never remember if you tried. He blended. But then, that was perfect. "I don't know what kind of man I am, Agent Mellin."

"I know about your friend Remus. But no one seems very interested in hearing it."

"Everybody's getting rich, are they?"

"Except for me."

"You and me, brother," said Dodge. "You know D.C.?"

"I've been once or twice on the job, is all."

"Come on. I'll show you your capital."

"HE WAS FROM NEW YORK CITY," DODGE TOLD THE prosecutors. "Remus had had two financial partners

early on, named Hess and Landau. He'd sent them
packing, but paid them so much that when they got
back to New York, they began to set it up for him to
ship into that city. That's where Mellin heard about
him. He knew it was big, so he pulled some federal
warrants and began tailing Remus around the country, listening in on conversations, trying to turn witnesses. He got nothing for a month. Remus was paying everyone. Then, in Columbus, Mellin managed
to conceal a sensitive condensor microphone under
Remus's bed and rewire the telephones. He comman-
deered some government typists."

ONE TRANSCRIPTIONIST WORE HEADPHONES CONNECTED
through a series of switches and tube amplifiers to the
microphone. The other wore a set wired into the
phone. The first visitors, two deputy federal marshals
based in Columbus, accepted envelopes. A thousand
dollars each, Remus told them. A thousand dollars.
He said those words.

Mellin picked up the phone when it rang for the
first time, held the mouthpiece on the base against his
shirt, and the receiver to his ear. The caller was a man
named Stratton. Six carloads, he said, had moved
from Louisville through Covington, and then into
Cincinnati. Whiskey, he said. He said that word.

How much whiskey must six train cars hold?
Mellin wondered.

By 10 P.M., forty-four men had visited Remus,
nearly every one receiving a thousand dollars. Treasury agents. Cops. Revenuers. City and state officials.
Mellin couldn't believe the mother lode of corruption

and bribery he'd struck, or how big this Remus must be. This was only Columbus, Ohio, after all, and the sixth city he'd visited in a month.

"Still," Dodge said. "I don't see why you came to me." They sat on the steps of the Capitol Building.

"Well," Mellin said, "I did what you'd expect."

High, happy from it, he reported to the chief Prohibition agent for southern Ohio in Cincinnati, a man named Robert Flora. The regional Internal Revenue director, also based in Cincinnati, sat in on the meeting. Mellin's good feelings lasted as long as it took Flora to flip through the transcripts, toss them back onto the table, and say, "Go home, Agent Mellin."

"What?" He looked from Flora to the IR director.

"In a few days," Flora said, "a man from this state—Warren Harding, of whom you may have heard—is going to be inaugurated into the presidency of the United States. How do you think the men named in these transcripts got their jobs? They're appointees, Mr. Mellin, damn near every one of them. Now are you gonna lift the lid from all this, these men, and the men who appointed them, and the men who appointed those men, who are about to be installed in the White House? In the week of the inauguration? Are you, a revenuer, gonna set off this bomb?"

Mellin stared. He felt flushed and slightly dizzy.

The IR director said, "Son, nobody wants these men arrested."

"But Remus—" Mellin started.

"Or him," the director said. "Do what Mr. Flora says."

Mellin stood up. "Has he paid off everyone?"

"Go home, Agent Mellin. You know they're going to broadcast this inauguration? Listen to it. And get yourself ready for spring. It promises to be most enjoyable this year."

DODGE SAID, "I HEARD ABOUT ANOTHER MAN, IN Kentucky, Sam Collins. He was the dry boss there. Tied up all the trucking so it was hard to move whiskey. Remus's people came on to him, offered him a hundred thousand to resign. He turned it down. Another fellow in Indiana, Burt Morgan, same story. They offered him two hundred. The point is, there were honest men out there, working on their own. I began to pull them together. Then, finally, the Justice Department named its national Prohibition director, a woman named Mabel Walker Willebrandt. I fixed it so I got to drive her around when she first came to town."

HE KNEW A LITTLE ABOUT HER—THAT SHE WAS BORN A Kansas sodbuster; that she had taught school in Traverse City, Michigan, where she met her husband; that after moving to California with him, she put herself through night law school; that after divorcing him, she had managed anyway to somehow adopt a baby daughter; that she quickly became one of the rising stars in the Los Angeles legal arena, finally creating and being named to the position in that city of Public Defender for Women in Trouble. She managed to build, in addition, a successful private practice, and made a good deal of money in a fairly short time. Dodge knew these facts, but he wanted to know only one thing about Mabel Willebrandt, and planned to use his time with her to find out.

All that she knew about him was that he was an agent. For the first day he just drove, helped her into and out of the car when she let him, carried her bags, commented on the various capital sights they passed. Finally, that first evening, as she stood exhausted in a crowded drawing room in the Justice Building, he took her elbow and nodded toward a side door.

"Escape?" he said.

She smiled gratefully and followed him out. The next morning she asked if he'd have breakfast with her. It was the one meal she would take on this trip that was not the venue for another meeting. She suggested they could eat in the hotel, but he took her instead to a little hash house he knew in Georgetown. It obviously delighted her, and he felt the time had come.

"You don't know it yet, Mrs. Willebrandt," he began. "But I'm no junior agent lackey. You can ask about me. Anyway, I pulled a few strings to get this assignment."

"And why would you do that?" she said.

"I wanted to talk."

"So I'm apparently having a meeting even over this breakfast." The circles beneath her eyes seemed to have deepened and become heavier in the night, her coarse-featured face grown a little coarser.

"Apparently," he said. "I apologize. I know you're tired. But this is important. It won't take long."

"Well," she said, smiling at her handsome companion. "Talk to me, Agent Dodge."

❧ ❧ ❧

"SO I TOOK THE CHANCE," HE SAID. "TURNED OUT SHE was untouchable, too, a tough, honest lady. I don't know what Harry Daugherty was thinking when he appointed her, but I think he got more than he bargained for. She gave us the go-ahead on Remus."

"It's interesting," Charlie said. "It's all interesting. But it doesn't really help us directly. Shook will only let us go on so long with history. What matters is Remus and Imogene."

"Well," Dodge said, "it all leads to them."

IN INDIANA, BURT MORGAN'S MEN ARRESTED A DRIVER who'd rolled his Packard with a backseat full of bottles. When pushed, the man told them he'd got it from Death Valley, outside Cincinnati, run by a fellow named Johnny Gherum. Collins had been hearing about Gherum and Death Valley. Word was that Gherum worked for one George Conners, who was connected in turn to George Remus.

In the spring of 1922, in Cincinnati, Robert Flora, the well-remunerated Ohio dry-boss, received an early-morning call from an agent named Dodge who was staying at the Sinton, a hotel Flora knew well, having visited a certain suite many times before its operations were moved to a building in the warehouse district.

"And how can I help you, Agent Dodge?"

"I need to see you here, as soon as possible."

"I'm very busy, you must understand—"

"I understand," Dodge said. "Believe me, I wouldn't ask if it weren't important. I promise it'll only take a few minutes of your time. And I think you'll find it . . . worth your while."

"Ah," Flora said, interested now. "I can be there at noon."

"That would be fine, sir," said Dodge, with all due respect.

When Flora knocked, the door was opened not by Dodge but another man Flora knew—his own Indiana counterpart.

"You," he said.

"Get in here, Flora," Burt Morgan growled.

Flora found the room filled with men. Here was Kentucky Sam Collins. Here, William Holman and George Winkler, two of Morgan's lieutenants. Here, D. O. Simons, a federal Prohibition agent out of Chicago. And a tall man in a cocked fedora, standing back in a corner with his arms folded, watching the proceedings, a smile playing across his face. Frank Dodge.

"What's the meaning of this?" Flora asked.

"We got us a raidin' party," said Morgan. "Only we need your help to see it off, this being your state, after all. We gonna visit your friend George Remus's farm up there by Cheviot, and we need you to pull us a warrant. Since, as I said, this is your state. Now, Robert, you got a problem with that?"

Flora looked at the men. He did have a problem with it. He'd taken money, given his word. But he knew he couldn't refuse now, in the face of these men, without risking at least dismissal, and possibly prison time, himself.

"I'll reach the U.S. Commissioner."

"Well, there you go," said Burt Morgan.

❧ ❧ ❧

"WE'RE STILL NOT TO IMOGENE," CHARLIE SAID.

Dodge said, "I didn't actually meet her for nearly two more years, until Remus was in prison. And that's a whole story in itself."

"Well, not for today. Shook's got hearings, so the trial doesn't start again 'til Tuesday. I'd say we could come in tomorrow, but my wife will skin me if I miss another Sunday—"

Walt said, "Why don't Frank and I get together tomorrow, just the two of us, to smooth it out. Then you can hear it on Monday."

"Good," said Charlie. "Good."

BUT ON MONDAY MORNING, CLYDE BASLER CAUGHT HIM as he came into the offices. "Remus got his petition. They're opening the bank box at eleven."

"Do we have the warrant?"

"It's coming."

"Hurry it, Clyde. I'll meet you there."

At the bank, Charlie stood back and watched. The press was waiting. Elston and Conners pulled up in a long car and waved the petition at the bank president, who met them. Cameras flashed. It was a big show until Clyde Basler and three city cops stepped forward with the warrant. Charlie wished someone had taken a shot of the look on Conners's face when he saw it. That's one picture Charlie would like to have had framed. Even more than that, he'd like to have been there when they told Remus.

But then Charlie got to experience the sensation himself. In a back room, they saw immediately that the box contained nothing Remus had sought—no cash, no certificates, nothing really having to do with Remus's business at all. It was only letters, notes, correspondences. Charlie felt a thrill run through him. But then, Clyde said, "Oh, no," and handed Charlie a letter he'd lifted off the top of the stack.

It was addressed to J. Edgar Hoover, the young new head of the Justice Department's Investigation Bureau, and signed by Franklin Dodge, Agent. "Dear Mr. Hoover," it began, "I'm afraid the time has come for me to tender my resignation."

"Why would this be in *her* box?" Clyde asked. "And why didn't he send it?"

Charlie felt it in his knees. He sat down. He knew what the letter meant. The son of a bitch had lied to them, lied utterly, baldly, over and over again. He'd thought he could cover it all up, now that she was dead.

What a fool I am, Charlie thought.

"She's under your skin, isn't she?" Dodge had asked him at the diner. "It doesn't surprise me."

Of course not, Charlie thought. Of course it didn't surprise you. Because she got under yours a long time ago.

"What do you want to do?" Clyde asked him.

"Get men on him," Charlie told Basler. "If he so much as looks like he's going to leave town, or talk to anyone involved in this case, arrest him."

As he left the bank, and the crowd of reporters shouted at him and fired their flashes, his stomach tightened with the sickening knowledge that he might lose this case. It had never before occurred to him in any meaningful way that this was even a possibility.

❦ ❦ ❦

He was glad he'd spent that Sunday with Eleanor and the children, because now he knew he'd have little time for anything outside this case. That evening he called Eleanor to tell her that it had gone bad, that he was going to be late, not to wait up.

"I read in the evening paper that you found some more of this woman's possessions," she said.

"Yes."

"And what were they?"

"Various things."

"Papers?"

"Mostly, yes."

"More of her writing?"

"Some of it."

"You're staying late to read it, aren't you, Charlie?"

"Yes, Eleanor."

"Good night," she said, and hung up.

Now, again, he had Imogene's voice. It was more scattered than it had been in the diaries, rushed, jaded, frightened, finally. But it was her voice. In notes, in letters, in thoughts jotted on scraps of paper, she'd come back to him:

April 15, 1922

I finally convinced George to sue the pool room contractor, but the contractor's lawyer was cagey. We lost the suit. So then I mentioned to George that he might think about hiring this lawyer. He just snorted. But a week later, that's exactly what he did. I said what a good idea that was, and he seemed to believe that he'd thought of it. He makes me smile.

As spring approaches, so finally does the completion of the pool room. It will have cost, in the end, some $150,000. "The final touch on our little cabin in the woods," I said. "You wouldn't be planning a party?" George asked. "Only a very large one," I told him.

THE END OF
SOMETHING

THE GUEST LIST HAD GROWN. INSTEAD OF JUST THE SOCIETY
people, those old friends and acquaintances from her
father's circles, many of whom she knew saw her as
fallen, she included now a fresher crowd—nouveau
businessmen, artists and writers, gangsters, politician
friends of George's. The papers never mentioned the
events, but what did that matter anymore? She'd
helped establish a new society, the jazz circle, they
called it, and the old guard could choke on it for all
she cared. But they never stayed away.

Instead of cash this time, everyone received an
engraved 24-karat-gold Elgin watch. A team of photographers shot each guest on the parlor porch, the
photos to be posted as mementos. A twelve-piece jazz
orchestra played on the far side of the pool room as
teams of women divers and synchronized swimmers
created balletic designs in the air and water. Near the
end of their program, Imogene herself emerged from
a dressing room in the white bathing outfit she'd
ordered from a Paris designer she loved. It was a single
piece, like a man's, but cut so low that it revealed not

only her clavicles but her cleavage as well. The skirt came down only a few inches over the tops of her thighs.

The guests gave a collective murmur and several left.

"Now she's an exhibitionist," someone said.

Remus stepped forward. "It's lovely," he said. "And you're beautiful in it." He kissed her.

Imogene fitted a rubber cap over her hair and climbed the ladder to the diving board. She raised her arms and pointed at the glass ceiling, laying one hand over the other, and stepped to the end of the board. As she dove, she twisted in the air.

When she climbed out, the thin pale fabric and the cool water combined to put her nipples on display. She saw Remus staring at them, the conflicting emotions of desire and jealousy written on his face. He wrapped a towel around her.

"You must tell me where she got it," a woman said. "It looks so . . . comfortable."

"But where would you wear it?" asked her husband, a motorcar dealer from whom Remus had bought, in the last two months alone, twenty-four Packards.

"To the beach."

"I don't think the beach is ready yet."

"She could wear it here."

"That settles it, then," the woman said.

"Can we have more drinks now, baby?" said Imogene.

"More drinks, my love," he said, and clapped his hands.

❧ ❧ ❧

IT LASTED ALL NIGHT, AS THESE THINGS OFTEN DID, AND
the next day they paid for it. At noon, the two of them
rested in Remus's study, Imogene still coming down
from the drinks, Remus just tired. He slid lower into
the leather of his chair. Imogene lay on a matching
couch, a forearm covering her eyes. They listened to a
Rhythm Kings 78 he'd brought her from Chicago.

> You got a big limousine
> You're standing real pat
> You're living on Broadway
> In a steam-heated flat.

A motorcar, its engine winding out, tore up the long
drive. Too quickly, too high-pitched. The tires shrieked
with the braking. Remus stood and looked out.

"Conners," he said, simply. She knew from his face
that something was wrong. More trouble to manage.
She didn't want trouble right now. She wanted this
quiet, just the two of them. But now it was going to be
ruined.

"One final moment," she said.

"What, baby?"

"Of stillness," she said.

> Since I found you, everybody wants you
> But I'm gonna see about that, you dirty
>   lady
> I'm cert'ny gonna see about that.

Remus looked at her and said, "You are so beautiful."

"You just like me naked."

"It's true. I'd keep you that way all the time."

He had a problem, she told him. He was oversexed. He had an obsession with her body.

She heard footsteps running across the front porch.

The things he liked to do with her breasts, the nape of her neck, her labia, her toes, her knees, her pubic hair, her anus, her lips, her tongue, her ears, her fingers. He was demented, she said. He needed to see an alienist. She'd giggle, then, and strip for him. One piece at a time, slowly, across the room. She'd set that rule. He had to wait. He had to watch, as she teased and took it off. A blouse. A belt. A stocking, which she'd roll down neatly. A brassiere. She would show herself to him. She would hold her breasts in her hands, hold them up to him, an offering. The breasts were always the last thing he could stand before coming across to her.

Conners ran in, breathless. He had always been so smooth, such an iceman. Now his hands shook.

"They hit Death Valley," he said. "Feds. At sunrise. They're all over the goddamn place." He did not excuse himself. He did not even look at Imogene.

"What feds?" Remus said. "Who are they?"

"That son of a bitch from Kentucky was there. I saw him when I came in. And Flora, the double-crossing shit. Johnny and me, we just drove up by chance. These goons were busting things up. They found the bottling room under the barn. There were only a dozen cases and some barrels, but what the hell. And Johnny and Ida had some in the house, I know. I played dumb. I said I didn't know nothing about nothing, like I was just some customer. Then I said, 'Let's go, Johnny,' and they jumped on him. 'You're Johnny Gherum,' they said. 'We got a warrant for you,' and they cuffed him up. I just got in the car and drove."

"It's Sunday," Remus said. "I thought we agreed you wouldn't hold there this weekend. I warned you." He'd gotten word of some strange federals in town. He'd told Gherum and Conners that they just had to clean it up for a few days, until they could test the wind. Sell all the stock and sit clean.

"I know," said Conners. "I could have got rid of every drop of it Friday night, but Johnny held some back."

"Held it back?"

"He was selling. On his own. Skimming."

She could not believe it. George already paid them so much.

"So it was there. But the bottling equipment was all there, anyway, the soaking boxes, the newspapers for wrapping, corks. They're confiscating it all. Dater was there. They arrested him. Maybe half a dozen men they got."

"I sent word this morning," Remus said. "It was all over town, about these men. I sent Babe out and told him to tell you to make sure you were clear."

"Well, he didn't tell me," Conners said. "Message like that, you should'a delivered it yourself. We have a telephone out there. You can't trust some simpleton, George."

Remus sat at first and took it in. But then she saw the color come up in his face. "They can't do this," he said. "We're protected." He stood.

"Where are you going?" she said.

Remus ran upstairs, and came down carrying a shotgun and a box of shells. "We'll take them," he said. "You and me." He went out to the garage and started one of the Packards.

She had watched all of this in silence, but when she heard the machine start, she began to scream, high and thin and wavering. She ran into the driveway, into the path of Remus's car. He stopped hard and even then nearly hit her.

"George!" she screamed. "You'll be killed! Where will I be? Don't go, don't go. Please. Please." She opened the door and flung herself on him. "They'll kill you." She wept until finally he calmed down and put the gun away.

"Dames," she heard Conners mutter under his breath.

THEY TOOK GEORGE FIRST, AT THE OFFICES. THE NEXT DAY they came for Conners. Altogether the federals arrested fourteen men, including Johnny Gherum, George Dater, and Babe. At the arraignment before the federal commissioner, the prosecutors asked that the bond on Remus alone be set at fifty thousand dollars. Remus slammed his hands on the table. No one had never heard of such a bond except in a murder case. Remus railed until the bailiffs removed him. The bond stayed at fifty thousand. He was home in time for dinner, but Imogene couldn't eat. She just wanted him to hold her. She sat in his lap with her face on his shoulder and cried.

❧ ❧ ❧

THE STRANGEST THING OF ALL WAS THAT THE NEXT morning they awoke together, Remus swam and dressed and went to the offices, and the business went on. Money still came. Not as much, now. They'd been hurt. Death Valley was out of business, and the big Squibb distillery in Indiana, for which Remus had paid half a million dollars, was sealed. He was forced to put off, for now, the series of deals Conners had set up that would have given him the corner on the market.

George went back to New York, to meet with Elijah Zoline, who would represent him in court, and Jess Smith, to whom he took another twenty-five thousand in cash. When he came home again, he sat across the dining room table from her.

"It is fixed," he said.

LAURA

THE PROSECUTION CALLED LAURA PETERSON, WHO HAD now become their big finish. When Basler escorted her in, the room hushed. The jurors sat up straighter. Even Shook seemed particularly focused. Laura, her black hair highlighted with its first white strands, sat on the edge of the seat in the box with a handkerchief clutched in her hand. She had always been thin, but looked thinner now, as she hunched forward on herself. Charlie saw Remus busy himself with writing, making a point of not looking at her.

Long before the crime, Walt said, there was the history. He talked with her about the year 1910, when she had met the fifteen-year-old Imogene Ring.

"She was a lonely girl. She had many friends, but none who were true. I became her sister. She'd always wanted a sister, she said. I loved her. She loved me."

Walt asked about Malcolm Coffey, and Laura told that story, especially about the day the news came that he'd been injured in France, and the day he came home, and she and Imogene had seen him, and realized the truth of his condition.

"I thought we would lose her then," Laura said.

"She couldn't function. I took care of her for a week."

She told about George Remus, what a nice man he'd seemed. She told about how in love Imogene had fallen, but how it had gone so wrong so quickly. "Not between them," she said. "But with the whiskey. It fascinated her. He drew her into it. She would never have done anything like that. It killed her father, you know. I think the end was always there, in the beginning."

"Did you still know Imogene then, in the way you had?"

"Well, no," Laura said. "I mean, she was very busy. They led a big life. The parties and the cars. Oh, they didn't shun me, I don't mean that. I was invited to several of those wonderful parties. And Imogene and I still had lunch now and again, as we had before. But it was different. She was different. She'd found her life, and it wasn't with some old spinster secretary."

"After the arrests in 1922, did things begin to change?"

"Yes, of course, but gradually. The trials dragged on for almost two years and the stress on her of not knowing, of waiting, was awful. But there was more trouble, too, you know. You'd think they'd have stopped with the whiskey."

"You're referring to the Jack Daniel's situation?"

"Yes, sir. And this time, she was involved."

"Objection," said Elston.

"Overruled. Proceed, Mr. Sibbald."

"So tell us, Miss Peterson, about life in those years."

❧ ❧ ❧

THE MONEY WAS DRYING UP. NEW LAWS HAD BEEN PASSED. Remus's operations were being closely watched. "It's dying," Imogene would say. "This beautiful life."

Then one day John Marcus, who had fled Cincinnati after the raid, showed up again. He came to see her. "St. Louis," he said. "It's like Cincinnati three years ago. Wide open."

That evening, when she and George had been served at the long dining room table, she said, "I have some money to invest. Twenty thousand dollars." Her words slid around a little. She'd had a couple of drinks.

"That's fine."

"I've heard of a distillery in St. Louis. The Jack Daniel's. What return could I get?"

He put down his soup spoon and looked at her. "So our old friend has talked to you."

"I want to know what kind of return I could get on an investment like that."

"If the men involved know what they're doing, and get a good price, and handle the product well, you could triple your money."

"That's very good."

"But it won't happen, because they don't know what they're doing, and they can't get the whiskey out anyway."

"Well, I hear they can," she said. "And I hear there's a man here they're trying to recruit who knows exactly what he's doing."

"Damn!" he shouted. "What business is it of yours?"

"Don't you talk to me that way, George Remus. It's

my business, too. I'm as deeply involved as you are. If it's your precious money you're worried about, then take mine. If it gets lost, you're out nothing. No risk. Isn't that the song you like best?"

"You don't know a thing about it," he said.

"I do know. You'd be surprised. And you could tell me. You used to tell me everything."

"I used to have a business."

"You have a fine business. Times change. You have to change, too. Can't you see that? Here's a perfect opportunity, and you won't even consider it." She'd begun to see him as something less than he had been. He was not all-powerful. He was no longer the maker, the man at the top whom everyone looked up to. He was just a man, like other men, hurt and confused and frightened. And she found that she loved this in him, more in some ways than she had loved the other.

"You don't understand," he said.

"I understand this—you need to do something. You've been terrible. I never see you, and when I do, you're unhappy. You're always unhappy."

"Well, then, take another drink," he said. "It'll pass."

"Oh, George," she said, and pressed the napkin to her lips. "I love you so much, but sometimes I don't like to be around you. What do we have to do to be happy again?"

"I don't know."

"You need to work," she said.

He looked at her. "Fine, Imogene," he said, and pushed his soup away. "I'll talk to Marcus. I'll meet with these men he's found. Just let's stop talking about it."

But the political winds had begun to shift. At the instigation of Samuel Gompers, the gnomelike head of the American Federation of Labor, a Minnesota legislator introduced a resolution calling for the impeachment of the attorney general, Harry Daugherty. The House went so far as to hold formal hearings, but when no concrete proof of any of Daugherty's misdeeds could be produced, and the Representative from Minnesota shat himself in public from the stress of it, the resolution was dropped. Still, a shot had been fired across the bow of the Harding administration. A week after Zoline's final presentation to the appellate court, in May of 1923, word came from Washington that Jess Smith, to whom Remus had paid nearly half a million dollars, had been discovered in his room with his head in a metal wastebasket. He'd fired a bullet into his right temple. It had passed through entirely and lodged itself in the heavy oak door frame. Most of the mess, though, had been contained in the trash can. Smith had remained a detail man to the last.

If there had ever been a fix in, the appellate court judges hadn't heard of it. They refused to overturn any convictions in the whiskey trials of Remus and company. Zoline went to D.C. immediately and filed a motion with the Supreme Court to hear the case. Amazingly, the court agreed, and put it on the docket for the fall. And so was more time bought.

In the summer, as the realization dawned that his administration was in trouble, President Harding vowed to quit his own drinking, to set a better example. He collapsed on a trip to Alaska and died that

August. Calvin Coolidge was sworn in. Harry Daugherty stayed on as attorney general, although the Senate opened hearings into his activities. Mabel Walker Willebrandt and Franklin Dodge retained their positions in the Justice Department.

John Marcus's Jack Daniel's caper, which Remus had agreed only to help finance and advise, was ill-conceived and run by fools. A local gang called Egan's Rats got wind of it and muscled in. Instead of removing the whiskey gradually, under cover, they and Marcus milked the entire warehouse, and refilled the barrels with diluted grain alcohol, so that it would pass the gaugers' routine chemical tests. But one of the gaugers was a drinker, and so the ruse was discovered. That fall, the Treasury Department opened an investigation. Remus and Imogene, though they'd had no direct involvement, were at its center.

"CAN YOU TALK ABOUT WHAT HAPPENED ON THE MORNING of the sixth of October?" Sibbald asked Laura.

She described the car chase from the hotel into the park.

"And then, after you were pulled over?"

"He got out and opened the door."

"Remus did."

"Yes. He opened my door. He said something."

"What did he say?"

"I don't remember. I don't think I knew then. I was so frightened—"

"Of course," Sibbald said. "Did he threaten you or Imogene?"

"I believe so. He kept asking her something. It was

hard to understand him, though. He'd mumble, then yell."

"The driver testified that Mr. Remus was cursing."

"Yes," Laura said. "I remember that. He was very profane. His face was red. That frightened me as much as anything."

"Did you see the gun, then?"

"No. I was afraid to look at him, to be honest. I looked at her, at Imogene. She looked so confused. Then she got out of the car. I told her not to. I reached out to hold her in, but she got away. Then I heard the shot."

She described the ride to the hospital and Imogene's death. As she spoke, eloquently and softly, she wept. Sibbald asked several times if she needed a break. She repeatedly said no, she would rather get through it all. And through it all she got, until the moment he lifted a paper sack and removed from it a piece of black cloth. Laura put her hands over her mouth.

"Do you recognize this?" he said, as he unfolded it. It was Imogene's blood-stiffened dress. The bullet hole in the left front had been circled in chalk. Sibbald held it up for the jury to inspect, then hung it over the railing around the witness box. Laura broke down and several of the jurors wiped away tears. Even Remus, who had looked up finally, pressed his fingers to his eyes. Sibbald hung the black-crusted silk stockings next to the dress.

When Laura had composed herself again, Sibbald asked her for any final thoughts about the victim.

"She was devoted to everyone she knew," Laura

said. "Much too devoted, sometimes." Here she looked directly at Remus. "She would have done anything anyone asked her. She had the biggest heart of anyone I've ever known, and I will miss her terribly."

When she began to cry again, Sibbald looked at the judge. "I have no further questions," he said. "Not for now, anyway."

ELSTON ASKED IF LAURA WANTED A BREAK BEFORE HIS cross, but again she refused. "I don't have much," he said. "Miss Peterson, did you ever visit Imogene in Lansing, Michigan?"

"Yes," she said.

"And why was she in Lansing?"

"She was visiting Mr. Franklin Dodge, Mr. Elston. Is that what you want to hear?"

"I just want to hear facts. Was this while she was living there with Dodge?"

"Objection."

"Overruled."

"She never lived there," Laura said.

"No?" Elston said. "Did you visit her there more than once?"

"Two or three times."

"Over what period of time?"

"I don't know. Several months."

"But she wasn't living there."

"Not that I know of. She went different places and stayed and moved on. After the marriage fell apart, she was unsettled, discontented. So she traveled. That was always her way. Sometimes she visited Mr. Dodge. He had become a friend to her."

"Do you recall making a statement to detectives, after the shooting, that Remus was a madman, and he had acted insanely in the park that day?"

"Objection!"

"Judge—" Elston said, but was cut off by Walt Sibbald, who said, "This is sneaky and backhanded, Your Honor."

Shook had the jury removed, and Laura as well.

"Your Honor," Sibbald said. "They're trying to establish the defendant's insanity through the cross-examination of a prosecution witness. That's not even allowable."

"Isn't it?" Elston said.

"The girl's not an expert, Mr. Elston," said the judge. "And she may well have been using a common figure of speech. In any case, I'll have to consider this carefully. It's tricky ground, and I'm not sure of it myself. For the time being, I'll have to disallow the question."

Elston, angry, said, "You're tying our hands. You're not allowing this man a basic defense. We'll come back to this."

"We certainly will," said Shook. "I'm still not sure what your claim is. Is Mr. Remus sane now? Did he get sane after the shooting? You haven't answered these questions. Yes, we will revisit this. But not now, not with this witness."

SHE WAS TIRED, AT THE END OF THE DAY, BUT WHEN Charlie asked her if she'd like dinner, she nodded. He took her to a chop house up on Mount Adams. It was dark, and there were booths in the back where they would not be disturbed.

After they'd ordered, he said, "I remember, after New Year's of '24, hearing about that jamboree they threw at the mansion. Everyone was talking about it. I'd just recently gone to work in the prosecutor's office. The rumors were so outrageous, the chief even considered opening an investigation into it."

"That was the end of it all. That moment. Imogene knew, I think. That's really what it was about. The last party."

BY TEN, THE GUESTS, OF WHOM THERE WERE AT LEAST TWO hundred, were well oiled. In addition to cases of Old Nine and the last of the Squibb Remus had stock-piled, there was vodka and gin, beer, and some of the most expensive table wines and champagnes available in America. One gentleman, with the help of three ladies, emptied twenty bottles of Dom Perignon into a bathtub, stripped, and climbed in. The three ladies then scrubbed him thoroughly.

The menus included such exotic fare as pork cheeks, venison butterflies in a truffle sauce, rattlesnake salad, and Beluga caviar. A local fifteen-piece jazz orchestra accompanied it all. Laura hadn't been to a party at the mansion in several years, and she was shocked at the change in the sorts of people Imogene had invited. She recognized a few faces, but most were strangers to her. When she wandered into the pool room and glimpsed a semi-public mating on a chaise behind a potted tree, she felt so embarrassed she nearly left.

Imogene drank and grew gayer by the minute, and Remus more sullen as he watched various gentlemen embrace her, dip her back, and plant deep kisses on her mouth. After midnight, Laura happened to pass by the library and saw Remus reading and sipping a glass of milk. When she paused in the doorway, he looked up.

"Laura," he said. "Come in." He smiled. "You'll take care of her, won't you?"

"Yes, of course," she said. "Is there no hope—?"

"I doubt it," he said. "I'm signing power of attorney to her over everything. She'll be in charge, but she'll need support."

"I understand."

"If you need anything, now—"

"No," she said. "I'm fine.

Conners came in then, and Remus stood and embraced him. They held each other for a long time. She felt uncomfortable.

"We should be going," Conners said, when they released.

"No," said Remus. "If you're tired, take a nap here. But you must stay 'til morning."

"And what's then?"

"You'll just have to see. But it'll be worth staying. I'd say your wife will kill you, in fact, if you leave early and she hears what you missed."

At the champagne breakfast, each couple found before their place a small hinged box. Assuming they contained rings, the women eagerly opened them. They found jewelry, all right, but men's: a diamond tie tack or cuff links. Remus laughed at the disappointed looks aimed in his direction, but said nothing until the breakfast was concluded. He then led his guests toward the front door, and outside.

There before them they saw, lined up along the entire length of the drive and out into the road, a string of one hundred new 1924 Pontiacs. One for each lady at the party.

TO CHARLIE, LAURA SAID, "IT WAS HARDLY A WEEK AFTER that, that we heard. Imogene collapsed."

"That was my father," Charlie said.

On January 7, the Supreme Court, led by the new chief justice, William Howard Taft, upheld all convictions in the case of *United States v. George Remus et al.* The following week, Remus and the thirteen and their families gathered at the Dixie Terminal before a private car he'd hired and outfitted with waiters and a chef to transport them and their wives to Atlanta. Most wives would return to Cincinnati, but Imogene had reserved a suite in Atlanta's Biltmore, just a short drive from the penitentiary.

In Atlanta, Laura heard, a crowd of spectators and press sent up a cheer when Remus appeared. He waved from the train, and shook the hands thrust at him as he was escorted to a waiting car.

DEFENSE

A PORTRAIT OF
MADNESS

WHAT DODGE HAD DONE CAME BACK TO CHARLIE IN STRAY
moments, an anger he'd rarely known creeping up his
neck. Walt found him once on the street, hands in
pockets, just staring off as he ground his teeth.

"I can't get around it," Charlie said. "It's not like
me."

Walt could barely speak of it at all. But there wasn't
time, anyway. "The issue," Charlie told Walt and
Clyde, in his office, "isn't what Remus did, but what
Shook will allow Elston to present. Their prospects
will be sealed in the opening testimonies."

"And what are those prospects, do you think?" Walt
asked.

"Better than they were," Charlie said, "but still
small."

"I hope you're right."

I do too, Charlie thought. Privately, he wasn't so
sure. The failed attempt to show a conspiracy, and
more than that, Dodge's betrayal, had hurt them
badly. The door was open for Elston. They had to shut
it, now, before he could come through.

In court, Charlie felt uncharacteristically nervous. His legs jumped under the table. It was like waiting for a game to begin. Or a battle. Waiting for the Huns, when you knew good and damned well what they were going to throw at you, but there was nothing you could do except wait for your chance to deflect it, and to begin your counterattack.

Elston wore the kelly green tie again. He hadn't worn it since the opening statements. It was his acknowledgment that this was the crux of the trial, the central moment that he'd been battling toward, that would either see his design come to fruition or wither.

He called as his first witness a local lawyer named Leo Burke, who had represented Remus in various matters. After establishing this, Elston wasted no time: "Mr. Burke," he said, "when was the last time you saw Mr. Remus?"

"Early last year. February of 1926."

"And how would you describe his mental condition then?"

The three prosecutors leapt up, slamming their chairs against the railing behind them and shouting, in unison, "Objection!"

So it was joined. In that moment, Charlie glanced at the other side. Elston merely smiled down at his papers. But Remus looked ill, as if he wanted nothing more than to stop this. For what Carl Elston was about to do was to try to clear the way to Remus's last chance at life by clearing the way to having him labeled, once and forever in history, as insane.

❧ ❧ ❧

AFTER HAVING THE JURORS AND WITNESS REMOVED,
Shook said, "My question, Mr. Elston, is, and has
been: is your client sane or insane?"

Elston cleared his throat and placed the tips of
each of his fingers carefully on the table. He said, "I
don't know, Your Honor. The point, as I have maintained, is that it's irrelevant to these proceedings. All
that matters is his mental condition in the period
leading up to, and including, the day of October sixth.
And that's what I aim to demonstrate."

"That he was insane."

"Then, yes."

"Before the shooting."

"Yes. I'd say for a period of about two years."

"And after the shooting, he wasn't insane anymore."

"I don't know. I'm not making that claim. I don't
care what his mental state was after the shooting."

Shook nodded and said, "Let's go on."

"Excuse me," Charlie said, "but then what? Judge,
you know he's going to ask whether this witness, this
lawyer, thought Remus was insane. And so you've got
the situation of a layman, probably several, being
asked to give medical opinions in open court."

Shook inhaled deeply and exhaled and said, "Very
well. I see that we're here already. All right. Listen:

"I've thought about this. I've been thinking for the
weeks of this trial. I've spoken with other judges. I
want you all to know that I have taken this issue very
seriously, for it lies at the heart of this defense, at the
heart of whether this man, George Remus, may live or
die. And this is what I've decided: I want to see facts—
demonstrable, concrete, specific actions. A lay witness

may not testify to a man's insanity, for that is a medical diagnosis. Any reasonable person, though, can describe the behavior of a man who acts insane. That may sound like a trivial distinction, but it isn't. I think we can all agree that certain actions or utterances have the hallmarks of insanity. So this is my point, Mr. Elston." And here he pointed his finger. "If you stick, in your questioning, to the facts of what someone saw, then I'll allow it. I do not want to hear opinions or diagnoses from people who don't know better. I want to hear concrete descriptions. If I do, I'll allow you to proceed in this direction.

"The subsequent point, then, is that before I'll allow you to go beyond this, into causation, I'll need to see clear evidence of a diseased mind."

Charlie saw Elston grip Remus's shoulder in celebration. Clyde Basler put it well. Under his breath, he whispered, "Shit."

"HE WAS FINE," BURKE TESTIFIED, "UNTIL I SAID, 'THE thing I wonder is what you're doing in regard to the divorce.' He stared at me. It was rather frightening. I asked him if it wasn't true that he was getting divorced. He said yes. Then he stood up and started pacing. It was as if he couldn't control himself . . ."

REMUS PUT HIS HANDS ON HIS HEAD AS HE WALKED TO THE office door and back again. "What do you hear about them?" he said.

"Who?"

"Imogene and Dodge. You've heard about the divorce. What else have you heard?"

"What else? It was you who told me about it—"

"What else!" Remus shouted.

Burke slid his chair back. Then, suddenly, Remus began pounding his fist into his own forehead. "God-*damn* her!" he said, through his teeth, as he pounded. "God. Damn. God. *Damn!*"

"Mr. Remus—" Burke said. He stood up.

Remus said, "I can't stand to think of them . . ." He held his belly and moaned and bent over the chair.

"Do you need a doctor?"

But just as suddenly as he had gone off, Remus straightened. His face cleared. "I apologize, Mr. Burke," he said.

"Are you sure there's nothing you need?"

"Can you have her followed?"

"What? No, I meant a doctor—"

"There must be detectives you use."

"Well, there are . . . are you sure?"

"Use them," he said, and his face reddened again and his nostrils flared. He said, "I almost had them myself, you know, in the Empire Hotel in Cleveland. I knew what they were up to. I bribed the clerk for the room number, but when I got there, it was being cleaned. I described them to the maid. She confirmed it. Oh, God!" His eyes bulged, and he beat himself again, in the chest this time, and pulled his hair until a handful came out.

ELSTON SAID, "HOW WOULD YOU DESCRIBE HIM THEN, overall? If, say, you and I were talking on the street, how would you refer to him?"

"I'd say he was insane. There's no question."

Walt stood, but Shook held up his hand to stop the objection. Charlie took the cross himself. "Why didn't you have him committed, then?"

"He was a client," said Burke. "Was it up to me to send him away? I didn't think so. As long as I stayed off the topic of his wife and Dodge, why, he was fine."

"Well, let me ask you, then, Mr. Burke, what sort of insanity did you think afflicted Mr. Remus?"

"What sort?"

"Yes."

"I wouldn't know, sir."

"You wouldn't."

"No, sir."

"Thank you."

"He was just crazy."

"That's all. Thank you."

A FORMER COMMON PLEAS COURT JUDGE NAMED BENTON Oppenheimer, another of Remus's attorneys, testified that Remus had trembled and clawed at his own face so viciously that he bled. Sometimes he cried out and fell to his knees. Elijah Zoline, once one of Remus's strongest allies, said he knew soon after Atlanta that something was wrong. Eventually he stopped representing Remus, because of the outbursts and manic episodes.

But more damning were Elston's next series of witnesses: government lawyers. Lee Beaty, chief federal prosecutor in the later trial concerning the Jack Daniel's case in St. Louis, said, "Well, to begin, he was convinced there was a conspiracy against him. That various groups were plotting to have him killed. The Justice Department—Mabel Willebrandt and Dodge in particular. The Egan gang in St. Louis. Even his own men."

"Mrs. Remus?"

"He didn't mention her in that regard and I sure didn't ask."

"Why is that?"

"Why, he'd go crazy. I made the mistake once. We'd just put him on the stand. I brought up a conversation he'd had with his wife. He started to shake, his hands then his head. He turned blue. The judge called a recess. I never went back to it."

Alan Curry, another Jack Daniel's prosecutor, testified to Remus's obsession with Dodge, and the disturbing expressions and sounds this obsession produced. Curry said he clearly remembered thinking that this was what a lunatic looked like. "I had never been this near one before, and frankly it fascinated me—"

"Objection!"

The judge looked up at Charlie, but Charlie hadn't said anything. It was Remus who had objected. The room grew still.

"Mr. Remus," said the judge. "This is your own attorney you're objecting to."

"It's lies," Remus said. "It's all damned lies."

Now the room broke, sound pouring forward from the gallery, the judge pounding, Walt and Clyde laughing, the jury standing to leave. Elston came back to the table. Charlie watched them.

"George," Elston said. "Don't do this. Please."

"But it's not true."

"Don't you want to live?"

After that, Charlie couldn't make out what they were saying. Elston pointed toward the door. Remus shook his head.

"Gentlemen?" the judge said, finally.

Elston said something else, and then Remus shouted, "I know, I know! Just go on!" Remus sat with his hands over his ears, and stared at the table while Elston turned back to his witness.

CHARLIE HAD FIRST MET CARL ELSTON WHEN THEY WERE both assistant prosecutors. Elston had been good enough. He'd gotten his share of convictions. But he was never the man they'd go to in a tight spot. He'd never been a Walt Sibbald or a Clyde Basler. Or a Charlie Taft. But some attorneys were simply not made to be prosecutors. They harbored an instinctive mistrust of the system. Where a man fit best was probably decided early in life, long before any of them became attorneys. In any case, Elston had clearly found his place now. He was an artist, and as the parade of defense witnesses stretched out, Charlie could sometimes merely sit in nausea-tinted awe and admire the bizarre and moving portrait that was being painted, a portrait for which Elston had brilliantly and single-handedly stretched the canvas.

THAT NIGHT, ELEANOR TOLD HIM SHE WAS TAKING THE children back to New York, for a visit with her parents.

"Now?" he said. "Ellie, they're in school."

"They can miss a few weeks."

"Weeks?"

"A month."

"Eleanor, please."

"Until this thing is over," she said. "Until you're through with . . . her."

"For God's sake," he said. "She's dead. She's dead, Eleanor. She was shot to death."

"I know that, Charlie. Don't yell at me."

"I'm not yelling. I'm . . . I'm sorry."

"It's just that you're not here, even when you are. I don't want to be here either, until you come back."

He looked at her. He held out his arms and she came over to him and put her face against him.

"Frank Dodge has betrayed us in the worst way," he said.

She nodded.

"I need this woman's help. I need to know what she knew."

"I understand," she said. "But we're still going, tomorrow."

The children were excited. After he'd helped tuck them in, he sat and talked with them about the trip, about New York, which they hadn't seen in more than a year.

Later, when Eleanor had fallen asleep, he sat in the study and smoked and read. Imogene had written often in the beginning of the Atlanta incarceration to Laura, and had drafted some of the letters first. He began with these:

March 3, 1924

My Dear Laura:

Even here, in a federal prison, George makes it

the way he wants. The warden was open to "suggestions," as George says. George has his own set of cells, one just for his clothing. His chef is here, too, and we all eat together several times a week, George and I and Mr. Conners and the warden. But the best thing is that I'm allowed to stay over when I want . . .

A LAST AND ONLY HOPE

S HE HATED IT THERE, WITH THE DISTANT SOUNDS OF lonely men howling and electric light streaming in through the gated window, but loved still curling into him in the night. George held her and said it didn't matter where they were. But then something went wrong, and it all stopped. The Justice Department, George said, bitterly. This Agent Dodge. She wasn't allowed to stay with him anymore, and all the nice clothing he'd had shipped down was boxed. The warden was arrested and made a guest in his own house. The chef was sent back to Cincinnati.

Her visits were limited to twice a week. She met him at a desk in a cavernous room where other prisoners sat across from their wives and mothers. She wanted to hold him, but had to sit across like the others, so she reached over and took his hands.

T HAT SUMMER, IN A CROWDED ROOM IN THE CAPITOL Building in Washington, the Senate began looking into the doings of Attorney General Daugherty. Writers scratched and photographers set off flashes while

George talked. She sat behind him and he reached back for her hand now and then.

They'd traveled together on the train, though he was always accompanied by federal marshals. In the hotel they made her stay on a separate floor. The reporters shouted when they came out together, "Give us a shot!" or "A moment, please!" George just naturally paused and showed them a confident smile. In the papers, later, she looked with horror at her own pinched face. She didn't want to be like that for him, so after that she forced herself to raise her chin and hug her husband's arm more tightly.

Before the hearings one morning, he pointed a man out to her. The man was attractive enough, but she immediately disliked his smirk, even before George told her it was Franklin Dodge. She watched him, willed him to turn so that he could see in her face how she felt about him, but he didn't. He just smirked. Then one day she glanced over and found him staring at her, the little smile playing across his lips. She glared with all her hatred, but he didn't look away or stop grinning. Oh, she hated him.

Senator Wheeler was hard on George, but George took it all and gave it right back. He told the senators the story of his business, from the beginning, the trucks and the cases and the men, and he told them the truth about the attorney general and about Jess Smith. After he told that, they were nicer to him. Elijah Zoline gathered her up one afternoon and took her to George's room. A marshal was playing cards with George, but at the sight of Zoline, he went into the hallway.

"I'm into a negotiation with the senator's people," Zoline said. "You've been good for them and now I think they can be good for you. We'll see if they can't shave off some of your time."

"Oh," she said. "George, do you hear that?"

He nodded, but didn't look like he believed it. "The horse is out of the barn," he said. At some sign, Zoline went out.

"Should I—" she said, and stood up.

George put his hands on her shoulders and pushed her back so that she was sitting on the table. "They'll give us a few minutes. That is, if you want to—" But he didn't wait for her answer. He pulled at the front of her dress. His breathing grew deep and hoarse. He unclasped her brassiere and squeezed her breasts and sucked at them as if he were starving and they could feed him. She wanted at least to go to the bed, but he held her there on the table. As he sucked at her nipples, he pushed up her dress and stripped off the garments beneath it.

After, she sat with her arms around his neck, his forehead resting on her shoulder as he breathed. She said, "If we could just spend one night—"

"I tried," he said. "They won't give me that."

George had been right, of course, about Senator Wheeler. He didn't shorten the sentence at all. It was up to the Justice Department, he said, not the Senate. He had no control over it.

ONE AFTERNOON IN THE VISITORS' ROOM BACK IN ATLANTA, she found him more distraught than usual.

"Mabel Willebrandt is going to kill me."

"What is it?"

"Elijah went to see her. He told her I'd done what they asked. I should be given something for that."

"And?"

"It went the opposite way. Can you believe it?"

"What do you mean?"

"Think about it," he said. "Harry Daugherty's her boss. He hired her. She wants to protect him!"

"She's angry?"

"Furious. She won't listen to reason. She went as far as to say that if I wanted anything from her, I'd have to recant my entire testimony. Declare myself a perjurer."

She felt dizzy. She laid her head down on the desk and wanted to weep but she was simply too tired.

"Imogene," he said.

"I'm all right."

"You've got to be strong."

"I'm strong. George, recant it."

"What?"

"Recant your testimony. Please just do whatever they want so you can get out. Please?"

"REMUS LIED!" THE HEADLINES SAID. THE THING WAS, there had been so much other testimony to Wheeler's committee that corroborated George's that everyone knew he'd told the truth. But now, either way, he was a liar.

Though Willebrandt declared herself satisfied, a month passed, and another, and no word came. George said that Zoline had finally told him he didn't think anything was going to happen. Mabel Willebrandt was under no obligation. Remus was at the top of her list. She had him where she wanted him and she wasn't going to let him go now. So George called some reporters in and told them he was recanting again. Everything he'd told the Senate was true. He'd recanted to try to get Justice to help him, but now he wanted to set the record straight.

When Imogene read the story in her hotel room, she knew that any hope was gone. She knew it in a way she had not let herself know before. He wasn't getting out until the sentence ran its course, and maybe not even then. She lay on the bed and wept for an hour. Then she washed her face and she went to see him.

He gripped her hands. "I won't make it, my love. You have control of the business and the money. Sell what you need, and just take care of yourself. Do you hear me? I will not make it out of here. I'm sorry. I only ever wanted to make it good, and I've done just the opposite."

She walked, dazed, through the steamy streets of Atlanta, got lost in strange neighborhoods, wandered until she recognized a building. She called Laura and asked her to come down for a week, just to sit with her.

ONE AFTERNOON IN NOVEMBER HE SAID, "YOU MUST HELP me." He'd stopped exercising, she could tell. The flesh hung on his arms and under his jaw.

"In any way I can. You know that."

"I can't ask you."

"George—"

"I will not make it, Imogene. I'm crumbling. I feel it."

"I'll do anything."

He gripped her hands so fiercely that he hurt her. "Elijah called today. The federals have passed down indictments in the Jack Daniel's case. We're both named."

She couldn't speak, could not even breathe for a moment.

"Imogene," he said. "Will you help me?"

She nodded.

"You must go to Frank Dodge."

She watched his face.

"Find him. Do whatever you need. Find out what they want to hear. You know that I know more than I've told. I can deliver anyone they want. I'm connected everywhere."

"But you have Elijah—"

"They hate him as much as they hate me. I need someone who—I need you. You have the sense and the sensitivity and the wiles, and you have the strength. Do you understand?"

She looked at him. She was not sure she did.

"Imogene," he said. "You're the only person I know who has it in herself to do whatever it takes."

She stared at him, trying to fathom it, to comprehend. The guard called out. It was time. No, she thought.

"Whatever it takes," he told her. "Go. Make it right. You're my last and only hope."

HOW WOULD SHE GO ABOUT CONTACTING THIS MAN? Whom would she call? She didn't know what to do. She had no idea. And then, strangely, she saw him the next day talking outside the new warden's office. She approached, but stood off. He glanced at her but otherwise ignored her until, finally, he broke off his conversation and said, "Are you waiting for me?"

"I am."

"Can I help you?"

"I'm Imogene Remus."

He looked at her.

"I wondered if we might talk."

"Sure," he said. "We can talk."

He took her to a nearby restaurant.

"Just coffee," she said.

"Is that all?" He wore the smirk again. He would be attractive, she thought, if it weren't for that.

"So—" he began.

"You knew who I was."

"Beg your pardon?"

"When you saw me waiting there in the prison, you knew exactly who I was. Didn't you?"

The smirk faded a little. "I did," he said. "I'm sorry."

"No," she said, "you're not at all."

He laughed, but it was a nervous laugh.

"Tell me, Mr. Dodge," she said. "What exactly is it we need to do to get some consideration?"

"What sort of consideration?"

"You know what I mean. Let's not play around, please."

"Can I get him out, do you mean?"

"Yes. For everything he could give you, and that I could give you."

"I don't know," he said. "It would be difficult."

"And in the Jack Daniel's—"

"That's a different situation," he said. "In that case,

it'll be easier. There may be a deal we can make. But for now, in this term—I don't know. I'm simply being honest."

"I believe you."

"I'm sorry."

"You're not really," she said. "But thank you." She sipped at the coffee, which had grown cold. She signaled the waitress. "He's repented, you know."

"I don't doubt it. They all do."

"But he's—"

"In bad shape, isn't he? He sounded liked it."

"He sounded—" She stopped. "When was this?"

"A few days ago, when I spoke with him."

She didn't look at him. She could not. He had spoken with George. And then George had told her to go to him. How had he put it? To do whatever it takes.

"He would have promised me anything, I think," Dodge said.

And she knew then. She saw it all. What she was to do. How it was to work. She waited for the waitress to fill her cup, then said, "But what did he promise you, Mr. Dodge?"

Dodge shrugged. He lifted the creamer and passed it to her. As she took it from him, the tip of his little finger skated along the edge of her hand.

"Of course not," she said, and smiled. "He couldn't. It isn't up to him in the end, is it?"

Dodge looked at her. She looked into him, deeply. "No," he said. "I guess it's not."

"I would like to order some food, after all," she said. She found that she was suddenly very hungry. She remembered that she hadn't eaten in days.

HOMECOMING

ELSTON HAD WON ONE ESSENTIAL CONCESSION, THAT AS long as he stuck to observed fact, he could present the history of Remus's mental disintegration. But this was only halfway to his goal—he wanted also to show what Imogene had done. The prosecutors would fight it viciously, but, he said, "You can't have an effect without a cause. She's the cause." This was exactly what Remus had wanted from the beginning—to expose her—but now, hearing Elston state it so coldly, he felt a turning in his stomach.

He found himself, too, increasingly unable to bear the descriptions Elston elicited in court. George Remus as lunatic. But as he listened to incident after incident he little remembered, it occurred to him that Elston must be rehearsing his witnesses, working through the testimonies to pad and shape them to fit his illustration of insanity. Remus knew lawyers who coached clients or witnesses into lying. Oh, it was all subtle: "Are you sure that's what you mean? Couldn't it be that—" Until they understood what the lawyer was really after. "Well, yes," the witness might say. "Now that you mention it, it could be that—" And so

the lie was formed and planted, and so it was delivered
in open court. Maybe it was done so subtly that the
witnesses didn't even know they were lying. Remus
had thought Elston would be above that sort of ham-
fisted trick, but there was no denying it fascinated the
jury.

ELSTON CALLED REGINALD FOWLER. REMUS REALIZED
he'd never known the man's first name. It was always
just Fowler, who waited at the end with the warm
towels.

The facts were established: that Fowler had worked
for the Remuses for five years, from 1921 until 1926,
first as a personal assistant to Mr. Remus, then later,
after Mr. Remus had gone to prison, as caretaker of
the house.

"Mr. Fowler," Elston said. "Let's begin at the end.
Were you at the Remus home, the mansion in Price
Hill, on the afternoon Mr. Remus came home from
prison?"

"Yes, sir. I was living in the apartment over the
garage."

"Do you remember when he arrived?"

"I'll never forget it," Fowler said.

Nor shall I, thought Remus. Nor shall I.

CONNERS MET HIM AT THE STATION. AS THEY TURNED
from Eighth onto Hermosa, Remus felt a sense of
deliverance, of peace, the first such emotions he'd
experienced in ages. He savored the thoughts
of reading in his study, of swimming in the pool,
of eating together with Imogene. This place stood

for everything they were together. He had made it for her.

Her: in the past year, after she began meeting with Dodge, her prison visits had grown increasingly less frequent. But she told him that she was very busy, pulling it all together, as he had bid her to do. "It's delicate work, George," she said.

And then the federal prosecutor in St. Louis contacted Zoline to discuss a deal. So it was working. "This time, I'm putting in the fix," she told him.

"But I'm still in here," he complained.

"One step at a time," she said. He saw her even less that summer, so rarely that sometimes he thought she'd forgotten him. Then in September, four months before his sentence was up, Zoline telegrammed to say he was being released. She'd succeeded.

Now, as he approached the house, he imagined the homecoming she had planned. Not too many people, just close friends, maybe a small orchestra. When they pulled in, though, he saw that the drive was empty. She must have had the cars hidden, to heighten the surprise. Then he noticed that some of the statuary in the front yard was missing. And then he saw the boards covering the front windows.

"What is this?" he said.

"George," Conners said. "We have to talk."

But Remus leapt from the car before it stopped and raced onto the porch. The doors were locked. Everything was closed up. He drove his boot into the heavy oak, then ran around to the back. A window off the kitchen was open. He stood on a garden chair and climbed through.

In the great front parlor he cried out. Nothing remained but a pile of trash in the middle of the floor. No artwork, no golden piano, no furniture. The library shelves were empty. His desk and chair were gone from the study, and the safe where he'd left a hundred thousand in cash stood open and empty. Upstairs, he found only a single bed in one of the smaller rooms and some of his clothing in a closet. His jewelry was gone. His shoes and his suits were gone. Her jewelry and her clothing were gone, too. It was all gone.

He ran into the hallway looking for something to smash. There was nothing, so he attacked the wall, pounding his fist into it until the plaster cracked.

"YOU BECAME CARETAKER AFTER MR. REMUS WENT TO prison."

"Yes."

"And Mrs. Remus?"

"She was gone most of that first year. But then the following spring, in '25, she began staying at home more often."

"Alone?"

"At first. But I began to notice, at times, a man there with her. He tried to hide himself at first."

"Hide himself?"

"Yes, sir. Once they pulled up in a motorcar when I was outside working. He held his hand like this, over his face."

"But you saw him at some point."

"Well, yes. I came to know him."

"And who was he?"

"Franklin Dodge."

Taft stood up. "Your Honor, may we approach?" Remus went with Elston. At Shook's desk, Taft said, "This is precisely what we've been trying to avoid. I object. I want this entire testimony stopped."

"Judge," said Elston. "When it becomes clear where this is going—"

"Why don't you tell us where it's going, Counselor."

"To Mr. Remus's mental state."

"Yes, fine," Taft said. "So Mr. Remus gets angry and punches a hole in the wall. It hardly constitutes insanity. And yet—"

"It had a much more pernicious effect than that," said Elston. "And if you'd let me get to it—"

"What if he doesn't? What if you allow this and then it turns out Mr. Elston was wrong, or misleading us? Then he's presented it all to the jury, who will surely not be able to forget it, whatever their instructions."

"Your Honor," Elston said. "Mr. Taft. I give you my solemn word as an officer of the court that any testimony I elicit in this regard will be solely to show the cause or condition of Mr. Remus's mental state. I'll swear to it."

"And of course you, Mr. Taft," said Judge Shook, "retain the right to object wherever you see fit." He waved them back.

Elston said to his witness, "Mr. Dodge, then, began spending more time at the house."

"Yes, sir," Fowler said.

"Did he sleep there?"

"Often, yes."

"Did you notice other changes?"

"Things began to disappear. Mr. Remus's effects. Jewelry. Autos. One afternoon, Mrs. Remus asked me to take down a painting by a Frenchman named Seurat that Mr. Remus particularly loved. I refused. I said it was his and I couldn't remove it without his permission. Dodge came over to me. 'Don't worry about him,' he said. 'He's not even going to be around here anymore, after he's out of jail. He's going on a nice long trip to Germany.'"

Again Taft objected. He said, "Here we are, now, trying to show some conspiracy and nothing in sight regarding Mr. Remus at all, let alone his sanity, or lack of it."

"This all goes to cause," said Elston. "This is all a part of what—"

"Approach," Shook said. Remus went with Elston again, and this time Sibbald came with Taft. Shook said, "Mr. Elston, I told you I wanted facts of your client's erratic behavior, or what caused it."

"And that's exactly what I'm doing. Mr. Fowler was at the mansion when Remus first saw it. It was he who informed Mr. Remus of what had happened, and he who witnessed both the immediate and longer-term effects of this. If I could just continue—"

"But you must present it to this jury in those terms—what did Mr. Remus know? What Mrs. Remus did or did not actually do is irrelevant. What Mr. Remus was *told* about it, and how it affected him, even if it wasn't true, is *all* that's relevant."

"But that's absurd," Charlie said. "It opens the door to their putting the victim on trial. They've concocted some conspiracy between her and Dodge, and now, under the guise of showing how it made George Remus crazy, they're going to try her."

"I understand your concern, Mr. Taft," Shook said. "But the question I have to ask is this: is there evidence of insanity? If so, then the defense is certainly entitled to show cause. I think that so far, we have seen some legitimate evidence. I trust that we'll see more. If we don't, if this meanders off into a diatribe against the victim, then I'll stop it and instruct the jury to disregard. Now, let's continue."

"You told Mr. Remus everything you've told us here today?" Elston said to Fowler.

"Yes."

"That his wife and Frank Dodge were conspiring against him?"

"Objection," Taft said.

"Overruled."

"I told him that on the day he came home. They'd filed a complaint with the immigration bureau claiming that when he came over as a child the papers hadn't been in order. They were attempting to have him deported."

"And how did he react to this news?"

"He frightened me. He stopped breathing. His face grew purple, the veins in his forehead and throat swelled, and he made horrible sounds. I thought he was strangling. But then he began to yell and race through the house again. He sometimes stopped to hit his head against a wall."

"He beat his head on the walls?"

"I remember how it echoed in those empty rooms."

❧ ❧ ❧

BY THE TIME CONNERS FINALLY CALMED HIM DOWN, HE'D
opened a gash in his forehead. Fowler brought a wet
towel compress and they sat, the three of them, on the
parlor floor until the bleeding stopped.

On the day after his homecoming, Remus received
a telegram from his wife requesting a divorce. In that
week, he discovered that nearly all the distilleries had
been sold for pennies on the dollar, and the main
bank accounts emptied as well. The cars were gone,
too, all but the Cadillac, which Conners had had Babe
keep. Remus moved back into the Sinton, but came to
the house every day. Sometimes he grew violent. More
often, he just sat, sometimes for hours, in one of the
empty rooms.

"WHERE WERE MR. DODGE AND MRS. REMUS AT THIS
time?"

"Objection."

"Did you tell Mr. Remus where his wife was?"

"Yes," Fowler said.

"And did it have an effect on him?"

"It did."

"What did you tell him?"

"That she was staying at the Alms Hotel. She'd told
me, in case I needed to reach her. I knew that Dodge
stayed there, too. I told Mr. Remus this. He got very
angry, then started to cry."

AT THE END OF THE DAY, ELSTON SAT AFTER THE ROOM
had cleared. As Remus was being led away, he said,
"Are you coming?" Elston waved, but did not get up.

Remus the lawyer understood. They had miles to go, and the chances were still long, but Carl Elston had managed to shift the momentum. This trial was now as much about Imogene as it was about Remus. He had won a great victory in this room on this day, and he wanted, for just a moment, to savor it.

CONNERS'S STORY

"HE SHOULD BE IMPEACHED," BASLER SAID OF CONNERS. They were having Monday breakfast in Charlie's office. "He's a crook."

"The kind people love," said Walt. "A whiskey man."

Charlie said, "Just disrupt it whenever you can." He believed utterly that Conners knew Remus was going to kill Imogene and helped arrange it. But he could say nothing of that now. He believed Conners would embellish what happened to make Remus look like a madman, and paint Imogene as a demoness. But as long as Elston posed the right questions, and stayed within Shook's guidelines, there was little they could do but let it play out.

ELSTON SAID, "WE'VE HEARD, MR. CONNERS, OF THE beginning of the breakdown of George Remus in Atlanta, and then in Cincinnati."

Conners wore a fine flannel suit. His wavy hair was lightly oiled. "I had trouble believing it and I was with him more than anyone. That he could slip so quickly and so far from being the strongest man I had ever met, to being . . . what he became."

"When did you really know?"

"In Atlanta he wasn't all that bad. After, when he discovered what she'd done to him, he began to have episodes. But when he was taken into custody again, then he really cracked."

"Custody? Again? What had he done wrong now?"

"Nothing. It came out of his plea bargain over the Jack Daniel's case. It was outrageous, what they did—"

HE'D BEEN IN CINCINNATI ONLY A FEW WEEKS WHEN A federal marshal showed up at the Sinton to take him to St. Louis. Elijah Zoline met them in Remus's new cell, where he explained that under the terms of the plea the Jack Daniel's prosecutors had the right to sequester Remus before the trial in order to go over testimony and to keep him away from the other defendants. It was also to protect him. Word had it that members of the Egan's Rats gang planned on killing him before he could testify. The informant was an old associate of Remus's, John Marcus.

It was October. The trial was scheduled to begin in January. Until then, Remus would stay in protective custody.

"WAS THERE REALLY A PLOT TO KILL HIM?"

"Yes. In the hoosegow."

"This was in order to stop his testimony?"

"Right. The plan was for three or four of them to start a fight near him. He wouldn't have survived it."

"Objection," said Basler. "Hearsay."

"Exactly," Elston said. "Mr. Remus heard this, too?"

"Of course."

"Overruled," the judge said.

"The Jack Daniel's trial itself, then. I imagine Mr. Remus was to be the central attraction."

"He and his wife, yes."

"How was his behavior there?"

AS CONNERS AND REMUS AND ZOLINE ENTERED THE courthouse on the first day, a tall man walked just ahead of them. When he turned to say something to his partner, and they saw his face, Remus cried out. Later, Remus swore he hadn't planned anything. But when he recognized Dodge, he lunged. Conners managed to grab an arm, but Remus got his other hand on the back of Dodge's collar and began shaking him. Zoline, on the other side, held on as well, but neither was strong enough to dislodge Remus in his rage. Two bailiffs helped free Dodge, who coughed and rubbed his throat.

"You've made a terrible mistake!" Remus yelled.

"You've made the mistakes," said Dodge. "Plenty, and you'll rot for them." He hurried off down a hallway, and didn't come back to the courthouse until Remus was done testifying.

Imogene never appeared during that time, either. On the day she was to testify, he was kept in his cell. He begged the guards and later Zoline and Conners to let him attend, even to the point of weeping, but they all refused.

"I REMEMBER ONCE," CONNERS SAID, "HE GRABBED ME around the head, and started throwing me around the room. Then he let go and ran, like as if he had somewhere to go, and of course he ran straight into a brick wall and knocked himself out cold. Jesus."

"Mr. Conners," Shook said, "this is a courtroom."

"I apologize. But I mean, that rattled me. And the poor guy believed he was going to die. I had to bring a lawyer in because he insisted on writing out a new will."

"You witnessed this kind of reaction on other occasions?"

"I saw him go into fits of convulsions, lying on the floor twitching and foaming from his mouth, like a hydrophobic dog. I saw him attack people, strangers or guards that had nothing to do with anything. I saw him pass out cold. Once I came in, he didn't even know me. Me, who'd been with him for years. He asked me my name." Conners paused and wiped at his mouth. "His pupils'd go, you know. That's how you knew when it was bad."

"How do you mean?"

"They'd dilate so much you couldn't see anything but black. It was scary looking. He'd go wild. And it got even worse. In the jug at Dayton, he changed again. After, he was a different man. I don't think he'll ever be the same after that."

"We'll get to Dayton. After Atlanta, when he was taken back into custody and held in St. Louis for four months, Mr. Remus fulfilled his part of the agreement with the Justice Department by testifying in the Jack Daniel's trial in St. Louis. Is that so?"

"Yes."

"And the defendants in that trial?"

"Except for Mrs. Remus and Marcus, all of 'em were convicted on George's word. They're all in Leavenworth now. After all that, he finally got out in January. This was '26 now. But as soon as he came off the train in Cincinnati, the state of Ohio arrested him again. It went clear back to a nuisance charge stemming from the original raid on Death Valley, four years earlier." Conners laughed. "I couldn't believe it. All of us had been charged with the same thing. The charges were dropped. It was a setup. I know for a fact Dodge was behind it."

"Objection!"

"Sustained."

ZOLINE IMMEDIATELY FILED AN APPEAL, BUT REMUS WOULD spend at least a month in the Montgomery County jail, in Dayton, Ohio, which was not a federal prison in Atlanta or Missouri. In those places Remus had had a relatively clean cell of his own, decent food, an exercise yard. Here, he was left in a barred cage filled with men. Instead of going to a mess hall, a guard shoved some plates under the grating. The others scuffled and fought over them. Remus told Conners he'd be goddamned before he got down on the floor with these animals and fought for food. He lay on his cot for three days before the guards noticed he was fasting.

In the appeals hearing, Zoline argued that Remus had already served the time for this sentence concurrent with his time in Atlanta. The other men who had been convicted of this same crime, of maintaining a nuisance, had had their sentences commuted on those grounds. The state had not contested that decision. Yet in Remus's case, it insisted that he serve the time. The judge agreed with Zoline that this constituted double jeopardy, and Remus was released. But the Montgomery County prosecutor and Justice Department lawyers both immediately filed appeals.

In April, the appellate court overturned the lower court's ruling. Remus was arrested and driven north to Dayton, where he began serving a year-long sentence, with no allowance for the time he'd already served.

IN CHARLIE'S OFFICE THAT EVENING, WALT SAID, "WELL, they've got what they wanted. Laymen testifying to Remus's insanity, and Imogene as the defendant."

"Just keep picking away at them," Charlie said. "Something will break."

What, he had no idea. But the following evening he got a call from a federal agent in Missouri who'd arrested a man on liquor charges. The man claimed he could turn the whole case against George Remus in Ohio in exchange for some consideration. The fed said that the case against the guy was thin, anyway, and the alleged crimes relatively minor. If Charlie wanted to talk to him, that was all right. His name was John Marcus.

Walt said, "It's another of Remus's crooks, Charlie. Why listen to him? If we want him here, we can just subpoena."

"We don't know what he knows," Charlie said. "We can't just put him up there and hope something clicks. Besides, I'm sure he's not above perjuring himself."

"Maybe that's the point. How can you believe anything he tells you, under oath or not? He's looking for a deal here, another escape. He'll say anything."

Charlie nodded. "I'm sure you're right. It feels

funny, though, that he'd want to insert himself at this
stage into Remus's life again. Don't you think that's a
little funny?"

"I don't know, Charlie. I just know I trust that man
even less than I trust Remus and Conners. Which is
not at all."

IN COURT, CONNERS PRODUCED A COPY OF THE CONGRES-
sional Record containing statements regarding Frank
Dodge by Senator La Guardia of New York, an old
friend of Remus's. Dodge, it seemed, had been
charged in New York City under the Mann Act in late
1925 for inhabiting a hotel room with a woman not
his wife. The woman was Imogene Remus. La Guardia
asked J. Edgar Hoover for Dodge's file, but Hoover
and Mabel Willebrandt both refused to release it.

Walt objected to the introduction of this record into
evidence. Shook asked whether Remus had seen it.

"He did," Conners said.

"Then I'll allow it," said Shook.

To Conners, Elston said, "What happened when he
saw it?"

"He didn't burst out. This time he just went to bed.
That's when I mark it he started to change again. He'd
been crazy before, wild crazy, you know, like I said.
Now it was like he just wasn't there. He didn't make
sense. He drooled. He soiled his pants." Conners
looked at Shook and said, "I apologize for that."

Shook waved a hand.

"And so he was finally released in April of this
year."

"Yes, sir."

"Eight months ago," Elston said.

"That's right. Then this summer, we got word someone else had been sent after him."

"To harm him?"

Conners laughed. "If you consider killing to be harmful."

"How did you learn of it?"

"A lot of people out there still love George Remus."

A smattering of applause from the gallery caused Shook to shake his finger.

"How did this affect him?"

"He was going to do them the favor and kill himself, I think. I had to keep people with him 'round the clock."

"And was it true? Had his murder been ordered?"

"Objection," Charlie said. "This goes to the very heart of the accusations against the deceased. It may be that Mr. Remus heard of such a thing. But even if it were later proved untrue, the damage to the reputation of Imogene Remus would be so great that the jury couldn't be expected to overlook it."

"Let's clear the jury—"

"Never mind," Elston said.

They all—Shook, Conners, Charlie—stared at him in surprise.

"We'll move on," he said. "I'll come back to this."

It would be several more hours before Elston turned Conners over to the prosecution. In the cross, Walt hit hard on the history of the business Conners had been involved in with Remus. But Conners simply agreed with everything Sibbald said.

"Aren't you still in that business?" Walt said.

"Whiskey," Conners said. "I own a distillery in Kentucky. We only sell into the drug market. It's all aboveboard. You're welcome to come down and see it." A couple of jurors smiled.

Conners, grim and hatchet-faced and truculent, was as brilliant in his way as Elston. He painted the darkest picture yet of the state of mental decay that beset George Remus. The prosecution would keep him on the stand for two more days of contentious questions that more resembled interrogation than testimony. But through it all he never faltered and never altered a detail of his story, and never ceased to meet his interrogators with the steady gaze of those flat black eyes.

THE DEAD

ON THE NIGHT OF THE LAST DAY OF CONNERS'S testimony, Remus dined alone in his suite. This had become a rare occurrence. If it wasn't Elston or Conners, it was Romola or Babe or even the sheriff, sometimes. But this evening they all had other places to be. He sat at the window as he ate, looking out at the darkening city. When he was done and they'd taken away the tray, he lay on the cot with his hands behind his head and knew he would wait here for hours, thinking, unable to sleep. It had become increasingly difficult for him as the trial progressed. He wondered about this, if it wasn't another sign of mental slippage. He came back to these thoughts often now, replaying the courtroom descriptions of his actions. He hadn't remembered many of those episodes, but now, when he tried, he found he could recall some of them, and knew that they were all probably true after all. Another symptom. There were his visions of Imogene, the hysteria that had sent him to the hospital. He was not stupid. He knew when things added up. He recalled Elston's coddling, Conners's suggestions that maybe he shouldn't listen in court. They both knew it.

He slept, and awoke later into the silence of the smallest hours, and sat at the window and watched the city sleep. And he saw her again. It felt as if he had known this time she would come, as if he had expected it. She approached in the brilliant white dress, and she stopped at the corner again and looked up at him. Again she left the ground. But this time he held himself there, forced himself to watch.

She rose the seven stories to his window and came in. He breathed quickly and his heart thudded. Perhaps she had come to kill him, to seek her revenge. He deserved it. But she only looked at him, and smiled, saying nothing. And then, to his surprise, he realized that he felt a great contentment at having her so close again. Here she was, with him, as they had been. Her face was younger than he remembered it. It looked as it had when he had seen her those years ago in her father's office.

"I love you," he said, softly. She did not seem to react to it. She merely continued to smile. "I don't know what ever happened," he said. "How it all went so wrong." She turned away at this. A little later, he turned to sip his water, and when he looked back, she was gone.

THE LAST TIME HE SAW HER, BEFORE THAT DAY IN THE park, was during the time Conners had testified about that afternoon, of the appeal of the Dayton sentence, in early 1926. Two months, Zoline had predicted, after Remus was released, before the case came before the full appellate court. Until then he was free for the first time in more than two years.

A St. Louis *Post-Dispatch* reporter named Anderson Rogers, who had covered the Jack Daniel's case, traveled back to Cincinnati with him. Remus had come to like the man, and found that he enjoyed telling him the story. They sipped coffee into the night, in restaurants or Remus's room. Conners occasionally joined them. Rogers's profile of Remus that winter ran to some dozen installments, and Remus found that he was briefly famous again.

Men called to tell him what they'd heard about Imogene and Dodge. That they'd been seen out drinking and dancing, that it was Dodge who'd handled the sales of the plants and the cars—Remus even met men who had bought some of them. That they stayed together in the Alms Hotel when they were in town.

He paid a man there. One day the man called and said, simply, "Yeah, she's in." He took a cab up Mount Adams and waited beneath a tree across the parkway, leaving only to buy a sandwich for his dinner. She didn't come back until ten. When she stepped out of her taxi, he took her arm.

"George!" she said. "Oh, my God. You're here! Oh, George!"

He squeezed.

She said, "You're hurting me."

He pulled her into a shadow and said, "Where is he?"

"Where is who?"

"That son of a bitch you go around with."

"I don't know, George. What is it?"

"What is it?" He slapped himself in the forehead. "You can ask me that?"

"Baby, you got out of Atlanta early. And you walked away from St. Louis. Do you know how hard this was?"

"Sure. And then they put me in again at Dayton. And I may go back there. They're still trying to get me."

"What?" She seemed genuinely shocked. He felt an absurd surge of hope, of life, course through him, but forced it away.

"They're appealing the judge's ruling. They're working the hell out of it. They want me back inside for another year. What does your friend say about that?"

"George, I—"

"I don't care," he said. "That's the funny thing. Why should I? What do I have to care about? It was never for me, Imogene. Never. None of it. If you want it, have it all."

"You said none of it mattered. It didn't to me, either, George. Not as long as you could be free."

"So you could deport me. I know you were at Immigration."

"*He* was, George. I went there to stop it—"

He turned away from her.

"It's what you told me to do. Well, I did it. Now you're here. And it'll work in Dayton, too."

"We'll see," he said.

"It will," she said. "You'll stay free. Then we can go back. This is what you wanted. What you told me to do."

He stepped into the street.

She said, "George Remus, please don't leave me.

Not now that it's all working. Now that we can have what we want."

He walked away from her.

"We can make the money back, baby. We can fix the house. Listen to me, please—" She called after him. She was crying. "George," she said. "Please—"

AFTER THAT, ON A FEW OCCASIONS THROUGHOUT THE YEAR and a half that would pass before he killed her, she sent him things—a photograph of them taken on the front porch of the mansion during one of her parties; a stack of fifty-dollar bills and a note asking him please to let her know if he needed more; an engraved watch she'd given him one anniversary years before. His first instinct was to assume that she was taunting him, and so he threw it all away. But sometimes, especially at night, he wasn't sure.

Now, in the darkest hours in the cell suite, in the way she had once sent him tokens that maintained her presence in his life, she began again to come to him. Sometimes, in his cold bed, he said her name, and listened, and heard a rustling in the darkness. Sometimes, when he rose in the face of his insomnia and pored over his papers, his memories, his histories, writing, crossing out, he sensed her there, peering over his shoulder. Occasionally he felt her move the pen to correct a mistake he had made.

So he was insane. And he was very likely going to die. Elston was a genius in the courtroom, but Charlie Taft had said from the beginning that it was a simple case of murder, and he was right. What more was there to it, in the end, than that? He had shot his wife to death. He would be executed, in spite of the fact that he really was crazy. When this came home to him, when he allowed himself to know it, always at night, always in his cot, his throat constricted; his breathing grew so harsh and labored that he felt on the verge of losing consciousness.

In those strangled moments, she came. She did nothing but appear and watch. But as she did, his throat began to relax and open. He would breathe again and think of the dead: of her lying in the morgue, of his father on the table in the house in north Chicago, of crazy Leo Gillenbeck as he dropped from the gallows, of poor little Herman, his idiot brother, of Alfred Ring. And he would smile, for it did not frighten him anymore. He had always feared it. Even in those brave nights with his men, riding, he held the possibility in his mind. Nothingness. But it was not nothing, after all. She came to tell him that. Dressed in white, in light, she wavered before him, as beautiful as she had ever been. She gave him this message: it was not nothing.

Soon after that, he always fell into a deep and dreamless sleep.

KILLERS

After testimonies from the St. Louis reporter Anderson Rogers, Elston called to the stand a man named Harry Truesdale. When Walt looked at Charlie and shook his head, Charlie stood up and said, "Your Honor, we have not heard of this man."

"I'm sorry," Elston said, "but he wasn't easy to track down. I entered his name with the clerk this morning." Shook spoke with his clerk, then nodded at Elston to continue. Elston established, first, that Truesdale had once been a member of the St. Louis gang known as Egan's Rats.

"And have you ever seen George Remus before today?"

When Truesdale spoke, Shook said, "Speak up, sir. The jury has to hear you."

"I said, 'Yes,'" Truesdale answered. "Four or five times."

Sensing something momentous in the offing, the gallery hushed itself and the jury grew as rapt and focused as it had during the descriptions of Imogene's death. Charlie saw Walt cup his hands around his face.

"Where?"

"Oh, at the dog track at Springdale. When he left his building. Once, I just saw him in his car as he passed me. A couple times inside the Sinton Hotel."

"You were following him, then."

"Yeah."

"When did you start following him?"

"Right around the time of the Tunney-Dempsey fight. I remember that. September."

"And when was the last time you saw him, before today?"

"In his room at the Sinton."

"I'm sorry, I can't hear him," Basler said.

"Please," said the judge.

"You said you saw him in his hotel room?" said Elston.

"The door was open. He was alone, looking out the window."

"And when was that?"

"On the afternoon of October fifth."

"The day before he shot his wife to death."

"Yeah," said Truesdale.

Clyde Basler stood up. "Your Honor," he said. "Wherever this is going, I object."

The crowd, its collective attention broken, erupted into laughter. The judge laughed, too, and even Basler allowed himself a smile. "Well," he said, "we've had it hammered home that what matters is what Mr. Remus heard, not what actually happened. Now this man is testifying about clandestinely following Remus, which is obviously not something Remus would have known."

Elston said, "This whole trial we've been accused, directly or by innuendo, of fabricating stories and causes and situations. I want the jury to hear what really happened. And then, believe me, Mr. Basler, we will get to what Remus knew and how he came to know it and what effect it had on him."

"It's a trick," Basler said. "They agree to one stipulation, then try to change it. What really happened is irrelevant, Your Honor, according to your own ruling."

Shook opened his mouth to speak, but Truesdale, speaking loudly for the first time, said, "But I talked to him. I told him what I was doing."

Elston waited. The judge said nothing, and Basler sat down.

"Why did you talk to him?" Elston asked.

"The whole thing stank. They was supposed to pay me half up front, but alls I saw was expense money. I kept asking when it was coming. 'Just do the job,' they said, but they finally kicked up a couple'a g's. And hell, they had men on me half the time. They hire me, then put men on me? What gives? Well, at the end, I give 'em the slip and got through to Remus. I had him dead to rights, alone in his room. I looked at him and I thought, You know, Harry, you're the one being set up here. They've give you nothing but talk, and you know good and damn well that's all you're gettin'. So I told the man what I was doing there. I guess I was thinking maybe I'd get something outta him for not doing it."

The judge, in his rapt focus, failed even to comment on the profanities.

"And why were you there?" Elston said.

"Why, to kill him."

The room stirred. A cloud of utterances rose and fell.

"You told Mr. Remus this?"

"Yeah."

"And how did he react?"

"Honestly, he looked like he just didn't care. Like if I'd done the job I'd'a been doing him a favor."

"How much were you to have been paid, Mr. Truesdale?"

"Ten g's."

"Ten thousand dollars."

"Yes, sir."

"You told Remus this?"

"Yes."

"Who hired you, sir?"

"I was contacted by a man I'd met before, called Jew John Marcus. But he didn't hire me. That was another man he took me to see, who said he represented Remus's wife, Imogene."

"And what was this man's name?"

"Frank Dodge."

Now the bubble in the great room burst, pierced by the scream of a woman in the gallery. People shouted at each other. Even the deputies yelled back and forth. Several reporters ran from the room. Shook hammered and hammered and finally stopped until the noise died on its own. Elston went on:

"Tell us how it was to happen."

"They knew where he went, where he stayed, his habits. I was s'posed to get him alone, away from his men. Maybe in his room. And put a bullet in his head.

That's how Dodge said to. But there was always people around him, 'til that last time."

"And when—" Again Elston was interrupted, this time by a great wailing moan from the defense table.

"Your Honor," Remus said. His face was wet. "Could we—?"

Clyde Basler said, "Oh, Jesus." One of the jurors, a woman, began to cry, then another.

"I apologize," Remus said, thickly.

"Let's recess," said Shook. The jury stood to exit as Remus came out from behind the table. Then, as if struck, he fell to his knees. He clutched at his chest, and collapsed. The three alienists rushed over to him. Elston, too, came over, but stood back a few feet, watching. Remus came to almost immediately, and struggled to get up, but as he did he began to wail.

"In here!" Shook said, indicating the door to his chambers.

"They'll hear him in the jury room," Walt said.

"Clyde," said Charlie. "See what you can do to get them to move the jury somewhere else for now. Get to Shook."

"It's an act," Basler said. "It's got to be."

"Well, the jury can still hear it. Now, go!" Basler hurried toward the judge's chambers.

"Marcus?" Walt said.

"Yes, make the call," said Charlie.

CLYDE BASLER MET THE TRAIN THE NEXT NIGHT. CHARLIE laughed as Basler told it. When Marcus stepped off in handcuffs, Clyde said, "We'll check you into the Commodore. Then we can start."

"I'm tired," Marcus said. "And I prefer the Sinton."

"The Commodore or the county jail. Your choice."

"Yeah, you're a tough guy, ain't you?"

Basler stopped and turned on him. They were about the same height, but Basler had twice the girth.

"I'm cuffed," said Marcus. "You want a shot, take it."

Basler said, "You want to rest tonight? That's fine. We'll start tomorrow afternoon."

"You guys are gonna love me."

"Yeah," Basler said. "I can feel it starting already."

THE DEFENSE BEGAN WRAPPING UP WITH A SERIES OF character witnesses, most notably Chicago's famous Clarence Darrow. "I've known George Remus for years," he said. "And I'll tell you this: that of any man I've ever met, he was, and remains, the staunchest opponent of the death penalty, of any kind of sanctioned murder. It is inconceivable to me that he could premeditate and execute one himself. Inconceivable. If he killed his wife, the only viable explanation, the only one, is that he was out of his mind. I will never believe anything else."

Charlie watched Remus wipe his eyes as the testimony concluded. The character witnesses would continue for another couple of days, but the defense was essentially over. Charlie had now to gather and plan his rebuttal.

IN A ROOM IN THE COMMODORE HOTEL, MARCUS SAT backwards on a wooden chair, his arms hanging over. In addition to a gold wristwatch, he wore a gold bracelet and two gold rings. The veins in his hands were distended, and his nails shined. His teeth, Charlie noted, were small and pointed and yellow.

"What I gotta tell you, it's gonna change everything," Marcus said. "But I gotta know what kinda deal I get."

"I'm only a local prosecutor," said Charlie. "But the U.S. Attorney in St. Louis tells me that if you cooperate and if you plead to a misdemeanor, as a courtesy to me, he'll ask for a suspension of your sentence. Isn't that what you were told?"

"Yeah. Fine."

"But that means you cooperate. My word is it. If I say you pussyfooted around, that's it. No deal."

"I'm glad to talk," Marcus said.

"Then do it."

Basler lit a cigarette for him. Marcus dragged on it and exhaled and hung his arms over the chair again. "Picture a lady," he said, "who was so in love with a guy, she'd do anything for him. And I mean anything."

Walt said, "What I want to know is whether Dodge really fell for her, too, or was it just an act?"

Marcus looked confused. He shook his head and said, "I'm not talking about Dodge, for Christ's sake. Dodge was the mark."

Walt said, "What?"

"It was all a setup."

"What was?"

"Everything, from the beginning, from Atlanta. Remus told her to do whatever she had to to get him out. Well, that meant sucking in Frank Dodge."

"But this gun from St. Louis, Truesdale—"

"Part of the con. The last touch."

"I don't follow," Walt said. "They hired him to kill Remus."

"As far as Dodge and Harry knew," said Marcus. "But it was never gonna happen. Imogene set it up to make it look like Dodge had put the finger on Remus. But Remus believed it, too, see. Just like he'd believed it all along when she'd played it so well with Dodge." Marcus laughed. "Jesus Christ," he said. "Smart as he was, he could be so fuckin' blind."

Walt and Basler looked at each other, the shock of disbelief written across their faces. Charlie just smiled.

He'd sat up late the night before, reading. His wife and his children were gone, and he had nothing to do but read. Of course, he'd have read anyway, even if they'd been there. He'd have read the letters and notes and plans of Imogene Remus. They were all fascinating, but the best, the most revealing, the richest, were those he'd just discovered, those he'd just begun to sort through, from the depths of her days with Frank Dodge.

November 1925

The strangest thing is that we both know it's a game, Frank and I. He said as much the other day. He asked me if we might make love sometime. "Physical love, I mean," he said. I told him I didn't know if I was ready yet. That's when he said, "It's different, now, isn't it? Us. It's not the game, anymore."

I turned and looked at him . . .

A PLAN

He said, "You don't think I believed, at first, that you were really attracted to me?"

"I don't know, Frank," she said. "I'm sorry for playing."

"We had to play. But it's been hard to be this close to you for this long, and yet to never . . ."

"I know," she said. "I haven't meant to tease you."

"Yes, you have."

"Well, perhaps, at times."

"It's changed, though," he said. "Don't you feel it? I love you now, Imogene. I'm in love with you."

"Don't, Frank. Please don't."

"I needed to tell you. I won't say it again."

"You're sweet."

"Will you think about it?"

"Yes. Of course."

"You've done what you said you would. For him, I mean. You don't owe him anything else."

"Frank."

"I know. I'm sorry. I'll be quiet."

"Shh," she said.

❧ ❧ ❧

SHE WAS KEPT FROM SEEING GEORGE IN ST. LOUIS. THIS crushed her, and she knew Dodge could tell. In the new year, when George began to berate her in the press through that fool mouthpiece Anderson Rogers, she knew Dodge was watching her reaction, waiting. She was careful to give him no sign of anything. But one night he knocked until he woke her. She peered out, then took off the chain and went back to the bed. He slipped into her dark room. She said, "What is it? Is something wrong?"

"No."

She heard him undressing. She said, "What are you doing?"

He pulled back the covers and got in next to her. He slipped an arm beneath her neck and began kissing her face and her neck.

"Frank," she said. "Don't."

"Shh," he said. "Just kiss me back, Imogene. Just kiss me, please. That's all."

She kissed him a little. He rolled so that his weight was against her. She pushed back, but he kept kissing her. She kissed him back and tried to push him away. He got his knee between her legs. She struggled against him, but she did not stop kissing him. He held her on her back, and spread her legs with his legs. With one hand he held her slender wrists over her head as he kissed her and bit her. She shook her head, but she did not say no. She wore a thin silk chemise with matching drawers. With his free hand, he pulled at the drawers until he ripped them.

She pressed up against him with her hips and

squeezed him with her legs and she tried to free her arms but she could not. Still, when he kissed her she kissed him back. When he pushed into her she cried out but she did not fight him anymore.

THE SECRET WAS THAT SHE COULD MAKE HERSELF GO AWAY. After the first time, it didn't matter anymore, so she let him come and do what he wanted. But always, when he was on top of her, grunting and licking her neck, she kept her eyes closed and left.

Sometimes she convinced herself she was purely a martyr, that she had done it all just for George. But in other moments she knew that she'd felt something for Frank. Perhaps, for a time, it had just been her hope, her belief, that Frank would help her secure George's release. Perhaps it was nothing more than the excitement of the illicit, the rush of the bad. Or simply the reflection of her anger at George—some days she woke up hating him so thoroughly she could taste it, and there was nothing better for it than to let Frank climb on and have at her.

Or perhaps it was that, in some way, in some small place in her heart, she felt something genuine for him. She wondered about that. Here was this powerful agent, seen by the world as an untouchable, who was nothing if not touchable. She had done what money, what whiskey, what power could not—she had corrupted him. And she knew that if she loved any part of him at all, it was that part, that weakness, that flaw.

Perhaps it was one of these or perhaps something else she couldn't name that led to this extended liaison that had so ruined everything. Whatever it was or had been, she knew when it was over. She knew on the day George confronted her in front of the Alms, knew it in the moment she saw him and felt him go through her that she loved him still as much as she ever had, and that she had to have him back. Of course, he hated her. He wouldn't listen to anything she said. She'd played the game too well. But she knew she could win him back. Because she knew when she looked into his face, through the hatred and the anger and the pain, that underneath it all, he loved her.

That afternoon, she went to Frank's room, where he sat cross-legged on the bed, playing solitaire. He looked up from the cards and said, "Something's happened. You look different."

"Frank," she said, and lay down on the far side of the bed, careful not to disturb the cards. "Is it true that you're fighting to put him back into jail, in Dayton?"

He lay down a card and said, "Wherever did you hear that?"

"I just heard it. Never mind where."

He played a few cards, then lit a cigarette and put it in the ashtray on the table. He said, "The department is."

"Are you?"

"I don't care anymore, Imogene. They could withdraw all the charges tomorrow, I wouldn't give a damn."

"Is that true, Frank?"

"Yes. It's Mabel who wants him gone again."

"Well, then," she said. "Can I—"

"You want to stop it?"

"I . . . feel like I should try."

"Why is that, Imogene?"

"I don't know, Frank. I just feel I owe it to him."

"Because you've cuckolded him? Because you feel guilty?"

"Maybe that's it."

"Did you see him?"

"Yes."

"And?"

"He hates me."

"Do you hate him?"

"No, Frank."

"Do you love him?"

She didn't answer. She looked out the window though she couldn't see very well.

"Do you love him, Imogene?"

"I don't know, Frank," she said. "I just feel sorry."

"For all you've done for him, he hates you. And you feel sorry."

"I'm sorry," she said.

"I just don't understand either of you. I never have."

"I'm sorry."

"I can't help with Dayton, Imogene. I'm sorry, too, but it's out of my hands."

IN APRIL, SHE MET WITH HER ATTORNEY ABOUT SOME TAX affairs. He told her that two days earlier the appeals court had sent George back to Dayton for a year. She wondered why Frank hadn't said anything. And she thought what a terrible waste it had been.

She had done everything Frank asked. She wrote to

George asking for a divorce. Frank had smiled as he read it. She went with him to the immigration bureau to launch that investigation, though later she sent them papers she knew would clear George. She stripped the house and sold some properties and hid others inside shells. She destroyed her life, and for what? A few months' early release, and that just so George could sit in a jail in St. Louis, and then Dayton? John Marcus told her once that even without her help, George would probably have gotten a deal in the Jack Daniel's case.

It made her sick to think of what would happen to him locked up for another year. He might be lost altogether.

The odd thing was that, even after all that destruction, and her own ambivalence, and after she cried when George went to Dayton, she knew that Frank was still in love with her. That he had fallen hard, and that nothing she did would change it. She saw it in his face. She could hear it in him when he made love. She knew men. She liked men, and she knew that this man had, after all this time, come over to stay.

Then, that summer, after George had been at Dayton for three months already, she had lunch with her old friend, the reporter Hinky Dolittle. They talked about George as friends talk about another friend they've lost touch with. When Dayton came up, Dolittle said, "Frank Dodge really nailed that one."

"Frank? No, it was all Mabel Willebrandt."

"Well, sure, she was after him, too. They both were. But Dodge was just vicious about it. You hadn't heard this? I got it that he was up there screaming at those prosecutors to keep this alive, to work the appeals, and he was writing to D.C. and doing a lot of the legwork for the background they needed. He's the one that kept it alive. I have that on very good authority."

She left the Alms that evening without seeing Frank or saying good-bye. She paid the night man to keep her departure hidden until the next day. She rode to Dayton first, to see George. He refused her, but she talked with a prosecutor there who verified Hinky Dolittle's story. She went to New York and met with George's friend Senator La Guardia, who hated Frank Dodge and Mabel Willebrandt and who gave her more information than she could digest. She went to Chicago and St. Louis and Atlanta and back to Cincinnati to find out what had really happened, and saw, finally, the degree to which Frank had hounded and persecuted her husband. She sat for days after this and just thought.

Months passed and she did not see Frank, though she had reports that he was still looking for her, tracking her. Then, near Christmas, she made a phone call, and left again. In St. Louis, she stood freezing at the curb in front of the depot. Marcus arrived, half an hour late, in a run-down Packard, its engine sounding throaty and raw in the cold air. The times had not been easy for John Marcus, either, apparently, though he was still here, still free. He leaned across and popped the passenger door open for her, letting her lift her own bags.

He took her to a small overheated room on the third floor of a walk-up hotel. It held only a small bed with an iron headboard, a table, and two straight-backed chairs, and looked out over an alley and a tarred rooftop. Marcus lifted the window, and the smoky St. Louis December air swirled in.

"Nice," she said.

He offered her a chair. She sat on the bed, adjusted the pillow so she could lean back against it, then swung up her legs and crossed them at the ankles.

"You wouldn't have anything to drink, would you?"

He smiled, and fixed her a bourbon and water.

"No ice?"

"Sorry," he told her. "It ain't that kind of place."

He already knew much of the story, but now she told him everything. She said, "He's hounding me."

Marcus slid a Chesterfield from the packet on the table, lit it, and flipped the match out the window. "Why do you think he's after you? Whiskey?"

"No," she said. "I don't know. He's angry."

"Well, sure, on the surface. But deeper down, that ain't why, and you know it."

"All right," she said. "But so what?"

"So what?" he said. "Why, you got all the power, now. You can steer it any way you want. Choose a direction."

"I want to tell him how I really feel. How I've felt all along, for every second I've been with him. That every time he touches me it turns my stomach."

"You could do that. It'd feel good for ten minutes, and cost you everything you been workin' for. And he'll never stop comin' after Remus, then, even after Dayton. He'll put everything he's got into destroying him."

"He's already destroyed him."

"Not entirely. Not yet."

"Then what?"

"What do you really want?"

"Will you help me?" she said.

"You gotta go back, play it out. Can you do that?"

She drank the last of the whiskey.

He said, "Of course you can. You know who you remind me of? Me." He smiled that frightening smile, but she did not look away from him. "I'll help you," he said, and shot the cigarette out the window. "But I need money."

"I can't pay you much."

"You control a few properties, still, don't you? Some stock. You can set it up for me to make some withdrawals."

"And then you'll kill him?"

He watched her a moment, then smiled. "You got it wrong," he said. "I ain't gonna hit a federal. Even one who's dirty."

"But you said—"

"I asked you what you really wanted. You want him dead? Is that it? Would that be satisfying? Or is it somethin' else?" When she didn't answer, he said, "I'd think you'd rather see him where Remus is. Reverse the situations. Remus with you. Dodge on the inside, looking out, chewing his teeth."

"Yes," she said, breathing a little harder. "But how?"

"They call him an untouchable, but you already shown that ain't the case. Go back. Let him into the business, let him smell that money. Then he'll have it all, a big income and you. But, in the spring, Remus'll get out and threaten the whole game. Then you turn it once more. That's when you'll need me."

SHE DID NOT LET DODGE CATCH UP TO HER. SHE CAUGHT him, in Washington. She knew she had to be the one who knocked. When he opened his office door, she simply put her arms around him. That was all she needed to do. She felt his tears on her neck.

Three months later he gave her a draft of his resignation letter to check over. She knew then she'd won, and just in time for George's release. She didn't understand yet how it would play out, but she knew it would. She put the letter away, for when she needed it. But when Remus was released in April, Marcus was preoccupied selling the whiskey she'd set him up to steal from a Covington warehouse she still owned. She had Frank involved in pulling whiskey from this same warehouse, using certificates and selling it to fronts who then sold it into the black market.

In June, she received word that George and Conners had shown up at this warehouse and tried to withdraw some stock. When the gauger refused to accept the certificates they presented, George had threatened him. "This is my property," he said. "Either you'll let me in, or I'll get past you any way I have to." Instead, the man telephoned the police, but by the time they arrived, Conners had gotten Remus into the car and left. The irony was that, though George couldn't know it, the money from this warehouse would all come back to him.

In July, her attorney, Judge Dixon, telephoned to say that George had filed several suits against her, not only for divorce, but claiming that she owed him millions of dollars and that she illegally held properties belonging to him. It was all getting uglier and more out of control, and she knew that the time to pull it back together was nearly past. She instructed the judge to give no reponse yet, and one afternoon had her driver take her to the Sinton Hotel.

It had not changed much in the years since she'd practically been a fixture here, though there was a huge pink candy shop and soda fountain off the lobby now, and she'd heard they were adding a dance and supper club on the top floor. She inquired as to George's room number, and rode up. It was the same suite he had kept at the beginning, and as she walked down the hallway she heard voices coming from the open door. He always kept the door open, for whoever wanted to stop in. Conners was there with two men she didn't recognize. He stood up when he saw her.

"It's gone too far," she said. "We need to stop this."

He looked at her, then told her to wait a minute. He went into the bedroom. She heard a bellow then, and the noise of glass smashing. When Conners came back, he just shook his head.

She began to cry. She said, "I'm sorry. This is all such a mistake. I need to see him."

"I'll talk to him about it. But not now. You'd better go."

She smiled at him through her tears, and left.

But she heard nothing from Conners or from George, and so in August she went to St. Louis to see Marcus again. She found him in a restaurant near his hotel, with a couple of other men, but when he saw her he waved them away and said, "Well."

"Enough," she said. "It's going to be too late. Are you going to help me or not?"

"I'll help."

"Have you worked out how?"

"I think I have," he said. "See, it's not Dodge we need to kill. It's Remus."

ALWAYS, WHEN FRANK WAS ON HER, SHE CLOSED HER EYES. He did not apparently think this strange, for he never commented on it. One afternoon, as they lay in bed, he said, "I have an idea. There was this woman, Old Mother Hubbard. She claimed to know things that Remus had done. She could cause him a lot of trouble. Maybe she could send him away again."

She sat up and said, "He'll still divorce me and take what's his." She lifted his hand and held it in both of hers. "Have you thought," she said, "of something more permanent?"

His eyes widened, then narrowed. "What are you saying?"

"Never mind," she said, though of course they both knew exactly. "It's just, someone like you, who knows about these things, ought to be able to figure something out."

She smiled and put the end of his finger into her mouth.

MARCUS'S STORY

"YOU'RE SAYING THAT YOU AND IMOGENE WERE FRAMING Dodge all along? That Dodge planned to have Remus killed, but she didn't?" Walt stood before Marcus, his thumbs hitched in his vest pockets.

"Yeah. I'm tellin' you that."

"And this gunman, Truesdale, he was in on it."

"No, he wasn't. He couldn't be."

"But you say the hit was designed to never happen."

"That's right. That's just what I'm sayin'."

AS ALWAYS, MARCUS WAS AT THE CENTER, CONNECTED IN all directions, knowing more than anyone, and yet less involved, less exposed. This was where he lived, where he had always lived.

At the meeting he'd arranged between Dodge and Harry Truesdale, he sat off to the side, arms hung over the back of a chair, listening but not speaking. They talked as if he weren't there. He knew Dodge would be nervous, wary of any unnecessary exposure, but he also knew that Dodge believed that he, Marcus, hated Remus because Remus had tried to sell him out over Jack Daniel's. In truth, Marcus bore Remus no ill will.

Remus had just been trying to save himself. He couldn't have known that Marcus had already done the same. But Dodge, believing Marcus had some stake in seeing Remus dead, let him stay and listen to the deal: ten g's for the hit, half up front, half afterward.

Dodge's hands shook. He chained his Lucky Strikes. Marcus sat with a cigarette burning in his own hand, but he did not drag on it much, so as not to draw any unnecessary attention to himself.

HARRY TRUESDALE WAS NOT QUITE AS BIG AS THE BABE, but he was still a big man. And he was not quite as simple as the Babe, but he was still simple. Harry liked to follow a program. The kind of guy who'd keep all his black socks in one drawer, and brown in another. Harry liked it when the game was all set up, and he just went in and knocked it down. He was good in those situations. He never missed. He never thought about it. He did the job, and went home and took a nap.

So maybe it was a bit of a joke that Marcus had set it up to be Harry that Dodge met with. It could have been someone else. There were plenty around. But in addition to the joke, Marcus liked the feel of Harry in this situation. He needed someone he could predict, and Harry was about as predictable as they came. The trick, in the end, was controlling Harry enough so that it didn't accidentally happen.

"Don't pay him the half up front," Marcus told Imogene. "Don't let Dodge give him nothin' but expenses. Tell him to tell Harry he gets the whole thing after."

The deadline, the last day for the hit, was October 5, the day before the divorce proceeding was to begin.

"It's perfect," Imogene said, when Marcus told her. "I'll arrange it for us all to meet at my lawyer's, as if to finalize the divorce. And then we'll get the news about Frank's arrest. And you must be there to tell George. The real truth, I mean. Not in front of the lawyers. I mean, we'll have that story, too, but I think he'll have a hard time believing it."

The story was that she had learned, by accident, that Dodge had hired the hit, and she called the feds in to stop it.

"You have to be there," she repeated, "to tell him how we put it all together, you and me."

"Sure," he said. "I'll tell him."

"And then it'll be like it was again, John. You and me and Conners and George. And we'll just go on."

"Listen, just make sure Dodge don't pay that money, or Harry'll really do the job."

"You mean you haven't told him?"

"Somebody don't know somethin', they're believable."

"If they question him."

"That's right."

"But Frank told him my name."

"What's that prove? Frank was layin' it off. So what?"

"But mightn't he do it anyway? If he believes he's getting the money after—"

"I know Harry," Marcus said. "But I'll make sure. You just make sure about the money."

"And you'll tell the police what we said?"

"Yeah, yeah," he said. "Don't worry about none of it. Except makin' sure Dodge don't pay."

"I'll make sure," she said.

MARCUS MADE SURE, TOO. "HOLD UP ON THE FIRST HALF," he told Dodge, when they met to go over things one last time.

"What for?"

"Just trust me. You wanna make sure it gets done, hold off."

"But—"

"Listen, a guy like that, he gets his paws on five g's, what's to stop him from skipping out? You gonna chase him?" Marcus laughed. "You gonna call in your federal buddies, tell 'em the killer you hired stiffed you?"

"But I told him—"

"Listen, he knows he'll get paid, 'cause you don't want him comin' after you. Right? Think about it. Trust me."

Dodge didn't look too sure about it, but he nodded.

Harry was due in town the next afternoon, on the last day of September. Marcus had called him the night before. "Make sure you get the five g's up front," he said. "This guy seems nervous, like he ain't so sure now. If he don't pay, don't do it."

"Right," Harry said.

CHARLIE AND CLYDE AND WALT RODE BACK TO THE courthouse in the Pierce-Arrow. They did not speak, though they had many decisions to make. At the courthouse, Samuel held the door and the other two said good night. Charlie waved, then leaned forward and said, "Sam, I know it's late, but would you mind taking a spin through the park?"

"No, sir."

He'd heard they were giving nickel tours up here now, a bus ride from the Price Hill mansion to the Remus Building to this spot of the climactic moment, the murder site. He patted Sam's shoulder and got out and leaned against the car and lit the Uppmann he'd been carrying with him all evening. He sucked until the fat tip burned evenly all around, and took a few more, deeper draws, then began to walk.

He thought about a woman. A woman who perhaps loved her husband so much that she gave herself to another man. Who then planned the murder of her husband in order to frame that other man, to get her husband back. But who, in the end, was murdered by the very husband she was trying to save. What, in all of this, did the husband know? Was he merely acting out of a jealous rage? Had she driven him crazy? Or was the truth even darker than that—was it possible that Remus had found out somehow about the murder plan, and acted to prevent it? Acted, in a sense, in his own self-defense? If so, why had he not claimed that in court?

The more you find out, Charlie thought, the less you know. And what, he wondered, as he walked there in the darkness of the park, only footsteps from where she had fallen, what was more difficult: to seek the truth, or to know it? And had it ever really been about the truth at all? Or was it about something else instead, something related tangentially to the truth,

but different from it? He recalled the words of George
Remus himself, just two months ago, at the arraignment: no good lawyer remains unaffected by his emotions. At the time Charlie had scoffed, thinking that
while that may be true of defense attorneys, it was certainly not true of prosecutors. Now, he wondered.

VERDICT

DOGS

ELSTON CONCLUDED HIS DEFENSE BY OFFERING AN EMO-
tional history of the life of George Remus. Remus's
younger sister, Ann, told the story of the fourteen-year-
old boy going to work in their uncle's pharmacy to support the family. Of that boy growing up quickly and
taking over the business, and prospering, and selling
it to go to law school, and prospering more. Of how
George had always helped others, and how becoming
a bootlegger, violating the laws he so vehemently op-
posed, was just a continuation of it. Why else, she
asked, do you suppose he became so widely loved?

That afternoon, the prosecution was to begin its
rebuttal. But when court reconvened, Shook announced that the alienists had completed their report.
He wanted to put Dr. Wolfstein, the head of the panel,
on the stand to deliver it. Elston objected, arguing
that this should wait until after the rebuttals, but
Shook disagreed. The report was important, and both
sides should have access to it as soon as possible. The
defense could have the afternoon, he said, if needed,
to finish. Elston said, "The defense is concluded
though we don't rest."

"Very well," said Shook. "Dr. Wolfstein, are you ready now?"

"I am," the doctor said.

The report began by complimenting Remus, holding that he demonstrated admirable qualities of leadership and yet a respect for authority, that he exhibited no history of sexual perversions, nor delusions of any kind, and that he was neat and clean in his personal habits and generally respectful to those around him. He had for the most part cooperated with the alienists in their examinations of him. His reasons for becoming a bootlegger were explainable by his notable and unusual history.

At first Remus claimed he had not been at all insane, then later he modified this to say that, in the hours after the shooting, he felt himself come back into his head. Later still, he claimed to remember nothing of the incident. When asked whether he'd decided ahead of time to kill his wife, he first said yes, then later denied this, saying that it was Dodge he had wanted to kill, and that he didn't know why he'd shot Imogene. He stated that he had still loved her, and loved her even now.

In conclusion, the report stated, first, that Elston's term, Transitory Maniacal Insanity, was no longer used. The closest the profession came to defining such a state was delirium, usually associated with some organic cause: scarlet fever, for instance, or pneumonia. Second, regardless of the definition, such a diagnosis required the presence of three behavioral elements: frenzy, followed by a catatonic sleep, and amnesia regarding the event. Remus had exhibited none of these. He carried out the murder calmly, then surrendered himself to the police. While he didn't really describe the event to the police, he certainly knew what he'd done, even reenacting it in the park for them. Only later, after entering his plea, did he claim amnesia. Furthermore, he exhibited no signs of paranoia or any other clinically recognized mental imbalance. He had been, simply, consumed by hatred and anger, and acted to express and relieve those feelings. The episode of late-night hysteria, which landed him in Bethesda Hospital for a day, was most likely a response to the approaching day of judgment, and his possible execution. The breakdown in court was another instance of emotional hysteria. He was, the report concluded, judged to be sane at the time he shot his wife.

Remus gritted his teeth as he saw Taft and his dogs smile, nod, pat each other.

He remembered none of it. Why had they discounted that? What he'd reenacted in the park was a game, what the police told him to do. Hold the gun. Show us. How many ways are there to shoot someone? You point, you pull.

He looked at Elston, whose facade revealed not a ripple.

IN HIS ROOM, HE DREAMED SOMETIMES OF FREEDOM, OF walking or swimming again. But then he remembered the awful days of the freedom of the summer just past, when he felt himself gripped by a terrible ennui he'd never before experienced. Nothing anchored his days—no men to organize, no whiskey to sell, no appeals, no wife, no parties, no house, not even friends, really. Conners was around, sometimes, but he had his own businesses to run. Remus saw the lawyers who were handling the lawsuit against Imogene and the divorce. But he felt nothing, no involvement in it, no urge at all to help them.

One afternoon, Babe came to his room. "I'm goin' to the track," he said. "You wanna? Them dogs are somethin' to watch."

"You know," said Remus, "why not?"

He found there, that afternoon, an escape from his life. The smells of the animals and the people, the sunlight heating it all, the sounds of men screaming at beasts, shaking in the air fists that clutched cash or ticket stubs. On a great chalkboard, they wrote the entries in each race, the history of that animal, its wins and places and shows, its bloodlines, the odds against it. You learned, over time, how much those bloodlines mattered. You remembered the name of a bitch who'd won a dozen races, and when you saw one of her pups, you thought you knew. You bet, maybe a quarter, maybe as much as five dollars. You laid it down, and they pulled the rabbit, and the dogs exploded from the gates, their muzzled jaws to the dirt, their hind legs coming so far forward that they nearly touched that muzzle, and though they were slight beasts, when they came past you could feel the vibrations in the dirt from the pack of them, and hear the pounding even over the screams and curses of all the other bettors. You lost plenty. But when one came—especially a longer shot, the one you'd noticed up there, a quality dog that had been injured, say, and had had enough recovery time but hadn't been tested yet, so you took the chance—when it came in at twenty-five to one, and you'd bet it across the board and you collected, for your few dollars, sixty or eighty in return, Christ you hadn't felt a thrill like that since the night those years ago when you swam into the blackness and crossed bridges and men came to kill you, and you and this immense man standing next to you fought back, and the money poured in like it was nothing more than water and there was never to be an end to any of it.

REBUTTALS

CHARLIE HAD DINNER WITH CARL AND WALT TO DISCUSS the redirect: which witnesses to reexamine, which points to clarify or sharpen, which to erode or muddy. Both argued for the most aggressive scenario. They'd lined up witnesses who'd known Imogene and would testify not only to her desire to reunite with Remus, but to his resistance to the idea. It was he, they would show, who abandoned her, and finally ended forever the possibility of a reconciliation. The capper, then, would be John Marcus.

"Are we sure about using him?" Charlie asked.

"Charlie," Walt said. "This is our bombshell. She was trying to save her marriage and he killed her. Given how this trial has gone, I think we need this—"

Charlie said, "I just want to think it through again. The fact is, she was involved in a murder plot. Elston can wring a lot of sympathy from that. What Remus knew, what he believed, was that they were both trying to kill him."

Basler said, "But she was doing it to get rid of Dodge."

"So says the gangster John Marcus. And Imogene

was a criminal. She nearly did time herself. This could be painted to look very bad. Elston can say, 'This made Remus even crazier. He killed her in what he believed was self-defense.' It's risky. I'm asking, is it worth that risk?"

"He shot her in cold blood," Basler said. "She had no weapon. She wasn't threatening him. He chased her down. This doesn't change that. What it changes is how the jury sees her. This is our chance to resurrect her image."

"That's it," Walt said. "That's exactly right."

"Yes?"

"Yes," they both said.

"All right," Charlie said. "Have we heard from La Guardia?"

Basler had been trying to get someone in the senator's office to verify that Imogene had, as Marcus claimed, called early on the morning of October 6 to report the doings of Frank Dodge.

"They're stonewalling."

"Of course they are," said Charlie. "With Imogene dead, they can't get at Dodge, but they can at least protect Remus. That means not helping us make Imogene look good."

"We thought of a subpoena—"

"Do you know who she talked to there? I don't. Are you going to ask to subpoena La Guardia himself? Shook'll laugh in your face. What'd you get from Hoover?"

"Nothing. He'll protect Dodge to the end."

Walt asked, "Are we even sure La Guardia's office contacted an agent after she called them?"

"No," Basler said. "It'll just be Marcus's word."

"It's risky," Charlie said.

"We need it," said Walt.

Charlie took a cigar from his pocket and rolled it beneath his nose. "Yes," he said. "At this point, it seems we do."

ON FRIDAY, DECEMBER 9, CLYDE BASLER BEGAN THE prosecution's rebuttal by informing the court that they'd need a full week.

A lawyer who worked for the Ohio and Kentucky Distillery, which Remus once owned, testified that Remus had been involved with the company throughout the period of his supposed insanity. It was even possible that Remus still owned a part of it. The testimony was dry, focusing largely on shells and fronts and legal maneuvers, and Elston managed to poke a few large holes in it. Enough, he said later, to let out the air.

An Atlanta friend of Imogene's said Remus was mean to her during his incarceration, and that if she had gone to Dodge, it was because Remus had forced her there, one way or another. This woman had twice found Imogene crying on the street outside the prison after Remus had made her leave.

Deputies, lawyers, jail guards swore they'd never seen him anything but pleasant and respectful. The rages, the breakdowns, the confusion, they said, weren't the Remus they had known.

Second Precinct officers described Remus's confession and behavior after the shooting. Elston, declining even to cross-examine any of these men, moved that the testimony be halted since it had no bearing on Remus's state of mind at the time of the shooting, and that the confession, such as it was, was already a matter of record. Shook denied the motion.

On Sunday, without informing the others, Charlie visited Marcus again in the Commodore. "I get the gist of it," he said. "Now I want details. How it was set up and how it went wrong."

MARCUS PAID A COUPLE OF PRIVATE DETECTIVES TO TAIL Harry while Harry tailed Remus, just to keep an eye, in case Harry got too close somehow and looked like he might do it. Then it was the fifth of October, divorce day eve. Imogene was calling him every few hours now, driving him nuts about how Dodge was wearing a hole in the floor, pacing, swearing that if they'd paid Truesdale, it'd all be over now. He wasn't handling it well, she said, considering he was an agent and all.

"Relax," Marcus told her. "Harry's frustrated. He can't get Remus by himself, and he's hot about the money. Make your call in the morning. I'll get Harry out of town."

"Then we'll tell George, won't we?"

"That's right," he said.

Later, Dodge phoned him.

"Trust me," Marcus said. "He'll do the job. He's gotta have an opening. Remus is always surrounded. But Harry's a pro, Frank. Let him work."

When he got back to his hotel that afternoon, the desk handed him messages from Imogene and from one of the detectives. He called the gumshoe first. They'd followed Harry, who'd followed Remus to the track at Springdale. Remus loved it there, throwing away what money he had left on the dogs.

"Remus left after a couple hours," the man said. "We were still both on the mark, this Truesdale. He's walking back to his machine, we're parked nearby, so's we can just follow. Then some other fellow pulls up between him and us, gives us the eyeball, like he knows who we are, like he knows what's going on. Then he says something to Harry, and next thing, Harry's getting in and they move some gravel getting outta there."

"You lost him?"

"Well, yeah."

"Who was it?"

"How would I know?"

"How long?"

"An hour."

Marcus hung up and the phone rang. Imogene said, "Frank said he should've done it himself, the right way. He said he was going to see that this man did his job. He went looking for him. He said if he couldn't find a big killer tailing George Remus, then he didn't deserve to be a federal agent. He was going to give Harry some money and see that it happened today. He only had a couple thousand, though, that he found here. John—"

Marcus hung up and ran for the door.

CHARLIE REMEMBERED READING SOMETHING THAT CORRE-sponded to what Marcus said. He had her papers in his briefcase, and thumbed through them and found it. It was hurriedly written on a sheet of Alms Hotel stationery. When he saw the date, October 5, a chill ran through him. It would have been the last thing she wrote, and what was sad was that it wasn't even about her, but Dodge, the man she despised.

October 5, 1927

What a fool Frank is. He can't even let himself be tricked without muddling it up. When he ran back here and told me his story, he was excited, like a child. And I, always the sucker, believed him—I thought George was dead. I wanted to scream. But I called John Marcus. Then I hated Frank even more than before . . .

WATCHING HARRY

It was warm for October and the track stank. Frank hated it there. It felt seedy, the dirt and the open bleachers and the stench of dog shit wafting on the air. He didn't like dogs to begin with, and these hairless skeletal creatures looked more like rodents than dogs, anyway. He knew if you tried to pet one you'd get nothing but a nip for your effort.

When he pulled up next to Harry on the gravel drive leading to the parking area, the man just looked dumbly in at him.

"You know you're being followed?" Dodge said, and tipped his head at the two goofs across the lot. Harry looked at them, then back in at Frank.

"You know that?" Frank said. "You have any idea at all what's going on?"

Harry just looked in.

"Get in."

Harry got in. Dodge drove.

"You know about those guys?"

"Sure," Harry said.

"So?"

"They're Marcus's, I think. So what?"

"Marcus is having you followed?"

"Looks that way."

"What the hell for?"

"I don't know. What're you following me for?"

"Because I want you to finish this. Now."

"Then whyn't you try paying me?"

"Paying—" Dodge swore, and reached into his jacket and brought out an envelope and handed it to Harry. "That's two g's. The rest when it's done."

"You said half up front."

"You think I won't pay you?" Frank said. "You think I want you coming after me? I look nuts to you?"

Harry looked out the window. "This is the craziest damn thing I ever seen," he said.

"Crazy," Dodge said. "How long do you have to follow a fellow before you can shoot him? Does it require a certain number of days? Jesus Christ."

Harry didn't answer.

You couldn't rely on anyone, that was the thing. He kept telling Imogene that. He should have just done it, but pulling on a man in cold blood, looking him in the face, Frank didn't think he had that in him. He didn't want to have it in him. He just wanted the people around him to do what they were supposed to do. That's all he'd ever asked.

"I'll drop you at the Sinton," he said. "He'll show up there sooner or later. Just go in and do it. Then we'll come back here and get your car."

Harry just sat shaking his head and looking out.

HE FOUND A SPOT ON OGDEN PLACE A BLOCK AWAY FROM the hotel. He could see the front doors. He turned off the motor and watched Harry shuffle up the street and cross over and go inside. Dodge closed his eyes. He told himself to be calm, that this would be over soon and he and Imogene could do whatever they wanted. They'd have plenty of money and plenty of time and the whole world to play in. It was a thing he hadn't ever thought he'd know, but now, here he was, on the verge of it. He'd told her he wanted to make love to her in every country in Europe.

He lit a Lucky Strike and tossed the match out the window. If Remus hadn't already come back here, it might be a while. But then Harry should come out and tell him that. There was no point in his sitting here all night. He could leave and come back.

Harry came out. Dodge checked his watch. It had been half an hour. Harry stood on the steps a moment and lit a cigarette. He looked up the street at Dodge with that dull blank expression. Then Harry turned and disappeared around the corner onto Vine.

What the hell? Dodge started the machine but had to wait for traffic. When he finally got around the corner, Harry was gone.

He thumped the wheel with the butt of his hand. Harry must have done it. That's all that made sense. He didn't want to draw any attention, so he just vanished. Good man, Dodge thought. Someone would've heard the shot. Soon the cops would arrive. He drove around the block, listening for a siren. None came. He drove around again, and saw Marcus hurrying up the street. He watched as Marcus ran into the hotel.

That was it, then. Harry had done the job. Marcus got the call from someone, probably Conners, and had to act like he knew nothing about it. He was hurrying over here to see what needed to be done. Now the cops would come.

Frank still had some questions for Marcus, like why was he having Harry followed? And for Imogene, like what had she and Marcus been talking about behind his back? He knew something was going on, but couldn't figure it. Well, he was going to lay into her when he got back to the Alms. She needed to know, now, that he was in charge. He'd get it out of her what had been going on, and then they'd leave it behind. Already, he could feel the pressure of it, the whole nasty business, being released.

Now, it was over. Now, it would begin.

DAWN

Charlie said, "I need to know what Remus knew about it."

"It was Conners who figured it out," said Marcus.

"Then they all know it, now." He sat and crossed his legs and laced his fingers around his knee. "How did it play out?" he said. "Tell me about that."

When Marcus ran up to Remus's room that afternoon, he saw him through the open door just sitting. Not dead, not bleeding. Quietly, Marcus backed away. He posted the detectives in the lobby of the Sinton, to watch for either Harry or Dodge and to stop them from going up to Remus's room. They sat there all night, but no one showed. Remus left early, they said.

So now it was time to come clean, to lay it out and take it down. It was the dawn of divorce day, the sixth of October, the day the feds were to get a call from Fiorello La Guardia's office, which had gotten a frantic call from Imogene Remus in Cincinnati about a contract she'd discovered on her husband. The day Frank Dodge would be arrested for conspiracy to commit murder. Just after sunrise, Marcus got the call from Imogene:

"I called. Like you said. There was no one in the office, of course, so I called him at home."

"You talked to La Guardia himself?"

"An assistant, a man I know. He'll do what needs done."

He dressed in a good suit and tie. He had a breakfast date with George Conners, except Conners didn't know it yet. But when he walked into the Grand Café at the Sinton and saw that Conners was already having breakfast with someone, and that that someone was none other than Harry Truesdale, Marcus felt crystals of ice form and melt in his veins. "Fuck," he said, through gritted teeth, for he knew now that he'd made a terrible mistake. Somehow, Conners and Remus had found out about the contract.

When he came up behind Truesdale, he overheard a little.

"Honest," Truesdale was saying. "I get the feeling it was never s'posed to really happen. Or else I was bein' set up. It was just all screwy from the start."

Conners said, "What do you think it is?"

"I dunno," said Truesdale. "I know I ain't seen nothing but a couple'a g's and some expense money. Marcus was running it but he had me going all over, giving me screwy directions and orders. That ain't like him a t'all. He just goes and does a thing."

"Yes, he does," Conners said, then looked up and smiled. "Well, maybe we should just ask him."

"This how it works now, George?" Marcus said. "You hear about a new killer in town and you take him out to breakfast? I always said you guys were soft."

"Actually, Mr. Truesdale was glad to hear from me, weren't you, Harry?"

"I dunno," Truesdale said.

"C'mon, Harry," Marcus said, touching his shoulder. "Time to go home. George, you sit a minute?"

"Oh, I'll be here," Conners said. "I've got to hear this."

Marcus walked Harry out to the front of the hotel.

"You go on, catch a train," he said. "The hit's off."

"Waste of my time."

"Listen," said Marcus. He pulled Harry's jacket open and slipped an envelope into the pocket. "There's another g for your time. And I'll see to it you get one more. I know it ain't ten, but it's not a waste, either. This is just from me to you, to make it right."

"What's going on, Jew John?"

"I don't know, Harry. It's all strange. But listen to me: there's one condition on this. Anybody ever asks, and believe me they will ask, you didn't have this meeting with Conners, and you didn't get money from me. OK?"

"OK, John."

"I mean it," Marcus said. "I don't care if Jesus Christ himself comes down and asks you, you don't know about this. All you know is you were hired, and it went strange, and you went home. Yeah?"

Harry nodded.

"Good man," Marcus said, and patted his chest.

Inside, he sat across from Conners, and motioned for a waiter to clear Harry's dishes and bring clean ones.

"So how'd you hear?" said Marcus.

"Does it matter?"

"Thing is," Marcus said, "there ain't no hit."

"No?"

"Never was, 'cept in Frank Dodge's mind. A little birdie placed a call this morning to Senator La Guardia, who is, as we speak, contacting federal agents to arrest Dodge for conspiracy."

"What little birdie?"

"Does it matter?"

"I think it does."

"A little Jazz Bird."

Conners put down his fork. The strangest look came over his face, a look of pure surprise on a man who was rarely surprised by anything. Though Marcus couldn't know it, it was very close to the look Remus had seen on Conners on the front porch of the mansion when they first took Imogene to see it, when Remus revealed the secret of how he was restructuring the business.

"The whole thing?" Conners said.

"Her."

Conners shook his head. "I have to tell you," he said. "Your man Harry got through to Remus yesterday. Caught him alone in his room."

"Shit," Marcus said.

"Lucky for us he didn't like the way it felt. So now Remus is talking about finding Dodge and finishing it."

"Remus pull a trigger? Never happen."

"He's beside himself. Some days he almost convinces me he's nuts. I told him just last night he'd laid a good cover if he did it. I could line up two dozen people who'd testify that he was loco. He started yelling, 'I'm not crazy!'"

Marcus laughed. "He couldn't do it," he said.

"I don't know. This is Dodge we're talking about."

"Well, it don't matter now, anyway. He's goin' away. That's what she wants. That's how she's played it."

"Seems to me she's played it all ways."

"Lady's got to take care of herself, George. Remus treated her like dirt."

"*Remus—?*" Conners started, then stopped and laughed. He threw his napkin on the table.

"Whatever," said Marcus. "I don't really care. She's sittin' on some good stock. I got my hands on a little of it. I say we get them patched together and get the hell back in business. It's been too damn long."

"It has." Conners finished his coffee, then said, "We heard Dodge was talking to Old Mother Hubbard."

"Crazy bitch. She stills thinks we killed Eli."

"Did we?"

"Well," said Marcus, "if we did, it was because he needed it. But even so, Remus wouldn't know nothing about it."

"You'd be surprised. He had ways of knowing things."

"I suppose he did," Marcus said. "About a lot of things. And the ideas he had . . ."

"He had some pretty good ones."

They came outside together, Conners with his hand on Marcus's shoulder. It was a sunny morning in the city, the sky clear and deep and the autumn air cool and the world feeling full of new possibility. They stood for a moment, enjoying it, taking it in.

Marcus said, "So tell me what happened with Harry, and how you ended up having breakfast with him."

"Well, I had actually heard about it a couple days ago. I didn't tell Remus, but I got a finger on it, found out where the guy was staying."

"What were you gonna do, hit him?"

"Yes."

"Just like that?"

"Just like that," Conners said.

"So what happened?"

"Before I could do anything, like I said, he got through. He had the shot but didn't take it."

"Harry's got a nose."

"So get this. He sits and talks with Remus. For half an hour they chat. About life. Then Remus gives him a couple'a hundred bucks to help him out."

Marcus started to laugh.

"I figured I owed the guy a meal, at least."

Marcus was about bent over when Conners said, "Isn't that the Babe?"

Marcus looked. "The hell—" he said.

The big man was sitting in Remus's Cadillac at the curb, his head on the steering wheel. Marcus rapped on the window. When Babe looked up, they could see that he was crying.

CHARLIE SAID, "SO CONNERS REALLY DIDN'T KNOW ABOUT Remus's going after Imogene."

"It was Dodge," Marcus said. "That's who Remus went after. I don't know why he did it to her. I don't know if anyone does."

Charlie walked to the window. He said, "All she ever wanted to do was help him. Help them. She wasn't the sort to hurt anyone. I don't think she had it in her to have Dodge killed, even if you'd been willing. And then for her to just get gunned down in the street—"

"You're wrong," Marcus said. "Her blood ran as cold as a snake's, when it needed to. But that's another story. An old one."

Charlie turned and looked at him. "Her father, you mean?"

"Well, no. After that. After she left and came back, that next summer."

"Tell me."

"I'm . . . protected on this."

"Yes, of course."

"They wanted to get married, but her husband, or what the Huns had left of him, was still alive in a sanatorium up north."

SHE SPENT HER DAYS AT THE MANSION, AND HER NIGHTS AT the Alms. Even when the house was ready, she didn't move in. She would not sleep there. Not yet. One afternoon, when Remus had to be out of town, she knocked on the door of Marcus's Sinton suite.

"Mr. Marcus—"

"John," he said, standing aside to let her in.

"John." She took off her hat and sat on the sofa. She said, "I'd like to describe someone for you. A man who was injured in the war. Badly injured. In the brain."

"Why?" he said.

"Just listen," she said, and told him. Afterward, she asked, "If it were you lying in that bed, what would you want?"

"Someone to put a bullet in my head."

"I need help. I need a man who knows what he's doing, and who can be very discreet. No bullets. Someone who can make a thing appear to be something other than what it is."

"What're we talkin' about here, Imogene?"

"I want to hire you to do a thing I'm afraid I should have done a long time ago." She told him, then said, "Can you do it?"

"Someone like that, yeah. Easy."

"How would you get in and out without being seen?"

"You'll go there," he said. "Make sure the window's unlocked. Open it an inch. Take a white ribbon, like that one on your hat, and pin it so it hangs outside."

"And how much will I owe you?"

"Please," he said. "Let's call it my wedding present to you and George Remus."

CHARLIE STARED. "SO WHEN MALCOLM WAS FOUND DEAD—"

"I didn't do it myself, you understand."

"I don't care about that."

"I mean it wasn't like he was really alive anyway. A pillow over the face. A simple thing. I heard he didn't even fight it much. Maybe he was grateful."

"I just can't believe . . . Remus didn't suspect anything?"

"I think he knew. Sometimes I even thought maybe she told him."

"Why—"

"I don't know," Marcus said. "Just the way they were."

AS HE WALKED BACK TO THE COURTHOUSE, CHARLIE thought of a young woman walking these same streets, buying fruit, looking in shop windows. No one was clean, he thought. It was so dirty that they'd all been stained by it, and now he was stained himself. Where did a thing like this come from? he wondered. Where was the seed planted that grew into such a monstrous thicket?

It came to him then that he was going to lose the trial. It came in the way hard truths always dawn on us finally, not gradually, but as sudden knowledge. They land and settle, and bring with them not only disappointment or grief or despair, but a kind of deliverance, too. A deliverance from wonder, and hope, and not knowing.

He called Walt and Clyde into his office. "We're not using Marcus," he said.

"Charlie—" Basler started, but Charlie cut him off with a look. He'd thought it through a dozen times. If Elston knew from Remus that Imogene had ordered the murder of her first husband, and then had the chance to cross-examine Marcus, the case would be finished. The question was whether or not Remus knew. The answer was simple—it wasn't worth finding out.

"I'm sorry," Charlie said to his two deflated-looking lieutenants. "I can't explain everything. You'll have to trust my judgment on this."

✣ ✣ ✣

IT WAS DONE NOW, THE WRITING OF IMOGENE REMUS. He'd read everything, much of it twice. And he knew something—he was finished with it. Finished with her. The desire he'd felt, the urge to learn more, to uncover, to see her, hear her voice, to know her, was gone. Whatever the jury decided, it had nothing to do with her anymore. She was just a dead woman.

Charlie picked up the telephone and asked for New York.

"Ellie," he said, when she answered.

"Charlie," she said, and started to cry.

"What is it?"

"We miss you," she said. "I miss you."

"Then come home," he told her. "It's over."

HE POSSESSED SOMETHING, A PIECE OF THE TRUTH OF THE Jazz Bird that no one else would ever see. He had become, in a sense, the caretaker, the keeper of this small insight into her life. That night, as a kind of eulogy, a final gesture, a thing he thought that maybe she deserved, even in light of what she had been, he finished her story.

EDEN PARK

LAURA WAS SO GOOD, SO HELPFUL. SHE CAME WHENEVER Imogene asked, and stayed as long as Imogene needed her, and then went away until the next time. Even in the beginning, when Imogene was just a young girl and Laura was a woman, they'd had a kind of parity, though Laura hadn't hesitated to correct Imogene or chastise her. After she'd come back to Remus, though, after Malcolm died and she became the matron of a huge estate and a fortune, it changed between them. Laura said little, now, except to respond to something Imogene said. She never corrected or criticized. She didn't even look directly at Imogene very often. But she always came when Imogene called.

And so on this morning, she waited in the lobby of the Alms Hotel. She smiled when Imogene came down, aware of nothing that was set to happen, secure in the false belief that Imogene and George Remus would be divorced on this day. Imogene smiled back, and hugged her, and said, "Dear, sweet Laura."

Imogene held her arm, and the doorman held the door, and they went outside together, into the light.

❧ ❧ ❧

IT WAS LAURA WHO KNEW. THE DRIVER SEEMED UPSET AT something, though he couldn't know, yet, how dangerously wrong things were. When he reacted, Laura looked back. She said, "It's him." She said it flatly, as if it surprised her not in the least.

Imogene looked and saw the great black Cadillac running up on them. It didn't quite occur to her yet what was happening. She grew frightened only when her driver cursed and pressed the accelerator, and she saw Laura's face. They were going to get hit, she thought. She felt herself flung back into the seat, felt herself sliding down, so that all she could see, for a moment, was sky.

IN THE PARK, WHERE THEY FINALLY STOPPED, WHERE THEY had to stop or be wrecked, George wrenched open the door.

"Where is he?" he said. He looked so confused, so lost, but also so angry. "Where is he?" he kept saying, as if he had misplaced someone. Himself, perhaps, for this wasn't George. She knew his eyes, and when she looked at this man's eyes she could see that it wasn't him. It was some mad, distraught animal, but not him, not her baby. She couldn't stay in the car any longer. She felt her throat constricting, the closed space growing hot and stale, and she was suffocating and she had to move, had to get out of it, had to get away from this man who was not George. She ran.

She ran where they had walked so many times before. She would run to their spot, to Breezy Point, up the steep hilly pathways, that's what she thought. She would lead him there, and then he'd remember, and come back into himself, and it would be him. He would see her, and it would be them.

SHE HEARD HIM COMING, AND THEN HE HAD HER. HE gripped her arm, he hurt her.

"George," she said. "Don't hurt me. Please."

"It's not you I want to hurt." He squeezed her.

She looked in his face and it was not him.

"Where is he?" he asked her.

She told him she didn't know.

His face changed, but it was still not him. "See this?" he said. When she saw it, she screamed. She knew, then, and she screamed and pulled at him but he would not let her go.

"No!" she screamed at the man who was not George.

It was her gun. She recognized it.

"George," she said. "Don't." She screamed his name. She screamed at him. She pulled against him, but he held her. And then she was cold. On this fine warm day, she felt so cold.

SHE LEFT, THEN. SHE WENT BACK, YEARS BACK, THOUGH IT was really not so very long ago. It was not Frank she went back to, or George, but Malcolm. Malcolm. Poor Malcolm. He was so very young, and she was younger still. She had only been fifteen when they met, but somehow she had known. She had foreseen what would come. And there were her parents as she remembered them, her father in a tie and vest and shirtsleeves, reading the morning paper over his coffee (the one moment of his day when he did not work), and her mother, peering into the cup, waving her fingers at Dinty, the girl they kept to cook and clean, to hurry on and fill it again. She would have wept if she'd had the tears, but water kept falling from her to the paving stones, she did not know why. She heard it falling and it left her nothing for tears. She had cried, though, already and long ago, for each of them.

She came back to Eden Park. Somehow she was in the taxi again. He was after her, still, so she passed through it and out the other side, and she was so cold, so cold now, and wet, she was wet everywhere, and it was getting harder to breathe. She went out the other side and she ran once more back up the road. Back toward Breezy Point. Their spot.

Then she went out into the world where she had gone so often in the prime of her days, for months at a time. London. Gstaad. Rio. San Francisco. Marrakech. Chicago. Oporto. New Orleans. Jerusalem. My God, she thought, I did go.

And now she knew she was going again.

THE NIGHT

THE PROSECUTION RECALLED LAURA PETERSON, THIS TIME to address the issue of Remus's sanity. She had, after all, Basler said, known the defendant now for eight years and seen him in any number of situations. She was also the one person who could describe his appearance in the moments before he shot his wife.

"I was so frightened," she said, "I didn't really hear what he was saying. I must say he looked terribly composed, cool, and focused, and as if he knew just what he was doing."

"Objection."

"Overruled."

"Did you ever witness, before the day of the shooting, Mr. Remus abusing his wife?" Basler asked.

"I did," she said, nodding.

"That's nonsense!" Remus said, leaping up.

"Mr. Remus!" said Shook. "I have warned you many times."

"Your Honor—"

"Enough!"

Remus sat again. His face burned. He lowered it toward the table and pressed his hands over his ears.

"Several times," Laura said. "Especially after things started to go badly. It was generally how he talked to her that was so mean. But I saw him throw a cup of coffee at her."

"Did it strike her?"

"No. But once I was at the mansion, in another room from them. They were fighting, and he spoke very viciously, as if he wanted to strike her."

"Objection."

"Sustained."

Elston was brief in his cross. "Tell us, Miss Peterson, was anyone else around during the incidents you described?"

"No, sir, not that I know of."

"Do you know of anyone who can confirm your stories? Anyone you can suggest who might have witnessed such things? Household help? Friends? Relatives?"

"I wouldn't know."

"Now," he said, "isn't it true that during the spring of 1926 you traveled to Miami, Florida with Mrs. Remus and Mr. Dodge?"

"Yes."

"And while there, that Mrs. Remus rented you a hotel room next to the room she shared with Franklin Dodge?"

"Objection!" Basler shouted.

"And I object to you!" Remus shouted back.

"Mr. Remus!" the judge yelled, pounding his gavel. "I have had enough!"

"Your Honor, I apologize," Remus said, coming out from behind his table. "But I've had enough as well. I must say that you've done a remarkable job in this difficult proceeding. And the jury have held up well, and the alienists have been terribly professional. But these three buffoons have tried me to the limit."

"That's it," Walt said, throwing his pen down. He was halfway across the floor to Remus, face flushed, when several deputies managed to get between them. "This man," he said, shaking his finger at Remus, "cannot be allowed to continue to berate the prosecution. We represent, no, we are to be *considered*, the state of Ohio. This disrespect is beyond the pale. I'll stop him myself if I have to."

"You, sir," Remus boomed, "are a damned idiot!"

"Enough," the judge said. "Mr. Remus, the prosecutors have acted properly throughout this trial. You've acted shamefully. Now you've gone too far. I find you in contempt of this court, sentencing to be postponed until the trial's conclusion. Now sit down and keep your mouth shut." To a deputy he said, "I want two of you beside Mr. Remus for the remainder of the trial. If he so much as starts to open his mouth, remove him."

When it was quiet again, Elston, as if nothing had happened, said, "Judge, your ruling on the objection?"

"Denied."

"Miss Peterson, did you have a hotel room next to one that Mrs. Remus shared with Mr. Dodge?"

Laura did not respond.

"I'll remind you," Elston said, "that hotels employ many people, and some of them know what goes on in the rooms. I remind you that local law officials are kept apprised of situations that could involve the

breaking of laws, such as the Mann Act. I remind you
that I can subpoena any of these—"

"Yes!" she said. "All right? I had a room next to
theirs. They were together. Yes. Yes. And who could
blame her? Can you tell me that? Who, Mr. Elston?"

Remus could only stare at her.

ON OCTOBER 5, THE DAY BEFORE THE DIVORCE, HE'D BEEN
reading when he heard heavy footsteps approach. A
man looked in. He said his name was Harry. Remus
offered him a seat, and a drink. Harry confessed he
was a hired gun, but something was just screwy with
the job. Did Remus know that feeling? Oh, Harry,
Remus said. Do I.

Conners and Babe came up for dinner. Remus had
them send up four meals because Babe liked to eat
two. But nothing was settled, nothing was good anymore. He didn't know what to do. Conners said he
didn't know, either. The Babe just hummed to himself. Remus said something in jesting anger about
knocking off Dodge, and Conners surprised him by
saying, "No one would blame you. Besides, all we'd
have to do is say you were crazy. I could get a whole
line of men to testify to that."

"But I'm not crazy," Remus said. "Anyway, he stole
my wife. What jury wouldn't view that as justifiable?"

"Well," Conners said. "There you go." And he
laughed, as if it were a joke. But was it a joke, or
had he been serious? Had he been trying to tell
Remus something without coming out and saying
it? Babe had stopped humming. Remus knew he was
listening.

After Conners left, he had Babe drive him to the Alms. He wanted to see her, but when they got there, he changed his mind.

When she called later that night, his heart soared in spite of everything, the hatred and anger and betrayal, the years in prison. He felt that lifting, and feeling it made him angry all over again. She had such power over him, and knew she always would. He heard the liquor in her voice, the slurs and slides. She didn't have to speak five words before he knew.

"Baby, I miss you," she said.

"I met your friend today."

"What friend, baby?"

"The little surprise you tried to send me."

She said, "You know I wouldn't do any such thing. But I do have a surprise for you. Can you keep a secret?"

"What surprise? What are you talking about?"

"It's not going to be what you expect. Tomorrow's going to be nothing like what you expect."

He heard music. "Where are you?"

"At a club. In the office. Do you want to come here?"

Cincinnati was full of jazz clubs now. The Salvation Army had recently obtained an injunction against a new one because it was next door to a home for wayward girls. The babies born there, it claimed, would develop "jazz emotions" from hearing it.

"No," he said.

"You don't have to drink. Or we can just walk if you like."

"Feeling a little nostalgic? Is that why you called?"

"I called to say that you're going to be surprised tomorrow. That's all. Something to look forward to."

"I'll bet," he said. "You get someone who can actually pull the trigger?"

"I never wanted you hurt. Or in jail. I've done everything to get you out, to protect you. Don't you realize that?"

"Sure," he said. "You've been a peach."

"I have done everything—"

"What's the surprise, then?"

"It has to do with something Frank was planning."

Remus felt the pressure begin to build behind his eyes. "Don't ever say that name."

"That's the point, baby. It'll all be over soon. You'll never have to hear his name again."

"When I'm dead," he said. "Or buried so far in some prison I'll never get out. Is that it?"

"Stop, George."

"What's this about?"

"You'll see. Something Frank's been working on."

"Does this have to do with Marcus?"

"Why, yes. He's involved. What do you know about it?"

It had to be that old nonsense of the murdered sheriff. He'd heard this before and heard recently that Dodge was going around with Old Mother Hubbard, Eli's wife, who everyone knew was crazy. So it was a frame-up. Oh, to have Marcus back once more, to release him on Dodge and see the look in Dodge's face as the foul-mouthed little killer came at him wearing that death smile.

"George?"

"I know about it, Imogene," he said. "I'm just tired. You play your games, you and Dodge. Play whatever you like. Taunt me. I'll take you all down."

"George," she said.

He hung up, then phoned the desk and told them not to put through any more calls.

But he couldn't sleep, couldn't banish the demons he wanted so desperately to drive from his head. Imogene and Dodge. A St. Louis gunman who wouldn't pull the trigger. Mother Hubbard. Of course the stories were true. They were all true and he knew it. Someone had killed that sheriff. Someone had killed Eli Hubbard. And they'd undoubtedly done it for him, or in his interest, or in the course of doing his business. It made him sick.

Imagine her calling like that, to taunt him with it. Dodge couldn't even hire a competent killer, so now he was going to resurrect some old charge. Deep into that night, Remus came to know something: it was never going to stop between him and Dodge. For the rest of their lives they'd be after one another, Dodge trying to put him away again, to get rid of him so he could have Imogene free and clear. And he, Remus, hating Dodge and waiting for a chance to strike back. They both knew that chance would come, sooner or later, unless Dodge won first.

As he lay in his sweat and his foul thoughts and his waking nightmares, as the images of all those years poured back upon him, he began to feel a kind of purifying fist of light inside himself, a light that could burn away anything, the light of absolution, of the absolute gesture. Conners had told him how.

She'd always been good at these decisions, of when to act, when to give over to what was going to happen. Of when to commit everything to your cause, to lay it all down. In a sense, she'd done it again. That was why she'd called him. He knew it, now. She was warning him. Dodge was planning something, isn't that what she'd said? A big surprise. Maybe he'd have the police there to arrest him again. Or maybe a new gunman would try on the street outside the lawyer's office.

But Imogene must have meant something else, too—that Dodge would be with her. She must be bringing him to the hearing, which meant they'd be together on the way there.

It was as it had once been—Imogene telling him how it would be, what he must do, and Conners giving him the mechanism. As the last of the night waned, Remus knew the answer. At five, he called the club where Babe sometimes worked.

"You need to get me here at the hotel as soon as possible. We'll go to the house, first."

"Yessir."

"It's Dodge. He's going to be there, you see."

"At the house?"

"No, no. Just come quickly."

At the mansion, Remus dashed about, tearing open drawers and boxes and closets. Then he remembered something. "Babe," he called. He was in the study, kneeling in a closet and pulling at the wall. "Feel this, where this square of plaster is loose. There's a finger hole."

The Babe knelt and lifted out the plaster. Remus

shoved him aside and reached in and brought out a package.

"It was hers, you know," he said. "I gave it to her when they first came to kill me. Now, it's for Dodge. It's perfect."

Remus knew Babe didn't know what he was talking about. He didn't know what was in the package, and that was fine.

WHEN THE PROSECUTION FINISHED ITS REBUTTAL, SHOOK asked Elston if he needed to call anyone else. "Only one, Your Honor," he said. "Dr. Wolfstein."

Whispers passed across the room.

"Doctor," Elston said. "I have just a single question for you. Your report stated that—"

"It was not just mine."

"I stand corrected. The report from you and your two colleagues stated that there were certain clinical requirements for a diagnosis of, what did you call it?"

"Delirium."

"Delirium," Elston said. "Temporary insanity, you tell us, being no longer in vogue."

"It's not seen as a useful—"

"People don't go temporarily insane?"

"Well—"

"I mean, they do, don't they? Is that possible?"

"I suppose—it's just not a useful diagnosis."

"Useful or no," said Elston, "is it theoretically possible for a man or a woman to go temporarily insane?"

"It is possible for them to enter a state of delirium, which is almost always associated with an organic cause."

"Almost always?"

"Yes, sir."

"Could this delirium be called a type of insanity?"

"Well, yes," Wolfstein said. "The whole term insanity—"

"And it is temporary in its nature?"

"Yes."

"Thank you," Elston said. "I apologize, Doctor. It seems I have, after all, more than one question. But I'm getting to my point. Would you define insanity for us?"

"Well, simply put, it's a deviance from what we think of as . . . sanity."

Elston smiled. "Then define sanity."

"Well, there's a long list of— It's very complicated."

"Never mind," Elston said. "Let me ask you this—do all alienists agree on the definition of insanity?"

"Probably not."

"They don't?"

"Not entirely, no, but for the most part, concerning the central elements of a definition, I'd say most alienists would."

"Do they all agree on what constitutes insanity? That is to say, its symptoms, its . . . manifestations?"

"Again, not entirely, but also again, most would certainly agree on many of its attributes."

"Its causes?"

"Again—"

"Thank you." Elston paused and took a sip of water, though he watched the doctor over the rim of the glass. When he set it down, he said, "Dr. Wolfstein, can you state unequivocally that George Remus was not insane at the moment he shot his wife?"

Wolfstein looked back at him for some moments, then said, "Not unequivocally, no, sir. But—"

"That is all. I have no further questions."

Walt Sibbald was immediately on his feet. "Doctor," he said. "We've seen a number of Mr. Remus's emotional outbursts during the course of this trial. Was he ever insane?"

"Objection," said Carl Elston.

"Overruled."

"Your Honor, the issue is not his sanity now."

"Mr. Elston, the issue is the definition of insanity. You have raised it. Mr. Sibbald, I believe, is simply trying to illuminate the point."

"Thank you, Judge," Walt said. "Doctor?"

"No, he was clearly not insane during any of these outbursts. He was angry to the point of being hysterical. But simply and only angry."

"Thank you again, sir," Walt said. He sat, as Charlie stood up to say, "Your Honor, the prosecution rests."

Elston said, "The defense rests, as well."

It was just after noon on Saturday, December 17.

THE JURY

THE REMAINDER OF THAT SATURDAY WAS GIVEN OVER TO the beginning of the closing arguments. The first came in the absence of the jury, when Shook asked each side's opinion on the verdicts the jury should be allowed to consider, beginning with guilty without mercy, which carried the death penalty. Charlie argued that the jury should not even be given the option of a not guilty verdict, since Remus had admitted committing the crime.

Elston, clearly upset, said, "You can't preclude a jury from finding a defendant not guilty. Why have a jury at all, then?"

"There's precedent," said Charlie. "I can cite at least two cases in which the not guilty option was not given."

"Then what have we been doing here for two months? There at least has to be the option of not guilty by reason of insanity."

"But the court's alienists found him sane."

"They are not a jury!" said Elston, his voice rising. "We went over all of this at the beginning—"

"Exactly," Charlie said. "And Mr. Remus agreed then to accept their findings."

"—and the prosecution and the court agreed that we would waive a preliminary hearing and allow Mr. Remus to argue the insanity defense. Now you want to renege on that, at the end of it? To not allow the jury to even decide? Oh, the appellate court will love this, Mr. Taft. They will just love it."

"Enough," Shook said. "I just wanted to hear your thoughts. I'll take this under advisement. Let's get on with the closing. Deputy, bring in the jurors."

THE CENTRAL POINT OF CHARLIE'S INTRODUCTION WAS THAT Imogene's death was a great benefit to Remus because the divorce hearing would have revealed many things, financial and otherwise, that he couldn't afford to have revealed. Elston, in his own opening, blasted this, saying that the prosecution had already tried to make one crackpot theory of conspiracy fly, only to have it crash at their feet, and now this was just another way of saying the same thing. Nothing was going to come out in the divorce that was going to hurt George Remus any worse than he'd already been hurt. And if his motivation had been to quiet his wife, he'd have done it discreetly.

On Monday, Elston attacked Frank Dodge and the prosecution for not putting him on the stand. The implication, he said, was clear: Dodge had too much to hide. Remus, on the other hand, had no need to testify. He could have added nothing since his memories of the actual shooting were fragmentary at best. He'd never been able to talk about it, not even to his own lawyer, and his memories of the period preceding it were dim and confused, too, because of the very issue at the heart of the trial: his insanity.

When Elston finished, Remus himself stood. He'd made it known that he planned on delivering a part of the closing himself, so the courtroom was packed. The deputies had allowed additional spectators to stand along the back and sides. Outside, the first snow of the season began to fall. The light grew dimmer as Remus, a chrysanthemum in his lapel, smiled at the jury and began.

The crowd expected at least a powerful and compelling oration, and maybe another breakdown or outburst. Neither came to pass. Remus made good points in his speech: that there was more to insanity than a technician's definition, and that it is recognizable to the common man; that he, Remus, had lifted himself up while a man like Charlie Taft had been born into the aristocracy and had never had to do the things Remus did to be successful; that there were compelling reasons for his not taking the stand. But he also wandered, stopping to praise Conners or Babe or Elston or the judge or the jury; to reminisce about his life; to complain again about the Volstead Act; to rail against Frank Dodge.

Then he stopped talking, looking off into some distance only he could see. The room grew so hushed that the batting of the snow against the window glass was audible. The silence grew uncomfortable. Finally, the judge said, "Mr. Remus?"

"That's all," he said.

The press called it a lackluster performance although several writers pointed out that the jurors seemed fascinated.

Clyde and Walt finished for the prosecution, their

arguments carrying over through Tuesday morning. Basler blasted Remus for not taking the stand, and denigrated the character of most of Remus's witnesses, especially George Conners. Walt questioned the character of Harry Truesdale and the notion that Imogene and Dodge had had anything to do with a plot to have Remus killed, and then he attacked Remus's use of the insanity defense.

By one o'clock, then, on Tuesday, December 20, it was time. In his instructions to the jury, Judge Shook did, after all, include the option of not guilty on the sole ground of insanity, though not a straight verdict of not guilty. He reminded them again that while the burden on the prosecution was to prove guilt beyond a reasonable doubt, the burden on the defense, in an insanity case, was to demonstrate insanity by a preponderance of the evidence. This was a lesser burden, he pointed out, but still a heavy one. He spoke for some time about exactly what it involved.

"And now," he said finally, "you must begin your deliberations." A deputy opened the door but none of the jurors moved.

The foreman raised his hand.

"Stand up," Shook said. "It's all right. You may address the court freely."

"Your Honor," said the foreman, "well, it's already one. If it's all right with you, we'd, well, we'd like one more lunch."

The room cracked, laughter and hoots rising up to meet the flakes blowing across the windows. Shook laughed as hard as anyone, then said, "I suppose it'd be hard to decide anything over the grumbling of stomachs. I'm sorry, I'm just anxious to get this thing over. Of course you can have lunch. Deputy, these people will be escorted to a good restaurant. They're to be given—" here he checked his pocket watch "—an hour and a half. Which means their deliberations are to begin at two-thirty."

CHARLIE TOOK CLYDE AND WALT OUT FOR LUNCH. THEY spoke little during it, and afterward gathered in Charlie's office, though no one expected to hear anything for some time. Walt stood at the window, his hands clasped behind him, watching it snow. "I have other work to do," he said. "I don't know why I'm standing here."

Charlie lit a cigar and exhaled and watched the smoke rise.

"You're right," Basler said. "They've only just started. Might as well do something productive."

No one moved.

"Worrying won't change anything now," Charlie said.

"Not worry," Walt said. "Just wonder."

"At?"

"Twelve people."

A secretary knocked on the door. Charlie called her in. "Mr. Taft," she said, "the court just called. They're back."

Walt turned and looked at her. Charlie said, "Who's back?"

"Well, the jury."

He looked at his watch. It was a quarter to three. "They've been out fifteen minutes," he said.

❧ ❧ ❧

THOUGH CHARLIE HEARD THAT DODGE HAD SWORN TO
stay away from it because he was angry at how they'd
treated him, he couldn't, apparently. He was pacing in
the hallway outside the courtroom when they came
down. Walt strode past him without a glance. Basler
nodded but didn't speak. Charlie stopped.

"They're back already," he said.

"What does it mean?" Frank asked.

"I don't know. I've never heard of anything like this.
Not in a murder trial."

Dodge nodded. He acted dazed, drugged even. His
clothes hung loosely, and his face was drawn and
pale.

"Have you been eating?" Charlie asked.

Dodge shook his head. "I promised myself a cele-
bratory dinner," he said, "when I hear that Remus is
going to die."

"Frank," Charlie said. "Just after he turned himself
in, after he shot her, someone came into the precinct
house and screamed at him. It was you, wasn't it?"

Dodge nodded, then wandered away. He found an
empty spot on a hallway bench and lowered himself
to it.

IT WASN'T UNTIL 3:30 THAT THE PRINCIPALS WERE
reassembled, since no one had expected anything to
happen on this day. The room by then was filled to its
capacity. Men knelt in the aisles between the rows of
benches, and people again lined the walls. The doors
to the hallway were left open, the crowd shushing
itself so it could hear. When the room had grown rea-

sonably still, Shook nodded and the deputy opened the door for the jurors.

Charlie noticed first that they all wore red mums, like Remus's. He was sure they hadn't worn them that morning. He gripped Walt's arm to point it out, but Walt leaned over and whispered, "One just smiled at Remus."

"Does the jury have a verdict?" asked Shook.

"We do, Your Honor," said the foreman.

"The defendant will rise."

Remus and Elston stood. Remus got behind him, as if to shield himself, and watched over his shoulder. Though it wasn't required of him, Charlie stood as well.

"Mr. Foreman, stand, please, and deliver the verdict."

The foreman cleared his throat and said, "We find the defendant, George Remus, not guilty on the sole ground of insanity—" A tremendous, deafening cheer rose up from the single collective throat of the crowd. Papers, hats, scarves, gloves, all flew upward toward the high ceiling and rained back down upon the throng. "Re-mus, Re-mus, Re-mus," they chanted.

Remus collapsed into his chair, his face washed white. Elston merely smiled down at the tabletop, and then he looked over at Charlie. Clyde Basler had put his head down on the table.

Charlie watched a crowd gather around Remus, slapping his back, pulling at his clothing. The judge pounded and motioned for the deputies to clear the room if they couldn't get it quieted. Once they got the doors closed, the room slowly settled again.

"I remind everyone," Shook said, "that Mr. Remus

has not been exonerated. He's been found not guilty by reason of insanity, and so he will remain incarcerated at least until there is a sanity hearing, which I imagine will not be until after the holiday. That is up to the probate court."

"Your Honor," the jury foreman said.

"Yessir."

"If I might, we have a request."

Shook looked at him a moment. "Your duties are finished," he said. "You have no standing now in this court. But go ahead."

"We, all of us," he said, "wanted to ask you to recommend, or request, I guess, that Mr. Remus be released for Christmas, on bail at least. We think he has suffered enough, and that he deserves at least that."

Another huge cheer went up from the crowd. Shook looked angrier than he had at any point in the trial. "I could hold you in contempt," he said. "This is absolutely inappropriate. I don't see how, in fifteen minutes—" He stopped, collected himself, and said, "Your request is denied. You're excused."

"I'm sorry—" the foreman began, but Shook cut him off and left the bench. Later, several jurors told the press that if Shook had included the verdict of not guilty, they would have acquitted Remus entirely and let him go home.

WHEN CHARLIE CAME OUTSIDE, INTO THE COLD, THE PRESS seemed no longer interested in him. They swarmed around Elston. Walt and Clyde had gone back upstairs. Charlie tightened his coat and began to walk. Walking sounded fine, he thought. He'd walk awhile, then call home for Sam to come. But as he started, he heard a shout, and looked up.

The Pierce-Arrow was parked at the curb, on Main, Sam standing up on the running board, waving at him. As he approached, he saw Eleanor, too, watching him. And then the children poured from the back and ran to him. He knelt on the pavement and opened his arms. They all just fit in. It had been nearly a month since he'd seen them.

At the car, he gathered Ellie into his arms.

"It's over," he said. "The jury—"

"Shh," she said. She placed a finger over his lips.

Sam stepped down and opened the back door.

Epilogue

THE STONE ROOM

AND SO, THOUGH GEORGE REMUS SPENT CHRISTMAS IN his suite at the top of the courthouse, it was a fairly happy day. Romola was there, as were Conners and his wife, and Babe. Carl Elston brought his wife too to visit for a little while, though they didn't stay for the meal Remus had ordered. Eight of the thirteen jurors came up and the others sent their regards. The sheriff and some of the guards stopped in for eggnog.

As he was leaving, Elston took Remus aside and said, "The hearing's set for the thirtieth. Next Friday."

"You don't anticipate any problems?"

"No," Elston said. "What are they going to do, argue now that you were insane after all? Come on."

"HE HAS BEEN FOUND NOT GUILTY BY REASON OF INSANITY," Charlie Taft said to the probate judge. "The state feels it must insist, then, that he be treated as if he is insane. We recommend that he be committed to an appropriate institution."

"I can't believe this," Elston said. "Mr. Taft and his

cronies have just spent the last three months crying that this man is not insane. They have done everything in their power to prove it. Three alienists, appointed by the court and sanctioned by the prosecutors, swore to Remus's sanity."

Dr. Wolfstein, in fact, and the two other alienists were called to testify, this time by the defense. Each held that Remus was not now, and had never been, insane.

Charlie presented the transcript of the defense portion of the murder trial as evidence. He called George Conners to corroborate, under oath, some of the statements he had made regarding Remus's mental health.

The probate judge appointed his own panel of three new alienists. They found that, while Remus was technically sane, he was also psychopathic and dangerous to society. At the end, the judge declared, "This court finds George Remus to be not only insane, but dangerous. He is hereby remanded for an indefinite time to the State Hospital for the Criminal Insane at Lima, Ohio."

Elston began to file his appeals in Allen County, in northwestern Ohio, where at least he had a different set of prosecutors to deal with.

In early January of 1928, Remus was committed.

IN MARCH, AN APPELLATE PANEL OF THREE JUDGES FOUND that, though there had been a grotesque miscarriage of justice in Cincinnati, George Remus was clearly not insane, and could not be held as such. The Allen County prosecutor argued that only the administrator of the hospital at Lima could now legally make this judgment. He threw up one roadblock after another. He had surreptitious help—legal advice, manpower, funds to hire private lawyers—from the prosecutor's office in Hamilton County.

Remus settled into his life in the crazy house, where he lay for hours contemplating the probable fact of his own insanity. He had, after all, still not been able to remember any details of that last morning in the park with Imogene. He wondered about his visions of Imogene and the fact that they had ceased after the trial. He wasn't sure what to make of this, whether it was a sign of his improvement or his doom.

One day when he was out walking on the grounds, he noticed a patient hugging an attendant. As he looked, he realized that the patient had his hands on the attendant's throat. He raced over and threw his arm around the patient's neck and heaved back with all the strength still in his great chest and arms. The patient let out a cry and snapped into him. For this, he became a favorite of the staff. They gave him a room away from the general population, so that the screams of agony and madness were dimmed, though not entirely blotted out. They slipped him books to read, and better food, for which he expressed his sincere gratitude.

In June, finally, Elston's wrangling brought them to the Ohio Supreme Court, which upheld the appellate court's judgment: Remus was sane, and he was to be immediately released from the hospital. It was Conners, of course, who picked him up and drove him back to the empty house in Cincinnati.

Judge Shook declined to ever pass sentence on

Remus for the contempt charges he had leveled. It would not be for several years that Remus would find a place where he felt comfortable. Though it was a stone room, a cell, it was not, finally, at Lima or in any other prison or hospital, but on Greenup Street in Covington, Kentucky, at the back of a small house not far from the Roebling Bridge and the southern bank of the river where he could dive, still, and swim, if he wanted, across to Cincinnati.

IN THIS ROOM, HE WOULD REMEMBER HIS LIFE. IT CAME back to him, sometimes, in isolated images or scents or sensations, sometimes in whole cascading episodes that played on the inside of his eyelids. It wasn't that he had forgotten them, necessarily. It was just that now, here, in the quiet, with little else to do, he had time to let them recur. They would continue to come for many years, in ever richer detail. Some of them he tried to write down. Others he was unable to capture. They rode the currents back and forth, like his uncle's crisp dollar note, until they settled and faded again into darkness. But there remained one memory, one moment, that he had tried and failed many times to recall, of that morning in Eden Park.

And then, one day when he was out swimming, he glimpsed a piece of it. He wanted terribly to write it down, but by the time he dressed and got into the room, it had faded again, like a dream. All he could remember was that it began with Dodge.

DODGE HAD TO BE THERE, WITH HER. IT ALL DEPENDED ON that. They had to be together, the three of them, each of them a party to it. Himself, the avenger, the light inside burning with a white heat. Dodge, the thief, the home wrecker, the liar, deserving everything he got. And her, the object of it, and the witness. She had to see him do it, so she would know how he felt about her, so she would know what he'd lay down for her. They'd have to be apart for a while, yet, but then it would pass, and they would go on, this time forever.

At the Alms he saw her and Laura come out. But not Dodge.

"Where is he?" he said. "Where's Dodge?" Babe looked back. "Christ, I get it," Remus said. "He's driving. It's a trick. Dodge is the chauffeur. Go!" And Babe drove.

As time passed in the room, the past began to come too quickly for him to write it all down. Finally, he stopped trying. He just paced, or swam, or walked, and let it come. Until one morning he awakened from a shallow dream and knew that a piece of that central moment he glimpsed when he was swimming had come back again.

Babe could drive. Remus had always known he could count on that. Babe had the touch. The Cadillac was a heavy car, but he made it jump right up like a little dog anxious to please, or a child. The car leapt forward, practically into the back of the taxi, but Babe had too much control to let that happen.

"Get alongside," Remus said. "Pull up." They raced, Dodge gunning the cab to get away, but Babe staying right there, turning when the cab turned. Then they were alongside, and Remus looked, and he could see that the driver wasn't Dodge after all. He looked nothing like Dodge. Where was Dodge? What was this about?

Remus fell back in the seat, dizzy, lost, unsure even of where he was anymore, or what to do, or how, or who to ask to tell him. But Babe kept driving as he had been told, gunning it and pulling in on the cab. They could see the two women screaming in the back and the driver trying mightily to open a little distance. Then the cabbie cut a hard right onto the parkway. He would have lost an average driver, but he couldn't lose Babe. Babe touched the brake and eased the Caddy around and they made the turn practically on two wheels and they were headed for the park, right behind the cab, and then alongside it again. Cars came at them in the other lane, sounding their horns, but Babe didn't flinch. He'd brake and ease back just enough to get by, then pull up alongside again. The cab had nothing on the Cadillac. And then the driver just locked his brakes and stopped. He gave up. Remus wished he hadn't. It wasn't over. They should have kept going, right on down into the city, to the law offices.

He got out. He looked up at the trees and the sky, and breathed in the scented air. He had to ask her. That was the thing. He had to know. He opened the cab door and said, "Where is he?"

They looked at him, their eyes wide, their faces white.

"Where in hell is the bastard?" She shook her head. Laura wouldn't look at him anymore. "Where?" he said. "I came to do what I need to do. You know what I mean, Imogene."

He reached into his pocket and felt her gun there. She watched him touch it. She opened her door and got out and started to run. Why was she running? He wasn't after her. Is that what she thought?

ONE DAY, WHILE HE WAS SWIMMING, SHE APPEARED ALONG-side him. It had been years since the trial, years since he'd last seen her. Now, she simply stood on the surface of the water, moving with him. After that, some-times, she came to the room and sat beside him as he worked. In the dark she watched him, and though he might sleep, he was always aware that she had been there.

He didn't know why she'd returned until he awoke one morning and remembered that morning in the park. All of it. She had brought it to him. She whis-pered it to him at night as he slept, so that when he awoke in the morning, it was there, fresh and waiting.

HE CAUGHT HER.

"Why are you running?" he said.

"Baby," she said. "Don't."

"No," he said. "Stop this. Stop fighting me. You're always fighting me. Where's Dodge?"

She pulled against him. He said, "You know what I have to do. See what I brought?" He took out the gun. He took out her gun. "See? Look at it, Imogene."

"George, don't," she said. "George!" She screamed. She screamed his name. She screamed at him. She pulled against him, but he held her.

"Look at it," he said, and he pressed it to her so she could feel it. So he could feel her. He felt the flesh beneath her silky dress, the flesh he had not touched in years. He held her arm and with his other hand he pressed it against her, against her soft belly, the belly he had licked and bit and sweated upon. He gritted his teeth and pulled her body into his. He felt her breasts against him and her thighs beneath the silk and her breath on his face. Her hair brushed him. He smelled that old scent of lilacs, and he pressed it into her and he said "See?" He heard a noise and his hand stung and her legs went out from beneath her.

He looked at it in his hand, and he showed it to her. See? She fell. He held her arm. He pulled on it. He did not want her to fall. See it? He lifted her up. See?

NOW THE YEARS ARE GONE. HE CAN NO LONGER SWIM, except for an occasional few minutes in the middle of the high hot days of summer, and then only for a few yards. His old heart and his arms and his jaw ache with the effort. But still, he paces, though all his years of walking here have left no trace upon the stone floor.

And she still comes, though she has never spoken to him while he's awake. And though he speaks to her, he has never offered her an apology. There is none needed, he knows. They played out their destinies. Hers, in the end, was less painful than his.

As he paces, he watches it happen as it will always happen.

SHE RAN AWAY FROM HIM AGAIN. SHE RAN BACK TOWARD the taxi. Again, he went after her. This was not right.

Laura had gotten out, now. Imogene went into the car, and through it, and came out and ran away again, up the road. The seat was smeared with blood. It ran down her legs. It spattered along the red bricks. He followed her. See?

He had nearly reached her when Laura ran up behind him and pulled his arm and said to go away. She was crying, and it was over now, it was all over, he knew it was over. It was over.

Laura went on ahead and caught her and they got in a different car. It went away. He looked for the Cadillac, but Babe had gone away, too.

He walked into the park. Eden Park. He walked up the steep dewy slope of a ridge toward the crest, toward the impossibly clear sky into which the impossibly bright sun had now fully risen. It was all a dream. All impossible.

He walked, and he whistled a tune. It was a song she used to sing, a song she had taught him. It was a jazz song she had loved.

ACKNOWLEDGMENTS, NOTES, AND REFERENCES

I HAD THE BITTERSWEET TASK OF WORKING WITH TWO editors on this novel, and though the change in midstream, as it were, was disconcerting, it has proved to be a kind of luxury. My former editor, Leslie Schnur, was present at the conception and strongly encouraged me when I mentioned that I was thinking of writing a novel set in history. She saw the manuscript through huge early changes that were crucial not only to the development but to the very existence of the book. And even after our formal relationship ended, she continued to work on the manuscript simply as a friend. I owe her a great debt.

To my great good fortune, Geoff Kloske at Simon & Schuster saw some promise in what was still a bloated and fuzzy story, and took it under his able wing. He is a fine reader, a real writer's editor in what I imagine the old tradition to have been, and I look forward to working with him into the future. I've known David Rosenthal, the publisher of Simon & Schuster, for some years and I'm overjoyed to have been invited into his house.

As always, my agent, Gail Hochman, was the rock in the storm. She read many more drafts of this book than anyone should have been subjected to, and worked harder for it than any of the others. I thank her, again, again.

Thanks, also, to Vicki Flick, Samir Abu Absi of the University of Toledo English Department, Frau Margarete Walsh of the Steiner School of Ann Arbor, Scott Holden, Molly Behrmann, Mary Carol Stall of the Taft Museum in Cincinnati, and those various folks I met in and around Ohio who knew of Remus, or the Tafts, or old Cincinnati, or the twenties, and talked and told me stories they knew or remembered or had heard: Charlie Taft driving around town with a canoe on the roof of his car, the Findlay Market when horses drew the produce carts, the river in the days before the locks and dams brought the level up so that Front Street itself was permanently submerged.

Though this story was based on real people and events, it must be viewed strictly as a work of fiction. I invented freely, especially in the history and character of Imogene, and anyone who knows much of the actual history will realize this. But while I changed many things, the essential structure of Remus's life and of the legal trials remains. In no place did I quote directly from any transcript, interview, newspaper account, book, person, or any other source.

The story also required some minor changes or alterations to the city and its buildings, and sometimes a lack of information necessitated invention. But in general I tried to be as accurate in this regard as possible. There still exist a few of the physical settings of the story, and I felt at times haunted by them, or rather perhaps that they were haunted, inhabited by the shadows of what had happened in them.

East of Broadway in downtown Cincinnati, on the far side of Lytle Park, you can still find the Taft house, now the Taft Museum. It was owned by William Howard's half brother, Charles P. Taft, and his wife, Anna Sinton Taft, whose father was David Sinton, one of the original backers of the Sinton Hotel.

The Sinton and Alms Hotels were both sold to the same holding company. The Sinton was demolished in the early sixties. The Alms, though, still stands, known now as the Alms Hill Apartments, at the corner of William Howard Taft Road (formerly Locust) and the Victory Parkway. In the lobby hangs an etching of it made in its glory days.

If you drive out Queen City Avenue, once known as the Lick Run Road, toward the towns of Westwood and Cheviot, you'll find, just past the intersection with Gherum Lane, a curve that winds hard up along the crest of a great ridge. Though the hollow formed by this ridge now holds the redbrick towers of an apartment village, you can easily imagine, standing in the parking lot and looking up at the road, the cars of competitors or government agents parked there, preparing to rain down fire or mount a raid against what must be the place once known as Death Valley.

The Roebling Suspension Bridge, where Remus really did fight hand-to-hand with hijackers, still connects the downtown with Covington, though it is frighteningly narrow and seems to stand as much as an anachronism as an essential link.

The reservoir in Eden Park is smaller than it was in the twenties, and the brush on the hillsides appears heavier, but otherwise the park itself looks much as it must have on the morning of October 6, 1927.

MY THANKS, FINALLY, THEN, TO THE STAFFS OF THE following institutions, all of whom were most helpful as I dug my way back: the Bentley Historical Library and the Harlan Hatcher Graduate Library of the University of Michigan; the main branch of the Michigan State University Library; the research department of the *St. Louis Post-Dispatch;* the Public Library of Cincinnati and Hamilton County; the Cincinnati Museum Center; the Cincinnati Historical Society Library; the Taft Museum in Cincinnati; and the Cincinnati Recreation Commission.

Much of my research relied, of course, on other sources, which were: *The Last Days of Innocence: America at War, 1917–18,* Meirion and Susie Harris, Random House, New York, NY, 1997; *Rumrunning and the Roaring Twenties,* Philip P. Mason, Wayne State University Press, Detroit, MI, 1995; *Prohibition: Thirteen Years That Changed America,* Edward Behr, Arcade Publishing, New York, NY, 1996; *The Ohio Gang,* Charles L. Mee, Jr., M. Evans & Co, New York, NY, 1981; *The Long Thirst: Prohibition in America, 1920–1933,* Thomas M. Coffey, W. W. Norton & Co., New York, NY, 1975; *The City of Rivers and Hills,* Paul Briol, The Book Shelf, Cincinnati, OH, 1925; *The American Gladiators: Taft Versus Remus,* Albert Rosenberg and Cindy Armstrong, Aimwell Press, Hemet, CA, 1995; *The Year the World Went Mad,* Allen Churchill, Hillman Books, New York,

NY, 1960; *Cincinnati, Days in History: A Bicentennial Almanac,* edited by Nancy Berlier, The Cincinnati Post, Cincinnati, OH, 1988; *Floyd Clymer's Motor Scrapbook, No. 5,* Floyd Clymer, Clymer Motors, Los Angeles, CA, 1948; *Jazz Masters of the Twenties,* Richard Hadlock, Da Capo Press, Inc., New York, NY, 1972; *The Jazz Revolution: Twenties America and the Meaning of Jazz,* Kathy J. Ogren, Oxford University Press, New York, NY, 1989; *Franklin Simon Fashion Catalog for 1923,* Dover Publications, Inc., New York, NY, 1993; *Going to Cincinnati: A History of the Blues in the Queen City,* Steven C. Tracy, University of Illinois Press, Urbana and Chicago, IL, 1993; *The Cincinnati Crime Book,* George Stimson, The Peasenhall Press, Cincinnati, OH, 1998; *Then & Now: Cincinnati and Northern Kentucky,* Jim Reis and Robert A. Flischel, Scripps Howard Publishing, Inc., Gibsonia, PA, 1995; *Dining in New York,* Rian James, The John Day Company, Inc., New York, NY, 1931; *Cincinnati* magazine (Remus profile, November 1974); *The Cincinnati Enquirer* (especially the murder and trial coverage); *The Cincinnati Post;* the *Cincinnati Times-Star;* and the *St. Louis Post-Dispatch* (especially Paul Y. Anderson's ten-installment profile of Remus in January 1926, and the murder and trial coverage).

**POCKET
BOOKS**

ALTERED LAND

JULES HARDY

Your life can change in seconds . . .

Joan is a single mother – beautiful, talented and desired.
John is her adored son, her 'Merboy'. Growing up in the
West Country, his life is lived outdoors, playing in the creek
by their cottage in Devon, swimming, hunting for shells,
collecting bits of old boats. On his thirteenth birthday, Joan
treats him to a trip to London to buy his first pair of Levi's
jeans. Unused to city driving, she takes a wrong turn. The
repercussions of that moment's hesitation are devastating . . .

Their story recounts the life-altering effects of that one
moment. It is a story about a mother's heartbreaking love for
her son, the different ways people survive damage and the
endurance of a dream against all odds.

With sensitivity and compassion, Jules Hardy's lyrical prose
explores the strengths and flaws of this unique relationship
between a mother and her son. It is a wonderfully assured
debut from an extraordinary new talent.

ISBN 0 7434 2904 4

PRICE £6.99

**POCKET
BOOKS**

BIG STONE GAP

ADRIANA TRIGIANI

Big Stone Gap, Virginia, is the sort of sleepy hamlet in
the Blue Ridge Mountains where kids get married and
start families at eighteen, and stay forever. So thirty-five-
year old Ave Maria Mulligan is something of an oddity.
A self-proclaimed spinster, as the local pharmacist she's
been keeping the townsfolk's secrets for years.

Now Ave Maria is about to discover a scandal in her
own family's past that will blow the lid right off her
quiet, uneventful life.

With an unforgettable cast of characters and a heroine
with an extraordinary story to tell, *Big Stone Gap* is a
wonderfully vibrant, unashamedly feel-good debut.

'Funny, charming and original' Fannie Flagg, author of
Fried Green Tomatoes at the Whistle Stop Cafe

'Hilarious and romantic. I couldn't put it down – a real
page-turner' Sarah Jessica Parker

ISBN 0 7434 4012 9

PRICE £6.99

**POCKET
BOOKS**

ISOLDE
Queen of the Western Isle

ROSALIND MILES

The first in a magnificent new Arthurian trilogy from
Rosalind Miles, author of the bestselling *Guenevere*.

Only daughter of Ireland's ruling queen, Isolde has always
known that she will take over the rule of the sacred Island
of the West when her time comes. Until then she practises
her skills as a healer and struggles to hold back her mother,
a passionate, headstrong under the sway of her champion,
Sir Marhaus, who is determined to make war.

Attacking Cornwall, Sir Marhaus wounds the king's nephew,
Sir Tristan of Lyonesse, so badly that he can only be saved by
Isolde, the most noted healer of the isles. And when the King
of Cornwall decides to marry Isolde, unaware of the young
couple's growing love, the stage is set for the mythic tale of
star-crossed lovers that the world knows so well.

Set in Ireland, Cornwall and Camelot, *Isolde* offers a compelling
new version of the familiar legend rich in Celtic magic and
mythology, yet firmly grounded in the well-loved Arthurian
world. Merlin, Arthur, Guenevere, and all their knights appear
once again to delight those who enjoyed Rosalind Miles's
previous forays into this enchanted terrain.

ISBN 0 671 03721

PRICE £6.99

**POCKET
BOOKS**

CHOSEN PREY

JOHN SANDFORD

**The deadliest of crimes . . .
The coolest of killers**

In the mist and rain of a Minnesota spring, a shallow grave
is found. It contains the body of a young woman,
apparently strangled. When the murder is connected with
a brilliantly-executed erotic drawing, where the victim's
face has been grafted onto a pornographic internet image,
Lucas Davenport becomes involved. More of the drawings
come to light and Davenport, makes a grisly discovery –
the drawings may represent more murder victims.

The case begins to come together in Lucas' mind, but the
mixture of ferocious intelligence and madness which he
faces means that the deaths must continue, that the
chosen prey must be stalked . . .

'A brilliant writer' GUARDIAN

'Few do it better than Sandford' DAILY TELEGRAPH

ISBN 0 7434 1555 8

PRICE £6.99

POCKET
BOOKS

This book and other **Pocket** titles are available from your book shop or can be ordered direct from the publisher.

☐ 0 7434 2904 4 **Altered Land** £6.99

☐ 0 7434 4012 9 **Big Stone Gap** £6.99

☐ 0 671 0372 1 **Isolde** £6.99

☐ 0 7434 1555 8 **Chosen Prey** £6.99

Please send cheque or postal order for the value of the book, free postage and packing within the UK; OVERSEAS including Republic of Ireland £1 per book.

OR: Please debit this amount from my:

VISA/ACCESS/MASTERCARD ....

CARD NO ....

EXPIRY DATE ....

AMOUNT £ ....

NAME ....

ADDRESS ....

....

SIGNATURE ....

www.simonsays.co.uk

Send orders to: SIMON & SCHUSTER CASH SALES
PO Box 29, Douglas, Isle of Man, IM99 1BQ
Tel: 01624 83600, Fax 01624 670923
www.bookpost.co.uk
Please allow 14 days for delivery.
Prices and availability subject to change without notice.